YOUR PLANTATION PROM IS NOT OKAY

YOUR PLANTATION PROM IS NOT OKAY

KELLY MCWILLIAMS

LITTLE, BROWN AND COMPANY

New York Boston

Little, Brown and Company
Hachette Book Group
1290 Avenue of the Americas, New York, NY 10104
Visit us at LBYR.com

First Edition: May 2023

Little, Brown and Company is a division of Hachette Book Group, Inc. The Little, Brown name and logo are trademarks of Hachette Book Group, Inc.

The publisher is not responsible for websites (or their content) that are not owned by the publisher.

Library of Congress Cataloging-in-Publication Data
Names: McWilliams, Kelly, author.
Title: Your plantation prom is not okay / Kelly McWilliams.
Description: First edition. | New York : Little, Brown and Company, 2023. | Audience: Ages 12 & up | Summary: High school senior Harriet is still grappling with her mother's death when an unwanted property sale causes her to join forces with her new neighbor to stop Belle Grove Plantation from turning into a wedding venue.
Identifiers: LCCN 2022030023 | ISBN 9780316449939 (hardcover) | ISBN 9780316450133 (ebook)
Subjects: CYAC: Plantations—Fiction. | Racism—Fiction. | Friendship—Fiction. | Grief—Fiction. | LCGFT: Novels.
Classification: LCC PZ7.M47885 Yo 2023 | DDC [Fic]—dc23
LC record available at https://lccn.loc.gov/2022030023

ISBNs: 978-0-316-44993-9 (hardcover), 978-0-316-45013-3 (ebook)

Printed in the United States of America

LSC-C

Printing 1, 2023

For Bill, a true ally.
Thank you for making this book
your quest.

CHAPTER 1

L ET'S START BY getting one thing straight: I do *not* live on a plantation. Not the kind you mean.

Once upon a time, enslaved people did work sugarcane in Westwood's fields, but years ago, Mom, Dad, and I restored it into an enslaved people's museum—and that's a totally different thing.

Of course, there *is* a Big House at Westwood, white with columns like thick marble teeth, poised to devour everything in sight...but we don't sleep there. Dad and I live in a new home in the woods, because we're not about to be the Black family in the horror movie that doesn't leave the haunted house.

I've been a Westwood tour guide since my fifteenth birthday, when Dad gave me an ID card and his blessing to teach the hard truths we learned while restoring this place. I love what I do, but guiding tours can really take it out of you. It's the proximity to suffering, to a history that should feel ancient, but doesn't. In the long grasses, amidst the orchards and bare-floor cabins and whispering live oak trees, time collapses like a wormhole. Yesterday is today and tomorrow feels impossible. You know what I mean, especially if you're Black or Indigenous or otherwise marginalized. You don't even have to live on a plantation museum to breathe air soaked with history you can't escape.

At the end of today's long shift, I'm sitting slumped at my desk in the Welcome Center, vaguely staring at our exhibit on the Middle Passage. My last tourists have finished buying their books and postcards, the parking lot's emptying out, and I'm stuck here manning the phones, wishing to God that we'd invested in central air. Southern summers don't mess around.

But my biggest problem right now is a jackhammer.

Last year, a mystery woman purchased the plantation next door: a neglected cane farm called Belle Grove. All summer, they've been doing endless construction. It feels like I can hear every hammer striking every nail.

If I know anything about River Road, which is plantation central on this stretch of the Mississippi, there's zero chance that Belle Grove's being transformed, like Westwood, into a memorial. More likely than not, it's about to be some awful bed-and-breakfast—and I'd bet my right thumb the proceeds will benefit somebody white.

And *the jackhammering.* It goes on and on. I've never been so ready to clock out, get home, and fall into a Netflix-shaped hole.

With two minutes until closing, I slip a sweaty lanyard off my neck. The ID tag reads HARRIET DOUGLASS, VOLUNTEER GUIDE. Outside, a high voice spirals out of control, and that's when a bad feeling sinks its claws into me, familiar to anyone who's ever held a customer-service position. You get a kind of premonition that some bull's about to go down—especially when it's bound to make you late.

In my case, the premonition takes the form of a stout white woman—one of my four o'clock tourists—making her way across the grounds, a surly preteen in tow.

Please don't come in here, lady. I am not in the mood.

A silver bell rings, and she's arrived. Her hand's wrapped around her phone like a claw, and her kid, maybe twelve or thirteen, looks utterly resigned. Like he knows his mom's about to make a scene. I don't want to stereotype, but her Ritz-Carlton visor totally screams Vacation Karen.

Behind the desk, my spine snaps straight. *Customer-facing systems engaged.*

Meanwhile, I rack my brains, trying to remember if she looked this pissed on tour. But honestly, I didn't pay her much mind. I was too focused on Mr. Goodman, a Black retired janitor who came to our museum looking for his ancestors.

Long ago, he'd heard a rumor that one of his kinsfolk passed through Westwood. He wore an old-fashioned camera slung hopefully around his neck, and every time I looked at it, I felt like the red heart emoji, cracked in half. The group held their breath while he examined our memorial wall, inscribed with the name of every enslaved person who worked this land. The green-black marble shone, shivering like water...and there it was, his family name. Mr. Goodman let out a surprised huff, and then broke down in big, gulping sobs. Black men, tough all year long, often weep at Westwood, but I never get used to it. The sweet older white couple from Florida started crying right along with him, snuffling into their matching flamingo shirts.

But this lady I'm facing now? She looked straight-up inconvenienced—and she didn't shop like the other tourists. I bet she's been sitting in her rental car this whole time, just stewing.

"Excuse me, young lady! Where is your manager?"

I hate this part. "Ma'am, what seems to be the problem?"

She jabs a finger at me. "*You* are the problem. This isn't a plantation tour. It's an ambush."

Between my ribs, a critter I call the rage monster wakes up, flexing sharp claws. Ever since Mom died, I suck at controlling my temper.

"I mean, the *nerve* of trying to make us feel guilty for something that's not even our fault!"

"We never intended—"

"And what about the Westwood family, hmm? They built this country, but you don't have a kind word for them. Don't you *know* slavery used to be *normal*? There were good owners, too."

3

That phrase, *good owners*, explodes behind my eyes like a firework.

It's a tale as old as time: A white woman who's read one too many historical southern romances takes a vacation to Louisiana, then shows up at Westwood expecting to see the plantation from *Gone with the Wind*. She wants nothing more than to visit rooms full of antique furniture, maybe buy a cute parasol from the gift shop and call it a day.

But what we do here isn't like that at all. Westwood is more like the Holocaust Museum—or the 9/11 Memorial. Some ex-plantations will sell you a fairy tale, but here, we tell it like it is.

Why can't this lady see that?

Dr. Maples says that when I feel overwhelmed, I should look around. Remind myself what's real.

Outside the window, a willow sways in the swampy breeze, and the chickens nap in their coop. Dad's scared of chickens—I know, right?—but Mom always wanted fresh eggs in the morning. Now that she's gone, I take care of the flock.

I turn back to my angry tourist.

"At Westwood, we focus on the perspectives of enslaved people. I'm sorry you feel guilty, but that wasn't our intent."

The woman throws her son in front of her like a shield. "Look at my Brayden. Just *look at him*. He's traumatized."

Brayden slouches, obviously wishing he were anywhere but here.

Like I've been dunked in freezing water, I suddenly miss Mom.

As a museum operator, she never blamed white folks for the feelings they brought to our tours. She'd know exactly how to reach out to Brayden—how to calm his mother, too.

My mouth opens and closes, but nothing comes out. I just don't have my mother's irresistible calm. Don't have anything of hers, really, unless you count the tiny upturn of my nose.

"I know it's *cool* these days to be the victim, but this was a bit much. Those creepy statues of African children. This is not what we signed up for *at all*."

Though my smile stays stitched in place, fury mounts behind it.

Unlike Brayden, the enslaved children memorialized in statues throughout Westwood were *actually* traumatized—their childhoods stolen forever. One of the Lost Girls stands outside the office, overlooking the chicken coop. She's dressed in sackcloth, and her eyes are open, iron-forged sores.

Her name is Louisa.

In a snap, I tumble off script. "What exactly were you expecting from a plantation tour, ma'am?"

She's thrown. "You know—Civil War heroes and the antebellum life-style. The *real* history."

"Our mission, as clearly stated in our brochure, is to fight present-day racism with historical education. If we don't study the past, we're doomed to repeat it. There's no reason to be ashamed by what you don't know about this country's racial—"

"Are you calling me racist? My *best friend* is *Black*, young lady!"

Karen takes a threatening step toward me, smelling of sweat and sunscreen.

"Where's your manager?" She cranes to see behind me, then starts banging on the call bell. "Hello? Is anybody there?"

My "manager" is my dad, and he's a historian with a doctorate from Stanford. Right now, he's busy working on his new book. I'm not about to bother him for this Real Housewife of Wherever.

I snatch the bell away. "It's just me today."

"Well, I don't accept that."

"You're welcome to put your complaint in the comment box."

Her eyes drop to the old shoebox we keep as a decoy for aggressive guests. She snatches up a piece of paper and scribbles intently, sweat clinging to the hairs on her upper lip. Past her shoulder, the sailcloth of the Middle Passage exhibit shudders in the breeze, beckoning to those who care.

Brayden rolls his eyes upward, examining our ceiling—and my heart goes out to him. His mother's a lost cause, but Westwood might be a formative experience for this kid. He could use what he's learned to grow up differently from his mom. It's a slim chance, but not impossible. And it's one of the reasons Westwood exists.

While far-off construction workers holler, I try to catch his eye.

What would Mom say to him?

She always found grace under pressure. Even for racists. *Especially* for them.

Just then, my very favorite chicken, Rosemary, pecks the back door. *Tippity tap.* She's notorious for flying the coop.

"There." Red-faced, Karen punctuates her letter. "Don't be surprised if you find yourself out of a job. It's completely inappropriate to discuss whippings and—" She lowers her voice to a stage whisper. "And *sex* around children."

I blink. "What?"

She scowls. "That *woman*."

Face heating, I rear back. We don't talk about sex on the tour, obviously, but we do tell the truth about the women Westwood purchased specifically for the purpose of bearing children.

I think it's Anna's history that she objects to.

Poor freaking Anna.

I always save her story for the end, as I'm leading the group across the Freedom Bridge. According to Dad's findings, Anna was a teenaged girl who bore five children in five years—all of them sold away from her. Just think about that: She birthed her babies, held them, nursed them, and then handed them over to a stranger who would never, ever love them.

Anna ran from slavery three times. Louisiana plantations followed a very specific protocol for those who tried to escape. As punishment, she suffered ear cropping, whipping, and branding with the fleur-de-lis. But she never stopped running. Eventually, Westwood's enslavers sold her to a plantation in Barbados as a "breeder." They wrote her up like cattle, in scratchy, evil penmanship: *Anna, strong-willed, but an excellent breeder.*

Dad doesn't know what happened to Anna in Barbados. The historical trail went cold. Today, her sculpture stands proudly on museum land, her gold-brown back sprouting a pair of gigantic angel's wings.

"That *woman* was a human being," I grind out. "I only told her story."

"That's a fine way to spend your time, telling unsuspecting people nasty stories like that. What must your mother think?"

At the back of my throat, I taste blood. "Keep my mother out of your mouth."

"Are you *threatening* me?"

Deadass we're threatening you, lady! the rage monster crows. *You are everything that's wrong with this country! NOW SIT DOWN. BE HUMBLE.*

Self-preservation holds me back. Some women actually do find me physically threatening. Never mind that I'm only five foot four. Sometimes, I feel like white people live inside a video game.

"I want the price of our tickets returned. Right now."

"No refunds."

Rosemary pecks louder, clucking for corn.

"Well, make an exception."

I hesitate. "Hang on."

Karen smiles triumphantly, but I'm not about to return her money. I open the back door and let Rosemary in. She nips grumpily at my ankles. *That's my girl.* I pick her up—her white feathers velvety against my cheek—and carry her to the desk.

Brayden makes a sound in the back of his throat.

I think hard at Rosemary: *Do it for Anna.*

Like a good attack chicken, she spreads her wings and launches herself at my disgruntled tourist.

Vacation Karen stumbles back, hollering, "What is *wrong* with you people!"

And there it is: plain-as-day racism.

For the first time, Brayden looks directly at me.

"Come on, Mom," he whines. "I want to go back to the hotel."

On impulse, I reach for one of Dad's books—*Oral Histories of the Transatlantic Slave Trade*—and offer it to Brayden, whose preppy-ass name is not his fault. My heart's pounding. All that anger transformed into need. The rage monster rolls over, whimpering and showing her belly. After all, we don't run this museum for our health. We have a mission. *Mom's* mission.

"Take the book. Free of charge."

Brayden's mother is running from the now-grounded chicken, clutching her purse like the bird might steal it.

"Don't you speak to him! Brayden, *come here.*"

In the end, Brayden doesn't take the book. Sadness pinches my heart, watching him follow his mother out the door. Behind them, glass slams, shuddering.

I groan, regretting setting Rosemary on my unhappy tourists. Wishing I were more like Mom. After a while I glance out the window, making sure Vacation Karen's really gone.

Then I pull her letter out of the stupid comment box.

> Our tour guide should be FIRED for the way she
> spoke to me, and I WILL be leaving a Yelp review!!!
> Westwood Plantation doesn't deserve one more tourist.
> What a WASTE of an afternoon.

Poisoned by the toxic fumes of this white lady's rage, I sink helplessly back into my chair. A negative Yelp review would be trash, because we need tourists now more than ever. Restoring a plantation's not cheap— my parents took out over two million dollars in loans. We could lose money we don't even have.

At this rate, I'll never be out of therapy.

I don't know why I keep letting the rage monster win—except, I guess, that anger feels better than the sadness that yawns beneath. Sadness for

Brayden, for his mom's closed-mindedness. And sadness for me, because Vacation Karen's whole attitude means that I failed to make her understand the meaning of this place.

Outside, a sunray glances off Louisa's bronze, sculpted cheek. I wonder if it's weird that I feel more strongly about a little girl who died over three hundred years ago than I do about most living people. If there's maybe even something a little bit wrong with me.

Then again, what did Mom and Dad expect, raising a Black girl on a plantation turned slavery museum?

The jackhammer drones on, endlessly puncturing my sanity. I lift my best chicken, nuzzling her soft feathers.

She stinks, of course. Most chickens do.

I consider giving Rosemary a bath. But I'm just putting off the moment when I'll have to tell Dad about impending Yelp doom.

CHAPTER 2

I N THE KITCHEN, Dad unpacks sacks of Zaxby's, a southern fast-food chain specializing in "chicken, zalads, and zappetizers." Dad ordered the meal on Uber Eats, because he's crazy busy with work. It took the poor delivery guy forever to figure out where we live, here in a small woodsy cabin behind the towering white Big House. He had to pass just about every memorial in the place, and at night, those statues of enslaved children look full-on *alive*.

For the delivery guy's ordeal, Dad tipped 30 percent.

I plant myself on a kitchen stool. Dad pops open my buffalo wings.

"Hey, kid."

He's wearing the dorky history T-shirt Mom bought him when they were at Stanford. It says (brace yourself):

I AIN'T SAYIN' SHE A GOLD-DIGGER...

HOWEVER

SHE DID COME TO CALIFORNIA IN 1852

So, yeah, that's the kind of dude I'm dealing with here.

I can tell it's been a good writing day because Dad's eyes are glazed like he's just woken from a dream. He's already written three books, all histories. This one's different: a memoir about restoring the plantation with Mom. He's pouring his whole heart into it; it's also supposed to pay off some of our loans.

"How were tours today?"

It takes me half a second to decide to lie to him.

"Great. Mr. Goodman found his people."

Dad lights up. "Fantastic! Got his number?"

"He knows you'll be calling."

"And you finished your college spreadsheet this morning? Safety, target, and reach, like we talked about?"

On the calendar behind him, today's date is circled in red: *College Plans Finalized.*

I start senior year in a week, and applications aren't due until, like, January. But Dad lives for these made-up mini-deadlines. Getting me into a top college has been his hobby since I was in diapers. Deadass he used to sing me nursery rhymes about the Ivy League.

The thing is, my transcript isn't as strong as we'd hoped. Since Mom died, I've been struggling to breathe, let alone turn in my homework on time.

"I already know my first-choice school. So, yes?"

Dad puts his biscuit down. "If you're talking about Brown University, Harriet, you can't bet on it. You need to find at least six more realistic options."

My stubborn streak ignites. "So you think Brown will reject me. Is that it?"

"Your grades could be better, your attendance is poor, and you have zero extracurriculars. Brown's one of the most competitive schools in the world. You know this."

"I was in plenty of clubs and stuff before Mom. In the personal essay, I'll explain what happened."

Dad shakes his head. "You're tilting at windmills. What about LSU?"

Two years ago, Dad wouldn't've let me settle for anything less than a top-tier school. I mean, I finished ninth grade with a 4.1 and a bouquet of résumé-friendly activities: I wrote op-eds for the school newspaper, competed on the cross-country team, even founded the St. Anne's chapter of the Red Cross. I was a textbook overachiever...right up until the day Mom's cancer turned terminal.

Now, I look like a slacker on paper. But my record doesn't reflect the real me—the me I *should* be, if death hadn't come knocking.

I'm not ready to give up on one of my oldest dreams. Haven't I given up enough already?

Dad narrows his eyes. "Where did this obsession with Brown come from, anyway?"

Honestly, I don't have a great answer to that. Brown's one of the only colleges that doesn't make you take any prerequisites, which means that me and my nemesis—math—can finally part ways. And it's in the North, far away from neglected plantations and statues of Robert E. Lee. I have to believe the rage monster will chill out on the other side of the Mason-Dixon Line. Especially at a place like Brown. I've pictured myself walking its drop-dead gorgeous campus since I first Google Image–searched the word *college*. Even now, it's a stubborn dream I can't shake.

Considering Dad left a tenured position at Carnegie Mellon to restore a plantation, you'd think he'd understand a thing or two about unshakable dreams. But he's old—he has that whole salt-and-pepper thing going on. Maybe he forgot.

I change the subject. "So, I'm thinking of resurrecting Westwood's Twitter."

"Yeah?"

Dad can't hide his eagerness. He's hella jealous of those professors with a bajillion followers. Unfortunately for him, he doesn't know a tweet from a text message, so Mom always handled Westwood's social media, posting special events news and deleting comments from spelling-challenged trolls.

"I'm thinking of it, anyway," I say softly.

The truth is, Mom's old accounts, bursting with love for all things Westwood, never fail to devastate me.

Dad nods, but he's frowning, not really listening.

"Uh—Dad?"

"Sorry." He shakes his head. "I got a call today. About Belle Grove."

I brace myself. "What's the deal with all that construction? Did you find out what's going on?"

"I found out."

"*And?* Dad, the suspense is killing me."

I swear to God, when he looks at me, it's like he's telling me Mom died all over again. It happened in the middle of the night and neither of us was there. The hospital didn't call us like they promised. They said she just slipped away.

What's messed up is that to this day, I can't remember the last thing she said to me. I've searched every file inside my head, but it's 404s.

"An actress—Claudia Hartwell—is moving into Belle Grove Plantation. That's why we've been hearing all that construction. My friend at the county clerk's office says she purchased it under a commercial license." He squints at me. "Do you understand what that means?"

I don't, but Dad's just started talking to me like I'm a grown-up, and I want to keep that going.

"It's bad?"

"According to Toni at city hall, they're turning it into an event venue."

Shit. I'd guessed Belle Grove might become a bed-and-breakfast, but this is worse. It's one thing to stay in a not-so-woke historical hotel; it's a whole other thing to go to an old plantation, once home to thousands of enslaved people, *to party.*

"Are you sure?"

"It's registered as a *wedding* venue, specifically." He reaches for another wing. "Some celebrities are getting hitched there."

A special kind of cold drips into my veins, sludgy as antifreeze. It's the same feeling I get when I see a Confederate flag billowing from the back of someone's truck, or when "Sweet Home Alabama" comes on the radio. The feeling is hopelessness. The conviction that despite all the work we do at Westwood, nothing will ever, ever change.

Racism will keep thriving. Police will keep brutalizing. Black people will keep dying. You can draw a straight line between what happened at plantations like Westwood and Belle Grove to the racial violence of today.

"So you'll stop them. Won't you, Dad? You'll call the mayor or something—"

"It's not so easy."

"Why not?"

"This actress is about to be our neighbor, and what she does with the property is up to her. She'll inherit Belle Grove's historical legacy, just like we inherited Westwood's."

I gape at him. "That can't be right."

"I'm afraid it is."

In my stomach, the zappetizers congeal into zludge.

"What if *we* buy Belle Grove? We'll expand the museum, tell new stories—"

"We can't possibly take out any more loans. And besides, it's no longer for sale."

"But *an event venue*? How can that happen? People can't just do what they want to the 9/11 Memorial. They can't just up and buy it to throw parties."

Dad winces like he's swallowed a needle. "There're thousands of plantations across the South. We can't possibly save them all."

"But this one's right next door! Our people would've known those people. Anna and George and Samuel and Louisa...they wouldn't want this. Right?"

"There's nothing I can do about this actress's plans."

"It's an atrocity."

"Yes. And we've got to make our peace with it."

How can he give up so easily?

"But—*Dad*—"

He reaches for my hand. "You've got to be smart with your anger, Harriet. Or it'll get the best of you."

On the verge of panic, I breathe with my diaphragm, just like Dr. Maples taught me. Big breath in, big breath out.

If I squint, I can almost understand why white folks want to get married on a plantation. At Westwood, green fields span seemingly endless acres, ancient oaks form shady passages, and columned, white buildings rise on hilltops like triumph. You can walk for miles beneath a bright blue sky, hearing the trees rustle and the churn of the water—the mighty Mississippi. These plantations are achingly beautiful, if you can just forget about all those troublesome centuries when Black folks weren't considered fully human.

But blood was spilled across that endless green. Thousands of enslaved people suffered to build these white mansions, and before that, the land itself was brutally stolen from the Indigenous tribes by German farmers. The true history of a plantation is violence, plain and simple. Why would you want to get married in a place where the ground still screams?

"You said celebrities are getting hitched at Belle Grove. Anyone I'd know?"

"Couple of actors," he says. "Sunny Blake and Randy White."

My jaw drops. Those aren't *celebrities*; they're straight-up *movie stars*. Sunny snagged a role in that addictive CW show, and Randy plays freaking Marvel superheroes. Even I know they're one of the hottest couples in Hollywood.

A headache throbs behind my eyes; that's the rage monster, sending up a flare.

"You can't let them go through with it, Dad."

"I'm a historian, not an activist. Now, if your mother were here..."

"If my mother were here, what?" All my hope's knocking at my throat. "What would she do?"

Professor Douglass straightens to his full height—he's six foot four, and if I had a dollar for every white person who's asked if he plays pro basketball, I'd be richer than God. Gathering our plates, he doesn't look at me. I want to scream that he can't let this happen. There are exactly three enslaved people's museums in the whole damned South, and we're one of them. It's a huge responsibility. But Dad's already pulling that heavy metal gate across his ability to feel, shuttering his wounded soul.

"Magic." The spoon, scraping our empty plates, sounds like grief. "That's what your Mom would do."

CHAPTER 3

HORROR MOVIES ARE my weed.

I switch them on to zone out. According to Dr. Maples, it's a coping mechanism. Mostly, I stream psychological suspense like *The Others* or *Get Out*, though I won't say no to a creepy space flick or exorcism movie.

Anyway, horror helps, especially in the evening, when a terrible silence echoes throughout this house.

When Mom was alive, she'd start each night off with the same song: "The Impossible Dream" from *Man of La Mancha*, sung by Brian Stokes Mitchell. Like a sacred ritual, she always played the soaring ballad before pouring herself a glass of wine.

To dream the impossible dream . . . to fight the unbeatable foe . . .

Since she's been gone, the silence left behind is haunting. I fill it with horror movies; Dad eats junk food until he falls asleep.

A Korean thriller churns on my laptop while I scroll social media, taking my mind off what's happening to Belle Grove. My phone is like the sunken place. I fall in headfirst, and a half hour later, I can't even remember what I came here to do. TikTok's memorized all my rabbit holes, and the app feeds me just enough dopamine to keep me scrolling until something gives me body horror. (Like: Truly, what thoughtcrime have I committed to deserve a tour of this dude's moldy bathroom?)

While the movie's legit terrifying soundtrack thunders in my bones, my best friend in the whole world shoots me a text.

I turn the volume down on my computer, but don't shut it off. Even texting, I can't stand the quiet.

Sonya:
buona serata, Errichetta!
did you hear St. Anne's is getting a new senior?
some girl from LA?

Sonya's studying abroad in Italy. She applied for our school's World Adventures Scholarship last year, and flew out a week ago to settle in with her home-study family. I couldn't be prouder of her, but Lord, do I miss her.

Me:
a new girl? fr?

We rarely get new students at our tiny Catholic school, where tuition costs exactly one black-market kidney per year.

Stomach sinking, I connect the dots.

New girl. New neighbor.

New atrocity.

On my laptop's screen, the protagonist screams. Shit's going down.

Me:
hold up
last name Hartwell?

Sonya:
since when do you have hot tea?

I sit up in bed and dial her number, even though neither of us digs voice calls.

Alarmed, Sonya answers right away.

"Oh my God, what's the matter?"

In one breath, I tell her about Claudia Hartwell buying Belle Grove, and the sinister celebrity wedding.

"Let me fire up my Google finger," she says.

We Google together, and somehow, what we find is way scarier than the horror movie swooping into its bloody denouement. Claudia Hartwell's an ex-soap star, and her daughter, Layla, is an influencer—a real one, with sponsors like Fabletics and Peloton. Her mom's already set up a website for *Belle Grove Antebellum Weddings & Events.*

There's also a linked Instagram account: *@Antebellum_Weddings.*

Gross.

"This Hartwell lady is everything I hate about planet Earth," I mutter. "Like the climate apocalypse can't come soon enough."

"*Oh buon Dio*, her daughter's got enough followers to shut down a server farm."

Frowning, I click around her page. "This Layla seems like a jerk. Look at her, pretending to eat a bagel on her yoga mat."

"But Harriet, she's *gorgeous.*"

Sonya uses the tone of someone saying: *The call is coming from inside the house.*

Layla Hartwell, daughter of Claudia, is objectively beautiful in the way of coltish white girls everywhere: her skin pale, her hair blond, and her eyes glittering blue. She's as effervescent and wide-eyed as a Disney princess. All of her posts are tagged in Los Angeles, where she appears to live a perfect life surrounded by other pretty size zeroes. So why the hell is she moving here, to Louisiana, in her senior year of high school?

"I'm getting strong Blake Lively vibes from the daughter," Sonya says. "You?"

I scroll past Layla's *What I Eat in a Day*, her skin-care routine, and at least a thousand discount codes for weight-loss gummies. With every click, I'm navigating ever deeper toward despair.

"They're gonna love this girl at St. Anne's."

"You don't know that," Sonya says.

But I do.

St. Anne's is a supersmall, superwhite private school—and Sonya and I are the only Black girls in our grade. Though we've been there for years, teachers still confuse our names. I'm light-skinned and heavyset, with natural hair; Sonya's darker, thin as a rail, and in love with the weaves she gets at Ayana's Twist and Shout. We literally look nothing alike, but racism doesn't care.

Outside my window, the wilds tangle with the sunset, turning a dark, misty green. A half mile to the east, Westwood ends—and Belle Grove begins. For better or worse, Dad trained me to have a historian's imagination. When I close my eyes, I can hear the shouts of men and women next door, breaking their bodies in the cutting season; I can feel the desperate thrum in the captive air.

I mute my movie. Even Korean horror can't help me now.

"Obviously, people are garbage," Sonya says. "But Earth is a trash fire on a time limit. In thirty years, we won't have to worry about any of this. We'll all be running from, like, the cockroach tsunamis full-time."

Sonya always knows how to make me feel better.

"True. I'm still sad about it, though."

"Your dad can't do anything?"

"Can't, or won't."

Sonya makes an understanding noise. "Wish I were there, *Errichetta*."

"Don't say that. You've always wanted to be an international woman of mystery."

Sonya giggles. "Italian architecture is out of this world. The boys, too. Only thing I can't get over is this jet lag. I should be asleep right now."

"Your host family still cool?"

"Yeah, but they're killing my waistline…one perfect linguine at a time."

"Worth it."

"Damn straight it is."

From the Belle Grove website, a pop-up springs at me like an undead evil clown, asking if I want to sign up for *all the latest plantation destination news!*

"Sometimes I wonder if white people come from another planet," I grumble. "I mean, is it even possible to be friends with one?"

"Um, yeah," Sonya says sharply. "You've got, like, an avalanche of white friends at St. Anne's. So do I."

I bite my lip, knowing it isn't true.

At least, not anymore.

When I was younger, I was pretty chill, if you can believe it. I didn't let it bother me when Sandy, a classic blond cheerleader type, came back from Jamaica with cornrows in eighth grade; I shrugged off Asher's weird obsession with the word *bet*; and I didn't make a stink when Morgan started crushing exclusively on Black reality stars, like some kind of Kardashian. But after Mom died, all my patience unraveled. I can't control my anger around other people anymore. At this point, there's not a white kid at St. Anne's that I haven't managed to alienate, insult, or ignore.

"Hey, I have an idea." Sonya sounds dangerously optimistic. "Why don't you join prom committee this year?"

I snort. "What about me says *prom committee member* to you?"

"Well, the committee picks the prom venue, you know. And I don't want to be dancing at the zoo like last year."

Sonya's returning from Italy in time for prom; it'll be her last big St. Anne's event before graduation day.

"Also, it'd be good for you to get back to being social. People understood you didn't want to go out last year, but if this year's the same? They'll start to take offense."

My skin heats, prickling. Why should the St. Anne's kids get to decide how long I'm allowed to grieve?

"Don't you miss your old life? Your mom's been gone a year, and I'm in Italy. You have to hang with other people. You can't be a shut-in forever."

"I'm not a shut-in."

"Oh yeah? Who do you talk to besides me?"

Fair point.

"You used to love hanging out with our grade. Everyone's still really cool."

"They were never *cool*, I just had more chill. Did you forget about Chase's obsession with white rap?"

"Okay, fine, *some* of the St. Anne's kids can be annoying. But they're trying. That's what counts."

"Since when do you defend—wait." Now I know what this is about. "You're not still dating Graham, are you? *Long distance?*"

"Honestly?" Her delighted laugh is a death knell. "Sort of."

I sigh.

My best friend's been crushing on this boy, Graham Lucien, since forever. Last spring, they finally hooked up. I tried to warn her that St. Anne's is not the kind of place where it's cool to swirl, but Sonya shrugged it off. Then she jetted off to her study abroad, and I assumed—incorrectly, it turns out—that the distance would stop the relationship in its tracks.

In my chest, dark emotions gather like a storm cloud, a thunderhead of bitterness, jealousy, and wild, misdirected rage.

"Next time you talk to Graham"—I swear it's the rage monster talking, not me—"ask if he'd ever party on a plantation."

Sonya's shocked silent; my heart races, realizing what I've said.

"Holy shit, Harriet," Sonya murmurs. "You can really be the worst, you know that? Graham wouldn't party at a plantation, *not in a million years*, because *white people aren't all the same.* Get outta here with that! What would your mom say?"

Mom was all about building bridges. She had tons of friends of all races, and she never said anything as hateful as what just came flying out of my mouth.

"I'm sorry." My heart's still sprinting. "I don't know what came over me."

"Okay, Harriet? You know I love you. But."

My stomach twists.

"I can't let you be a jerk about my boyfriend. I talked to him yesterday. If he knew you thought such awful things about him…"

Oh my God. Has Graham been calling Sonya, too? How often are *they* talking? When did I become my best friend's second-choice person?

"Errichetta?"

I snap out of it.

I don't want to fight with Sonya, and I don't want her worrying about how I'll treat Graham Lucien while she should be practicing her Italian. Sonya's one of St. Anne's few scholarship students, and one day, she'll be a political science major at Yale studying to become a US diplomat. She's gonna make it happen, too. She'll travel the whole world in sleek black pantsuits, or I'm a buffalo wing.

"I'm sorry. This year *will* be different, I swear." I suck in a shuddering breath. "Harriet Douglass is officially turning over a new leaf."

"Well, good."

An uncomfortable quiet stretches between us, and regret floods me. For a year while my mother was dying, and another year after we buried her, I've been the flakiest possible friend, making plans and then canceling them, hiding in my house like I'm afraid of the light. I want to believe that I'll do better this year, but it's hard to get back to the world after shutting it out for so long. Like the door to my old life rusted with disuse, and now, it's stuck fast.

Miserable, I press my cheek against the phone, leaning against my last, best friend. "I really wish you could come over tonight."

"Me too. I'll be there in spirit. Okay?"

Lonely tears well up; I slam them down.

"Ciao, bella," she says.

"Ciao, Son."

After we hang up, I stare a little longer at the Belle Grove website.

Claudia Hartwell, the ex-soap star, smiles wide in her bio. I lap up the schadenfreude of her disastrously micro-bladed eyebrows.

This lady can't possibly understand what she's doing, turning Belle Grove into a fantasy wedding playground. She can't know what kind of history she's trampling on. Mom said it's the education system that's to blame. The lady just doesn't know. Right?

On the other hand, education didn't help Vacation Karen.

What would Mom do? I asked Dad.

And he said: *Magic.*

I know exactly what he means.

In fourth grade, when I started at St. Anne's, I was basically an outcast. It's tough being the new kid in a southern town, and even tougher when you're bussing in from the poorest stretch of road in all Louisiana. So one day, Mom hosted a welcome breakfast in our chapel. She invited my whole class, and about half of them came: Graham, Asher, Sandy, Morgan, and Chase. We were there to dedicate a memorial. Beneath an inscription in remembrance of slavery, my classmates pressed their handprints into molding clay, contributing to one of Westwood's most important exhibits.

Working with us helps them get over their guilt, Mom said. *This way, they'll understand that we're not just here to tear their monuments down. We're here to help them erect new ones.*

After that, I wasn't just the weirdo who lived at a museum. I had friends. *Good* ones. Even if they weren't perfect, racism-wise.

Now I flop down onto my bed, clasping my hands behind my head.

Dad thinks we can't stop the Hartwells, but he's wrong. My blood sparkles with the kind of hopes that can only ever lead to disappointment. I let them fizz, because it's better than the alternative. When Mom was dying, I did the same thing—hoping against hope until the very end, dreaming the impossible dream.

Dr. Maples has a word for this kind of thinking.

She calls it *denial*.

CHAPTER 4

M Y THERAPIST SHRINKS heads from a pretty French gallery house in Jefferson Parish. Like all old houses in this town, it's on the national historical register and probably haunted. I haven't read up on it, because if I were to find out that it was once home to an infamous slave trader or something, I wouldn't have any choice but to keep seeing Dr. Maples. Dad insists that I see the best, and Dr. Maples is the city's *premier pediatric grief therapist specializing in cancer trauma.*

She's also, unsurprisingly, white.

I have to take the bus into town. Since Mom died, I don't drive. Not ever. Behind the wheel, anxiety grips me, but what happens next is worse. Driving, someone will inevitably cut me off. After that—and this is 100 percent true—I see red.

According to secondhand reports, I roll down my window and start yelling, cursing, and pounding the horn. Sonya's seen it, and so has Dad. But I can't remember any of it to save my life. Last summer, Dad took away my license to keep me from getting arrested or worse.

Obviously, raging out on the road is, like, terminally entitled—and, trust me, I hate this side of myself. I've always had a temper—Mom used to call me Baby Alligator, because I got so snappy—but I never blacked out before the rage monster showed up. I'm pretty sure she came fuming into my life on the last day I ever saw my mother alive. Now she's settled into the space behind my sternum, and there's never an exorcist around when you need one. Only psychiatrists.

Then again, maybe blaming Mom's death for this rage is taking the easy way out. Like, what if I also wound up living with the rage monster in the alternate timeline where Mom's still alive? What if Irrationally Angry Black Girl Making a Scene at Walmart is just my personality?

I press Dr. Maples's buzzer once, twice.

My eyes linger on the red bricks beneath my feet. Enslaved people hand-produced the bricks that line these streets, which is why they're slightly misshapen, each one unique. Most people don't know that, or care to know. But Dad always says that a true understanding of history is like having a sixth sense: *I see dead people.*

There would be no New Orleans without slavery. No state of Louisiana. No United States, either.

The door's intercom shrieks like a banshee, and I march into Dr. Maples's office. As always, she's waiting for me in her wing-backed chair. Two fun facts about my psychiatrist: I've never seen her smile, and I've never seen her stand up, either. I guess she's comfy enough right where she is.

"How are you, Harriet?"

"Honestly? Not great."

I can't stop thinking about Belle Grove and the actress planning to desecrate it. It's like a furnace has opened up inside me. I want to tell Dr. Maples how torn up I feel, but I'm not sure she'd understand.

Dr. Maples is the whitest woman I've ever met. We're talking, like, translucent. Sitting beside a box of Kleenex and a small glass clock, I feel like I'm in the TV show version of a therapist's office. There's a diploma from Yale mounted like treasure on her wall, a Belle Epoque chandelier twinkling elegantly overhead, and an unlikable Klimt painting (a white woman's wearing, like, a very complex carpet?) that's probably supposed to make me think about the unconscious or something. Anyway, it's so boring it stings my eyes.

Or maybe I'm just disappointed that Dr. Maples definitely won't care about Belle Grove as much as I do. How could she? Whiteness is more than color. It's an honest-to-God way of life.

Beside me, the glass clock ticks.

"I take it the breathing exercises haven't been working for you."

"Yeah, no. And the grounding technique? Turns out, it doesn't work at an enslaved people's museum."

I'm trying to make a joke, but Dr. Maples doesn't smile.

In all the months I've known her, she's *never* smiled. Frankly, it's unsettling.

"We haven't found the right coping techniques. We'll keep trying."

"You say that every session."

My words come out harder than I meant, and her eyes lock with mine.

"What's bothering you today, Harriet?"

"An actress is buying Belle Grove plantation. That's the property next door. It's an old sugarcane farm, same as Westwood."

She raises pencil-thin eyebrows. "I see."

"She's turning it into a *wedding venue*. Like enslaved people didn't die there. Like it's okay to play make-believe with that part of history."

"And how does that make you feel?"

Yeah. Therapists actually say that in real life.

"It makes me *feel* like white people ruin everything. Like no matter how hard we work at Westwood, nothing will ever change."

"And is it up to you to keep white people from 'ruining everything'?"

"Not me *personally*. But slavery museums in general? Yeah, I'd say that's kind of the point."

Dr. Maples holds her poker face; the creature that lives in my belly growls.

Uh-oh.

Dr. Maples has never seen me Hulk out before, but I didn't sleep well last night and...well, I can't actually control it.

"Does your work at the plantation weigh heavily on you, Harriet? Do you ever have trouble sleeping, or focusing on your goals?"

Because she's determined to hit a nerve, the rage monster starts throwing things.

"I want to be a historian. Westwood Plantation *is* my goal. Essentially."

"When we first met—" She flips through her notepad. "You told me that you wanted to attend Brown University for undergrad and then pursue a doctorate in history. That's a demanding career path."

My vision narrows. The rage monster's now rocking out to death metal, and with every passing second, she cranks the volume louder.

"You think I'm not up to it?"

"My concern is that every time you visit me, you express angst related to Westwood. Specifically, the behavior of white visitors—which you can't control." She frowns. "You have to draw boundaries. Or you'll burn out."

You've got to be smart with your anger, Dad said. *Or it'll get the best of you.*

"Look, I've seen this kind of thing before. The Hartwells will hire Black waiters to serve appetizers at white weddings. They'll pretend the whole history of slavery was just a glossy, rich person's dream. It's offensive to me. It *should* be offensive to everyone. How the hell am I supposed to draw boundaries when my neighbor's hawking one-hundred-proof racism?"

"Perhaps the Hartwells will approach their work respectfully."

"*How?* What could possibly be respectful about what they're doing?"

"You can't tell the future. You're thinking catastrophically when—"

I leap to my feet. "It *is* a catastrophe! Why can't you understand!"

I'm not sure how it happens, but in the next second, Dr. Maples's glass clock hits the Klimt, shattering into shards.

I clap my hand over my mouth. If I didn't know better, I'd think a poltergeist had done this violent, awful thing. Not me.

Oh my God. Will she throw me out? Have I finally flunked therapy, just like I'm flunking everything else?

Dr. Maples is as still as stone.

"How did you feel just now, when you threw the clock?"

"I didn't—" The broken shards stare up at me, accusing. "I don't remember doing it."

Dr. Maples's head snaps up. "You don't remember? Like your road incidents?"

Collapsing back into my chair, I bury my face in my hands.

"I want to take us back to your first amnesiac event. Were you angry then?"

She's talking about my last conversation with Mom. Which I don't remember.

"I was never angry at Mom. She was, like, the perfect human."

Her eyebrows rise. "No one's perfect."

I'm shaking, shivering like I always do after an episode.

"Harriet." She leans forward, concerned. "Three deep breaths."

I take them, long and deep, and when I'm done I'm so ashamed. Toddlers throw tantrums; I'm almost eighteen. If I can't fix the rage monster, what will happen to me?

For what feels like eternity, neither of us speaks. I run a quick calculation while Dr. Maples studies me. These sessions cost three hundred dollars an hour—every penny coming straight out of Dad's second mortgage. Three hundred divided by sixty is...and divided again...

Forget it. I can't with math.

"We *will* find the right technique to manage your anger," Dr. Maples says at last. "You just have to trust me."

"I try every exercise." I need Dr. Maples to know I'm not some spoiled, hopeless little jerk. "Last night, I even tried journaling again."

"And how did that go?"

Desperate to vent, I wrote about helping my parents restore the plantation as a kid, crying most nights but feeling part of something, too. Then I had a nightmare about Claudia Hartwell (and her micro-bladed eyebrows), huffing and puffing and blowing the whole house down.

"I don't think journaling helped."

"What about medication? Are you willing to try an antidepressant?"

I flinch; Dr. Maples notices.

"What are you feeling right now?"

"Mom took all the meds under the sun. And there were always side effects, and meds to treat the side effects, which created more side effects. Nausea, skin peeling, crippling fatigue. I've seen it all."

"You don't trust medication. Is that what you're saying?"

For some reason, my belly tightens. "I guess."

"Trust is a big issue for you."

With one shoulder, I shrug.

"Antidepressants are highly effective for many people suffering from complex PTSD—and in general, there are few side effects. But I won't push you. In your case, I truly believe talk therapy and coping skills will benefit you most."

"Maybe we could just use meds, like, until I start college? Then I could stop?"

"Why do you assume you won't still need medication in college?"

I exhale. "Everything will be better when I'm at Brown."

When I'm at Brown, I said. Like that school's not a huge reach.

"How, exactly?"

My eyes wander to the perfect future in my imagination, hemmed in by stone towers and emerald-green grass. Brown University is in Providence, Rhode Island, well and truly out of the blast radius of the toxic South. I won't know who fired the bricks I walk on—maybe I won't even care. I'll be a calmer person up North. I have to be.

"Harriet, have you ever heard the phrase: Wherever you go, there you are?"

"Is this a riddle? Like you can't ever step in the same river twice?"

"It means your external circumstances aren't responsible for your reactions. *You're* responsible."

Funny how that rings hollow. Wealthy and white as she is, what external circumstances could possibly get Dr. Maples down?

My therapist sighs. "Our time's up, but I do want you to try a new technique this week: mindfulness meditation. Okay?"

"School starts tomorrow."

"There's an app. You only need ten minutes a day. Can you commit to try it for one week?"

Therapy is exhausting, and I hate trying new things only to fail. But at this point, what choice do I have?

"Sure."

Dr. Maples rises from her chair, moving to clean up the broken clock. To my surprise, she stumbles, limping.

Finally, I understand why she always stays seated.

Feeling like the slime behind the refrigerator, I hurry to help her, scooping shards into my bare hands. I dump the remains into a wastebasket. Then, awkwardly, I extend my arm to Dr. Maples. She leans into me as I help her to her wing-backed chair. She's light, birdlike—and as unsmiling as ever.

"I'm really sorry about this."

"Apology accepted."

"Why do you—" I frown. Is *limp* an offensive term? "What happened?"

"Pediatric bone cancer." She's buried her nose in her notes; she doesn't look up again. "See you next week."

Cancer.

I want to ask, *Did it hurt, like Mom's?*

And, *Did you get into therapy to help others survive what you did?*

And, *How do you turn your pain into something good—without losing your mind?*

In the end, I leave without saying anything at all.

My phone pings an alert in the waiting room.

Vacation Karen finally left that Yelp review.

> I'd give this place zero stars if I could!!! Totally
> unprofessional...terrible customer service...the
> tour guide was SO full of hate...I was ATTACKED...
> they'll be hearing from my lawyer...

A sick sweat trickles down my sides, knowing I messed up big-time. Lately, it seems I always do.

Because I can't stand to look that cold, hard fact in the face, I think about Belle Grove all the way to the bus depot, my feet striking brick.

All my rage, huddled in its dark, forbidding cave, focuses its burning gaze on this one travesty: that damned celebrity wedding, mocking everything I believe in, every truth that I hold to be self-freaking-evident.

There's got to be a way to stop this runaway train, despite what Dad says—though for the life of me, I can't think of one.

But I mean: It's 2022.

How hard can it be to cancel a *plantation*?

CHAPTER 5

O N THE FIRST day of school, the kitchen's a disaster zone.

All weekend long, Dad's been chowing down on every species of fast food: We've got KFC, Taco Bell, Popeyes, and Burger King, all representing up in this kitchen because Dad was too depressed to throw the wrappers away. The air in here smells as salty as a locker room.

I grab a KFC bag and stuff the remnants of old meals inside. Every few days, I find myself doing this: cleaning up the filthy kitchen because my poor dad won't. Or can't.

Who says I'm the only one in this family who needs therapy?

I'm nearly done when the front door slams. Dad must've hit up the drive-through again for breakfast. He stamps into the kitchen, fresh McDonald's in hand. His T-shirt asks: WHERE DID PETER THE GREAT GET HIS COFFEE FROM?

The answer (God save us): TSARBUCKS.

By the scowl on his face, I'm positive he's seen Karen's Yelp review.

"Harriet."

"Dad—"

"No." He cuts me off. "Today's the day. We're gonna visit your mother on your first day of school. No arguments. It was always a special day to her."

I clutch the fast-food sack. "No. I don't want to go."

Mom's buried in Westwood's northern field—and it's beyond weird that her body is so close to home. I don't know why Dad couldn't bury her in a city graveyard like a normal person, but for my part, I haven't been back to her grave since the funeral. Even walking in that direction, my blood pressure spikes.

Dad, on the other hand, never misses a day.

"Just come with me, Harriet. Your mom would've been so excited for you."

The past conditional tense kills me.

With more force than strictly necessary, I chuck the trash into the garbage can. Then my eye snags on the tea towel slung over the faucet.

Mom's tea towel, decorated with dancing narwhals.

A sound explodes in my head, a Nolan foghorn full of dread: *BAH-HHM.*

I rip the towel from the faucet; it comes away damp.

Goddamn it, Dad. "Um, why the *hell* is this here?"

"Language. And it's a kitchen towel. Where else should it be?"

My hand clenches, wrinkling the silly smiling narwhals. Mom purchased a set back when I was a little girl obsessed with unicorns, while she preferred mermaids. She decided narwhals were a good compromise, calling them "the unicorns of the sea." She cleaned our counters with these silly towels for years. After she died, I put them on the high shelf with our good china. There, I thought, they would be safe.

Now it's the first day of school, and my eyes already burn with grief.

"You can't use these towels, Dad. You of all people know how fragile textiles are. They rarely last a decade."

Gently, he takes the towel from my clenched hand. "I'd forgotten all about these."

"How could you forget?"

My father's brown eyes are steady, sad, and deep. The thing about dead people is that no one remembers them in the same exact way. The Mom of my memory is not my father's late remembered wife; since her death, Mom's no longer an objective self, but a relative entity. She exists only in relation to me, to Dad, to her friends and family.

In other words, she's *history*.

And I hate this fact so freaking much.

"Many things in this house remind me of her," Dad says. "The television set, the love seat, the birdhouse, the tire swing."

"The tire swing? That thing's barely hanging on."

"It's in need of a full restoration. And these tea towels—they need a tombstone. Don't you think?"

My head rocks back, wondering if Dad's lost his mind.

He snaps open his briefcase, pulling out a folder full of small, sturdy cards: labels. In the museum business, we call them *tombstones*. There are at least a hundred of them scattered about Westwood, marking relics of times gone by: sugar drums and cutting shears, sackcloth dresses and iron cookware.

"Tea towels, circa 2010," Dad narrates, while writing in Sharpie. "Crosshatch fibers. Fanciful narwhal design. Representative of a mother's love."

He hands the card to me, and my whole body softens. Tonight, I'll wash the towel by hand and put it back on the high shelf—with its tombstone this time.

"Take some blank ones, too. In case you want to mark anything else."

I'm so grateful. Sometimes, Dad just gets me.

"Baby, are you sure you don't want to visit your mom today? She'd love—"

UGH. "Stop, Dad. Just stop."

His face falls. "But why?"

I can't tell him it's the rage monster. She always rushes in when I'm scared, and Mom's grave scares me more than anything. If I visit that spot today, there's, like, a one in ten chance I'll morph into a supervillain hell-bent on destroying planet Earth.

And I need to get to school.

I head for the door; behind me, I hear Dad unwrapping his Egg McMuffin, the paper crinkling like despair.

●　●　●　●　●

On River Road, I wait for the 27 bus.

Across the street are the levees, the swamps, and the wide Missis-sippi. German settlers divided this land into parcels, which are basically pie slices that begin at the tree line and sharpen to points at the river. Westwood owns one perfect slice; the neighboring parcel belongs to Belle Grove.

In the orchard that runs along this road, colors blur together—green and sunset and violet blanketed beneath a humid haze. A lazy breeze blows, wrapping me in a memory I don't need right now: Mom and me playing tag among those trees.

I was nine when we moved to Westwood to build the enslaved people's museum. In our first year, Mom and I spent every minute together. I hung out with her while she made phone calls to construction companies and sculptors. Because we couldn't live in the Big House—seriously bad vibes—we camped out in the orchard while our new hous-ing went up.

In the mornings, we froze our asses off. While Dad cooked breakfast over a campfire, Mom and I played tag to warm up, running as hard as we could.

Got you! Mom would say, breath curling. *Can't catch me!*

When the peaches ripened, Mom ordered over a hundred laundry baskets from Amazon. We still collect peaches in those same mint-green hampers. Naima, my dad's research assistant, sells the fruit in the gift shop, and Dad gives the rest to Auntie Yates. Every year, she bakes our harvest into an improbable number of bitter-tart pies.

"Never want to sweeten these too much," Auntie Yates told me once. "These peach trees have stood since slave times. Our ancestors ate this same fruit, and I assure you their lives didn't have much sweetness."

Auntie Yates's pies taste of mournful memory, but as a historian I wonder how many peaches Westwood's enslaved people were truly able to eat.

Westwood's people received most of their meals in a metal trough. Even the children weren't afforded the dignity of a table, a plate, and a fork. It's one of the details that's almost too terrible to think about—master enslavers treating Black folks like livestock—but that's what makes it so important to share with our tour groups. When it remains abstract, horror's hard to catch hold of. Misty as a dream and all too easy to forget.

Finally, the bus rumbles down the wide gold road.

Reverberating in my head are Sonya's wishes: that I don't hide from life anymore, that I reconnect with our old friends. And she's right. I ought to make an effort. I've been a bitter recluse for way too long.

No more angry Harriet, I promise myself. *No more rage monster.*

With this mantra in mind, I tighten my backpack's straps, tug down the hem of my plaid skirt, and wait for a new year to begin.

CHAPTER 6

S T. ANNE'S IS an obscenely beautiful Catholic school in Metairie, the city just outside New Orleans. Its gilt iron gates and marble floors are the stuff of legend among Louisiana's private schools. Even I have to admit, this bastion of privilege sure is beautiful.

Of course, the people inside are mostly white—with a smattering of diversity for the brochures. Low-key racism aside, I've gotten a solid education here. I'll never be any great shakes at math, but I can write a mean ten-page paper. And I've always felt happiest surrounded by lots of Post-it notes, to the point where Mom used to worry.

"Go outside!" she'd holler. "Catch a fish or something!"

But like Dad, I prefer books to fishing hooks and a solid thesis to bait. My freshman year, while I studied like a demon for exams, he slipped me a bottle of vitamin D supplements.

"Scholars rarely get sufficient sunlight, so let's own that," he said.

Then, as an afterthought: "Don't tell your mom."

I'm not always happy at St. Anne's. It's hard to be "the only one" in most of my classes, and after years of leading Westwood tours, I know what too many white people think of me behind their smiles. Sonya says I'm too cynical, but I'm just being realistic. It's safer, emotionally speaking, to assume the worst from people. Hoping for the best is where you get yourself into trouble.

Unfortunately, that attitude is also why I spend most nights alone.

For three hours in St. Anne's hallowed halls, I don't hear a peep from my rage monster. Then the bell rings for AP American History, and I officially meet Layla Hartwell of *Belle Grove Antebellum Weddings & Events*.

She breezes into class, perching gracefully in the seat next to mine. She really *is* prettier IRL, willowy and impossibly blond, with an aura of... famousness, I guess. She wears it like a filter.

I wonder if she's moved into Belle Grove yet.

Wonder, too, if she has any idea that plantation weddings are not okay.

Luckily, I'm not blazing with rage anymore. On the bus, I practiced meditating with the mindfulness app. It calmed me down so much I almost missed my stop.

Now, the whole class bends toward the new girl like a tree toward sunlight. It's a small seminar, and I've known everyone but Layla for years: There's Graham, Sonya's boyfriend, who's baby-faced and white like Wonder Bread. He wants to be a journalist, and he published several of my op-eds in the school paper before I shrank into my grieving shell. Then there's Morgan, a girl with a pixie cut who's obsessed with the goblincore aesthetic. For years, she's been foraging in the swamps and filling her pockets with mushrooms.

And of course Asher's here—so far as I know, there's not an AP class in the universe he isn't taking. He's Jewish and gay (a real double whammy at a Catholic school), and probably the person in this room I trust the most, because our mothers were friends. He tears his eyes from Layla long enough to say, "Hey, Harriet, where've you been hiding? Want to go for a jog after school?"

Grief blindsides me, remembering what it was like to run with Asher. But those days, before Mom got sick, seem so long ago now—my old, carefree self lost forever.

"No thanks, Ash. You have fun, though."

Out of the corner of my eye, I see him sag.

Meanwhile, Sandy Chase, this year's prom queen contender, is looking understandably wary of the new competition. Her boyfriend, confusingly, is named Chase, and though academics aren't his strong suit, he goes wherever Sandy goes. Currently, he's staring fixedly at Layla Hartwell's chest.

For my part, I'm studying her hands, which she holds limply at the wrist even as she pecks at her phone.

"Hey," she murmurs in my general direction, fingers tapping.

Phones aren't allowed in class, but Dr. Heidel isn't here yet. I can't exactly hate her for breaking the rules everyone breaks.

But I *can* hate the tattoo on her wrist: *Live, laugh, love.*

How cliché can you get?

Layla Hartwell catches me staring. "It's the worst, right? I pretend it's post-ironic, but honestly, I just got wasted and made a bad decision."

I'm dying to ask this new girl about Belle Grove, and where the hell she gets off living in that house of suffering. But of course, I can't speak to her: The rage monster might hear. And this is my most important class.

My lifelong dream is to study history at Brown. The problem is, Brown U admits less than 1 percent of its applicants, and there are tens of thousands each year. I need straight As in all my APs, but especially this one. How would it look if I didn't ace the class I want to major in?

Legs crossed primly at the ankles, Layla leans toward me. "What's your name?"

I answer reflexively. "Harriet."

She sticks out one limp hand. "Layla Hartwell."

I stare hexes at her until she drops that hand. Confusion clouds her offensively symmetrical face.

Then Dr. Heidel blows into the room, and I put my phone down just in time.

Our history teacher is the scholarly, brilliant, overeducated type. Today, he's dressed in a brown velvet cardigan with elbow patches.

I've actually met Dr. Heidel twice at Westwood's fundraisers. At the Annual Donor's Cocktail Party, I found out that he attended Brown for undergrad. When Dad told him that I was applying there, he clapped me on the back like the good old boys do. Considering the poor state of my college application, I'm really hoping he'll write me a strong letter of recommendation.

I've been waiting *forever* to take Dr. Heidel's class. In fact, I've structured my entire schedule around it, ditching AP Anatomy for its noncredit version. Now that I'm finally in the room, my heart picks up its beat.

"Students who are looking for an easy A," Dr. Heidel booms, "this is your cue to leave."

St. Anne's is a competitive place; you could hear a pin drop.

"In this class, we'll study American history, yes." His voice is thickly southern, full of drawls and flourishes. "But we'll also learn to use the tools of logic and rhetoric to think in new ways about modern problems."

Breathless students are already taking notes, but I keep my hands in my lap. Dad taught me long ago that it's more efficient to take mental notes during a lecture, opening and naming file folders in your mind.

Logic and Rhetoric.

Subfolder: *Modern Problems.*

"We'll learn to set aside our current frames of reference to think objectively about the past—and especially about the social structures that emerged from the trajectory of the American South. Believe me when I say you'll read history until your eyes bleed."

After watching Dad comb through Westwood's records for years, I know a thing or two about research. This is my *jam.*

"Who can tell me what the word *history* means in the original Greek?"

My hand shoots up, the answer ready on my lips: *inquiries.* Herodotus coined the word in 500 BCE. We still use history as a means of inquiry, or *understanding*, today.

Seeing me squirming, Asher mouths, *Calm down!*

But after three years of taking notes on the Official History of

Everything, I'm eager to finally practice *real* history—a discipline that's more about asking questions than memorizing facts.

"Yes, Sonya?" Dr. Heidel drawls, calling on me.

The sound of my best friend's name punches the air from my lungs.

Sonya's the only other Black girl in the senior class, but she's not even in the country right now. Everyone knows she's in Italy.

I glance behind me, just in case she's magically appeared.

Then my eyes swing back to Dr. Heidel.

Even though he's met me twice, even though I'm the daughter of another history professor, he's confused me with the only other Black girl in school.

Though I don't want to—though I never thought I'd have to—I open a new subfolder under Dr. Heidel's name: *Racist Jack-hole.*

I'm hot with anger, but also a sticky sort of shame. If I don't get out of this room, I'm going to start yelling. Or crying. Probably both.

Gathering my things, I stumble up.

"Is there a problem, Sonya?"

Okay, this is just ridiculous.

Dr. Heidel can clearly see my face—*which is not Sonya's face.* Even if there's wiggle room here, a hypothetical, totally justifiable, non-race-related reason he'd confuse my best friend and me, that's two strikes. The rage monster won't give him a third.

Go for it, she urges. *Take him to the bank!!!*

"Actually, I have a question." My throat grinds words like gravel. "What exactly are the historical roots of racial face blindness?"

Beside me, Layla Hartwell gasps.

I whirl on her, but the expression on her face isn't what I expect.

She's not shocked; she's *outraged.*

"Oh my God." She looks straight at Professor Jack-hole. "Did you get her mixed up with another Black girl?"

Dr. Heidel puffs himself up. "What are you implying?"

I've heard that tone from white people a million times. Usually on a plantation tour, when somebody takes offense. White guilt's as unstable as dynamite.

"I'm not implying anything." Layla twirls a stick-straight strand of hair. "I'm asking if you made a racist mistake. And you did, didn't you?"

Dr. Heidel's eyebrows drop. "Both of you. Out."

"*Excuse* me?" Layla cries.

"You can't speak to faculty that way. I'm writing you up." Strangely enough, Dr. Heidel's fancy drawl's disappeared. Pissed off, he sounds like any old Yankee.

"I'm down for detention." Layla cocks a thumb at me. "But why should *she* get in trouble for your microaggression?"

At the front of the class, Graham holds up his phone, recording.

Leave, I command my feet.

But I'm frozen in place.

"Consider that this is a terrible impression to make on your first day, Layla Hartwell," Heidel says—and I purse my lips, because of course he knows *her* name.

Layla rises, a sassy hand on her hip. "Um, you can just apologize for messing up, my guy. You *should* apologize. Then everything would be cool, right, Harriet? I mean, we've all internalized racism. It's not that deep."

Her bright eyes, fixed on me, are mesmerizing. *Who is this girl?*

"Yeah. An apology would be fine," I mumble.

Stupidly allowing myself to hope.

But Dr. Heidel is already striding across the room, and I know in my bones that he's about to take his guilt and frustration out on us.

How the heck did Layla Hartwell and I become an *us*?

"Security," Dr. Heidel barks into the phone on the wall—and just like that, my stomach fills with molten cement.

So much for my most important class.

CHAPTER 7

AFTER A TENSE AF meeting with St. Anne's dour principal—who, for the record, is *extremely disappointed* in both of us—security escorts us out of the goddamn building.

In case that wasn't enough, Graham captures the whole thing on his phone.

Stalking out, Layla Hartwell looks incensed and graceful, like a social justice gazelle. I'm not particularly vain, but next to her, I'm going to look dumpy on TikTok. Especially when Graham sets us to some trend.

A redheaded security guard puts his hand on my elbow, steering me out the door, and my skin ignites in protest. This is, like, forreal, forreal.

Outside, the rage monster wants me to know that *this will not stand!!! We did nothing wrong!!! Dr. Heidel needs to CHECK HIMSELF, and by the time I'm through with him he'll wish he'd never been born, because I have a very special set of skills, and I am the Terminator, and always bet on Black—*

"Principal Benoit will call your parents to pick you up," the guard says. "Stay outside the gates, and don't cause any trouble."

Then he turns away, leaving Layla and me alone on the wrong side of iron.

Fun fact: These classic southern gates, with their swirling metal and arrow-tipped heights, are ubiquitous on plantations. The pointy tips kept enslaved people from climbing them to freedom.

And there I go, seeing dead people again.

Shocked by the turn the day's taken, I groan.

Dr. Heidel is a frequent donor to Westwood's cause—a longtime supporter. But still, it turns out he harbors a whole bucket of racist attitudes, and this is exactly why I can't trust white folks, even when I want to.

I think of my old friend Asher, asking where I've been hiding.

Think of Sonya, begging me to come out of my haunted shell.

Yearning twists my heart, but I can't take any chances. It's better to be lonely than hurt again. That much is crystal freaking clear.

In the bright sunlight, Layla slouches like a runway model. Her face is what would happen if Blake Lively and Emma Stone had a kid together. Right now, I want to punch it.

There's cypress swamp ahead of us, and ten billion biting flies out for blood. My phone's already blowing up with friends, acquaintances, and even enemies wanting to know what I did—and how I know beautiful Layla Hartwell.

Did you have a gun??? Briar-from-Calculus texts. OMG did somebody DIE??

Is that racism or hyperbole? My blood pressure spikes just in case. I take three deep breaths, flicking my phone on *Do Not Disturb*.

"Well, that was harsh." Layla elbows me like what happened is no big deal. "Wanna smoke?"

The joint appears like magic in her hands, and suddenly, I know two things:

1. I'm going to strangle Layla Hartwell, and 2. They're going to tear me apart on *Forensic Files*.

"Are you kidding me right now? You just torpedoed an AP!"

She shrugs. "You're the one who brought up *racial face blindness*."

You should never point at white girls—they don't like it—but my finger shoots out anyway. "You escalated the situation."

"I did, right?" Layla giggles. "Shit, the *look* on his face!"

I vividly recall Dr. Heidel's expression when Layla called him out. For a second, I want to laugh, too.

"Wait, are you high right now?"

"I'm about to be. Come on, what's the best place to smoke around here? At this point, it's self-care."

"You know that term was co-opted from—"

"Audre Lorde. Isn't she fire?" Layla slips on a pair of sunglasses, ignoring the way my jaw dropped to my chest. "But it really is important to take care of yourself, you know?"

Layla Hartwell watches me, beaming a gentle interest that reminds me, more than anything, of Mom.

This freaking LA micro-influencer is *holding space*, and God help me, I'm going to take it.

"I've met Dr. Heidel *twice*!" I bellow loud enough to scare the birds from the trees. "He's been to my house. He—he—" I gulp back tears that taste of phlegm and misery. "And *you*! Why did you even get involved? What was the point of *that*?"

Layla shrugs. "That pretentious snob should take several seats. Who needs that class, anyway?"

"I do!" My hands fly to my hair, tugging. "*I* needed that class!"

For a moment, Layla looks crestfallen. Then she shakes her mane of hair like a pretty, pampered pony and snaps out of it.

"If you don't want a smoke, what about a hug? That always makes me feel better. I promise, in an hour, this won't feel like such a big deal."

I stare at her, spluttering.

The *audacity* of this rando from LA telling me what I need!

And yet...there's a sweetness to her that feels—genuine. Like she came from a world of rainbows and unicorns where a hug fixes everything. A planet of pure sunshine.

Layla Hartwell is NOT your friend, the rage monster growls. *Her mom's turning Belle Grove into a goddamn WEDDING VENUE.*

"I don't want a hug, and I don't want your weed. I know who you are. You're the Belle Grove girl. You're the worst of *everything*."

Elbows deep in her handbag, Layla freezes.

Sweat trickles down my spine, wondering what Layla Hartwell's like when the claws come out.

"I was lying before, when I asked your name," she says. "I know we're neighbors. I've been googling you and your dad, like, obsessively."

She's been googling *us*?

"Those trees." She gestures with the joint. "Is that a good place to talk? We don't have to smoke if you don't want to."

"Horror movies are my weed," I find myself saying.

She arches a blond eyebrow. "Do you smoke them or vape them?"

Uh-huh, yeah, I get it now: Layla Hartwell's a manic pixie dream girl.

I didn't know there were any left in the wild, but I've read enough John Green novels to know that she'll only chase me if I play hard to get.

Slipping on my backpack, I light out for the swamp. "Hope you're not scared of gators."

Delighted, Layla laughs. "How great would that be! Wildlife!"

I shoot her a sour look. "They eat dogs, you know. And other adorable pets."

"But I'm sure they don't mean to. They're just trying to live, you know?"

If any animal on earth has truly bad intentions, it's a gator. But apparently, Layla Hartwell is set on seeing the bright side of damn near everything.

"Whatever. Just please don't light that joint. I hate the smell."

"How come?"

It reminds me of cancer, of Mom smoked-out and weeping on the couch, but Layla doesn't get to know that.

"I also have Adderall, if that's how you roll?"

Oh my God. I can't even imagine the rage monster on stimulants. We'd Godzilla the world.

In the cypress swamp, leaves and vines block out the light, enfolding us in shadows intermixed with misty sparkles. I'm reminded now, as ever, that the South is gorgeous. Like, nature really understood the assignment. But as always, people have ruined this place. Bored St. Anne's kids have left plenty of evidence of their bad habits: broken beer bottles, snarled cigarettes, a condom wrapper. If this were a museum exhibit, the tombstone would read: TRASH OF THE PRIVILEGED, C. 2022.

"Okay, Layla Hartwell, let's start from the beginning. You moved from LA to turn a plantation into a wedding venue. Do I have that right?"

"The wedding thing's my mother's baby." Layla perches daintily on a rotting tree stump. "She's had this fantasy of restoring a plantation for years, like she's Scarlett O'Hara or something. When her agent dumped her, she figured, like, *carpe diem*. It's totally twisted."

"Yeah." A healthy amount of steam curls from my ears. "It is."

"So I was hoping you and I would have a class together, of course."

"Why? Because we're about to be *mortal enemies?*"

"No, grumpy," Layla pouts. "Because I know all about what you're doing with your slave museum."

My eyelid twitches. "First of all, we don't call it a *slave museum*. It's an *enslaved people's* museum—emphasis on the *people*."

"Exactly. Slaves were *people*. My mom's being such an asshole. We've had a million fights about plantations and monuments and the Deep South...it's just—look, she's never going to pull it off. I just have to humor her until she gives up."

"There's a website," I say accusingly. *"Antebellum Weddings."*

Layla blows out a breath. "The raw food restaurant she never opened also has a website. Same with the gourmet food truck and the Alzheimer's charity. It's all wishful thinking. She's got no follow-through."

"Your mom *bought* Belle Grove, Layla. Seems like she's following through on this whole plantation thing to me."

"Yeah." She slumps. "TBH, Mom's really outdone herself this time. She took out all these loans...."

The rage monster, driven half-insane by recent events, begins to chitter: *We are not okay with this. We are NOT okay.*

Seething, I turn to go.

"No, wait, I swear to *God* it won't happen. Don't leave. *I have a plan.*"

"Oh really? Because so far, your plans suck. Facing off with Dr. Heidel? We could be suspended right now, for all I know."

Layla dips back into her bag and brandishes two sheets of paper. "I printed these before class. From the city hall website?"

My stomach clenches in recognition.

"Tickets for the Westwood Museum. We're going. Me and Mom. She's not a bad person. Just a little oblivious."

"Plantation weddings are beyond oblivious."

"She grew up in Texas. They didn't teach slavery in the curriculum, like, *at all.* I swear, she just doesn't know."

She just doesn't know.

The words stick in my heart like a splinter. Because that was Mom's dream, right? To fight racism with education.

On the other hand, this isn't *The Parent Trap.* A plantation tour isn't going to pay off Claudia Hartwell's loans or get her agent back. Why get my hopes up?

"Look, I don't want to hurt anybody," Layla says. "I just want to go back to LA."

Her voice breaks on the *A*, and all at once, I feel sorry for Layla Hartwell. Whatever her situation, it's not normal. Wearing those too-glamorous sunglasses and waving that unlit joint, damage rises from Layla like mist off the swamp.

"Please. Trust me?"

She has no idea how much I'd love to trust people like her, what a better place the world would be if only I could. For an instant, I allow myself to dream: What if I did join forces with Layla? What if we talked her mom into taking an enslaved people's tour, and showed her the error of her ways?

What if, together, Layla and I worked Mom's good magic, born of love and hope...and what if angry, broken Harriet Douglass finally saved the day?

I'm not alone in dreaming. Layla's right here with me, her eyes holding mine. In the grove, we have what can best be described as *a moment*.

Then I blink, and it's gone. "Sorry, but I'm not the trusting type."

Suddenly, Layla Hartwell doesn't look like a rich and powerful influencer anymore. Disappointed, she looks like a child playing dress-up.

I break eye contact first, switching on my phone.

Me:
sonya text me ASAP
also i miss you

No surprise, she doesn't answer. The time difference is a vast, lonesome borderland.

In the distance, Dad shouts my name, red panic in his voice.

Before he has a heart attack, I bolt for the gate.

CHAPTER 8

A S MY FURIOUS father bundles me into our car, I catch my first glimpse of Layla's mom—aka, the woman who's turning Belle Grove, a literal plantation, into some kind of fantasyland amusement park.

She's stumbling, drunk, out of an Uber.

"Oh, Layla," she slurs. "How can you do this to me? I had to come clear across town."

Behind the wheel of our Honda, Dad freezes.

"It's okay, Mom." Layla pats her mother's shoulder. "Nothing a vodka soda won't fix."

Dad and I swap a glance. Who day-drinks on their daughter's first day at a fancy new prep school?

"Y'all okay?" he calls out.

Claudia flashes Dad a dippy smile. "Fine and dandy. But who might *you* be?"

Um. Is Claudia Hartwell flirting with my father?

"Don't worry about us," Layla says. "Mom just took a champagne spa day at the Four Seasons. You know, because she's been working so hard?"

Layla oozes sarcasm, but her mother doesn't seem to notice. She only has eyes—and smiles—for Dad.

"All right." Dad speaks directly to Layla, like she's the grown-up. "Be safe."

Settling her mother in the back seat of the Uber, Layla winks at me.

I'm still deciding whether or not to wink back when Dad peels away, his face tightening again with anger.

"Do you know who they are?" I ask. "That's Claudia and Layla Hartwell. They bought Belle Grove. I think they just moved in."

"It's none of your concern."

I glance back, wondering if Layla's right that Claudia can't follow through. I mean, on first impression, she does seem like a mess. Outside of the French Quarter, I've never seen anyone that drunk in the daytime. And those sky-high heels she was wearing? They're so *unserious*.

"They really don't seem like they get along," I muse. "Honestly, they don't seem like mother and daughter at all."

"Your principal didn't call me to talk about the Hartwells, Harriet," Dad says irritably. "We're here because of you. How could you get kicked out on the first day of school?"

"This wasn't on me. That Belle Grove girl was the one acting messy."

"That the truth, Harriet Douglass?"

I grip my seat belt like a lifesaver.

"Because your principal told me that you called Dr. Heidel racist, which raised holy heck up in that classroom."

"I never called him racist. I just said that he..." Realizing my mistake, I trail off.

Dad looks at me sharply. "You'd best finish that sentence."

"I said that he had racial face blindness, okay? He confused me with Sonya, even though he's met me before. He didn't see anything about me except the Black."

I expect some sympathy, but Dad keeps scowling.

"It was racism, is what I'm saying."

52

He still says nothing.

"Dad? Are you listening?"

"How many times have I told you that you've got to hold yourself to a higher standard, Harriet Douglass? You can't talk back to teachers no matter what. You've got to be darn near perfect to get anywhere in this world."

I fight not to roll my eyes. "Respectability politics died in, like, the nineties."

"The internet's got you confused. Everyone seems enlightened behind a computer screen, but in real life? Nothing's changed. You want to go to college? Be successful? Don't snap every time you get your feelings hurt."

"You mean I've got to suck up to white people."

"I mean you've got to protect yourself. Even—and especially—when white folks disappoint you."

My head aches. "I thought Dr. Heidel was on our side. I mean, he donated a bunch of money to Westwood, didn't he?"

"You're old enough to know by now that racism has layers. His intentions are good, but that doesn't mean he's perfect."

"He hurt my feelings. Doesn't that matter?"

"Of course it does. You come home and talk to me. You talk to your friends. But you do not start shit in class. We clear?"

I sigh, wishing it were that simple. But of course, nothing's simple when it comes to the rage monster. "I'll try, Dad."

"Fine. Now listen to me. The school's not suspending you on *one condition*."

"What?"

"You've got to write a letter of apology to Dr. Heidel. For *implying* that he's racist."

The rage monster blows smoke up my throat. *Oh, hell no.*

"I didn't do anything wrong."

"Oh, yeah? You didn't—let's see—*lose your temper*—once again?"

Dad sounds so disgusted with me, I want to shrivel up and die.

"Write the apology, Harriet."

Ever helpful, my rage monster whispers: *Oh, hell to the* hell *to the no. We don't owe that racist hobbit a goddamn thing, and I'll tell you something else—he should be apologizing to us. AND DAD KNOWS IT.*

A mosquito splatters against the windshield; Dad switches the wipers on.

"I'm not apologizing," I say tightly. "I won't."

Lips clamped together, Dad swerves onto a side road.

"Where we going?"

"Dairy Queen. My daughter got herself booted from class on her first day of senior year, and I need something fried."

Well, that tracks.

The rage monster, still tugging at my brain stem, growls.

"It really wasn't all my fault. That Layla girl ran her mouth, too."

"Enough, Harriet! You're in trouble here. And it's not just school. Now let me get some fries in me. Okay?"

I lean back in my seat, wondering what other kind of trouble's about to rain down. Maybe Dad talked to Dr. Maples. She's not supposed to share anything from our sessions, but they do check in from time to time. Maybe she told him about my assault on the Klimt.

But probably, Dad found out about Vacation Karen's Yelp review.

We pull up to the Dairy Queen drive-through, where Dad orders enough from a gum-snapping girl to feed a small village. Then he pulls into the parking lot, rolls the windows down, and tosses me a bag of food.

I'm sick of burgers. Sick of fast food of any kind. Instead of eating, I watch my father from the corner of my eye. His face betrays nothing, but junk food quantities are a pretty good measure of his stress levels, and he bought two strawberry milkshakes that he has no intention of sharing. In the sun, the extra-large paper cups glisten, sweating.

"A lawyer called me this morning," he says. "She says you attacked a woman with a chicken. I'm inclined to believe her."

Shit. "Dad—"

"Don't. Her lawyer asked that you be fired from Westwood Tours, and I agreed."

"*Fired?* I'm a volunteer!"

"You broke my trust. You'll turn in your badge and focus on your studies."

Instinctively, I rest my hand on my backpack, where I keep my Westwood ID.

"Don't you even want to know what happened?" I flash on Vacation Karen's twisted snarl, insisting that *there were good owners, too.*

"I know exactly what happened. A white person disappointed you—again—so you lashed out, trying to get free. But that's not the way."

Somehow immune to brain freeze, Dad drains half a milkshake in a single slurp.

"When I was an assistant professor at NYU, police followed me back to my office. They didn't believe a Black man like me could work at that fine college. I was still a kid then, and mad as hell, but did I yell at them? Attack them? No."

"But you reported them. Right?"

"No!" He's honestly scandalized. "How could I expect to get tenure if I made a fuss over every little white thing that happened to me? I thanked those officers for their service, and then I locked myself inside my car and blasted 'Fuck tha Police,' just like every other self-respecting Black professional in America. I did not seek out conflict. I remembered the importance of *excellence.*"

"It's a different time, Dad."

He snorts. "Not that different."

"It was one mistake." I'm desperate now. Begging. "I'll do better. I swear."

"You'll turn in your badge. And then you'll write a heartfelt apology to Dr. Heidel. Understand?"

Dad holds out one long, smooth palm. Waiting.

Cold drains through me, thinking of how I feel leading my tours. How close to Mom. How *real*.

At Westwood, every tour begins at the Big House. I open with a brief history of chattel slavery—you'd be surprised how many people don't know the basics—and then I tell Westwood's story through the lens of enslaved people's experiences. I start with Sarah, who cooked in an outdoor shed from sunup to sundown for fifty years. According to Dad's records, the first Mr. Westwood whipped her within an inch of her life twice: once for stealing flour, and once for simply spilling it. Even Dad's precious *excellence* couldn't have saved her.

If I can't tell her story...or Anna's or Louisa's...then how can I keep living on this plantation land? How can I bear it?

"You can't punish me like this."

"I'm not punishing you. I'm *parenting*. You've got to focus on your education. Your mom would want that."

If he thinks he's the only person in this car who can play the Mom card, he's got another think coming. "Mom loved *Westwood*."

"She loved you more." Dad's palm is open between us. Waiting. "And so do I."

"Funny way of showing it."

"Your ID, Harriet. Now."

The suffocating reek of Dairy Queen turns my stomach. I have no choice, now, but to give up the thing I love the most in this whole backward universe.

With clumsy fingers, I unzip my backpack's pocket. My lanyard spills out, and then my laminated ID tag. I drop it into Dad's hand. He promptly whisks it away. Like these tours haven't kept me going since Mom's death. Like it's not the reason I wake up in the morning.

"You can have my tours. But I'm *not* apologizing to Dr. Heidel. Not in a million years."

"For crying out loud!"

Furious again, Dad starts the ignition. The engine turns over with an irritated cough. We drive in stubborn silence, both of us waiting for the other to break. But it won't be me who speaks first. My arm still burns where the security guard touched me. Telling me without words that I don't belong at a place like St. Anne's, even though I've been a student there since elementary school. And what did I do wrong? Nothing. I only told the God's honest truth.

We turn onto River Road, and I fix my gaze out the window. Plantations rise all along this famous stretch. Today, many are abandoned. We whiz by derelict houses, rusty silos, and neglected barns. Those crumbling plantations sadden me, because I hate to see history unmarked. But more than a handful of the River Road estates have been restored into tourist monstrosities—and those I consider enemy combatants.

Before Belle Grove, Miller Plantation and Resort was our fiercest adversary. We cruise past the opulent marble palace surrounded by tour buses. (Damn, they must be raking in the dough.) Every single person stepping out of those buses is white, and no wonder.

Mom and I once took the Miller tour together. Our guide was a white girl in southern belle attire—complete with a hoop skirt and bonnet. The tour was ninety minutes of straight furniture talk—Look at the molding on these doors! Look at these French banisters! And that fireplace!—with a smattering of family history.

Slavery wasn't mentioned once. Over and over again, the guide referred to enslaved people as *servants*.

In other words, it was all a lie.

They obscure the truth about slavery so white folks won't feel uncomfortable, Mom whispered into my ear. *But that's a mistake. People deserve a chance to know better—and do better.*

Outside St. Anne's, Layla said: *My mom's not a bad person, I swear. She grew up in Texas. They didn't teach slavery in the curriculum. She just doesn't know.*

Finally, Dad and I pull up to Westwood's oak-lined driveway. The Welcome Center's just up ahead, and the Big House behind it. We roll into Dad's Museum Director parking space.

"Write your apology, Harriet. I mean it."

"No," I say, firm. "I won't."

"Fine. Then grab a broom." Dad points in the direction of the janitorial shed. "Every floor in this place needs sweeping."

"Are you serious?"

"As a heart attack."

I stare at my father, and he stares straight back.

Since Mom died, we never fight.

"Fine. I'll sweep. What do I care."

"Harriet—" he starts.

But I'm already hustling out of the car and down the dirt path toward the shed, anger mixing toxically with shame, doubt, and fear. I tell myself I'm not still reeling from Dr. Heidel's bad behavior—the ugly attitude I never saw coming, thinking he was one of the enlightened ones.

Behind my eyes, traitorous tears bloom.

CHAPTER 9

ALL OVER THE plantation, tours are wrapping up. Westwood usually runs six per day, and there are twelve docents on staff. Some are volunteers, others salaried employees. When they're not leading tours, they roam all over the twenty-acre museum, caring for exhibits, statues, and monuments. The plantation relics need constant upkeep: The cabins of the enslaved have termites, and there's a soft patch of ground near Anna's statue that's swiftly becoming a sinkhole.

Our docents work closely with gardeners, archaeologists, and restoration experts. We also host historians, professors, and PhD candidates in our famous archive. Dad's running a serious operation here; it hurts so much to think it'll all go on without me.

I wave to Naima, who's taking final questions outside the Welcome Center. She waves back cheerfully, her ID around her neck.

Westwood's not a top-down operation. Every tour guide's allowed to script their own lesson. Naima leans into the legacy of the Middle Passage— the languages and memories enslaved peoples brought across the water; Henry, our oldest docent, focuses on the economic underpinnings of the slave trade. We collaborate with two members of the Chitimacha Tribe, who speak on the devastating loss of their land and the experiences of native peoples in enslavement. But my tours focus on women and children, because those are the stories that tug most strongly at my heart.

Who will fill that gap, now that Dad's taken my tours away?

I trudge across the field to the janitorial closet, grabbing a broom and dustpan.

Remembrance Chapel, sheltered beneath the frozen tears of a weeping willow, stands empty. I figure that's as good a place as any to start sweeping.

In the dust-spun silence, a series of chills, like ghost hands, strokes the length of my spine. I always forget about the feels in here. There's a pulpit at the head of the room, a memorial plaque decorated with handprints, and six pews for sitting in quiet reflection. And people do reflect here. Once, a woman sat down, thrust her hands into her hair, and wept until her eyes swelled up like tangerines. Dad had to call her a taxi home.

At the end of each pew, a bronze statue stands guard: a little girl with hands clasped behind her back, a boy crouched on the floor in abject sorrow, a pair of twins gazing warily at the door.

An etching of two live oak trees, their branches intertwined, decorates the plaque on the wall. It has a magical aura, this plaque, like it's ever-so-gently haunted. Actually, the whole chapel feels that way. Mom built the place with such care, overseeing the felling of the longleaf pines that became the roof, floor, and walls. After, she commissioned stained-glass panes from a Creole artist who wept as he made them. The finished product is stunning: The light that filters through those windows is as blue as the Atlantic, and no matter the weather outside, the chapel's always as cool as the grave.

I don't believe in literal ghosts, but I do believe in the almost unearthly power of some places—the *place-ness* of them, Dad calls it. I shiver slightly in the shadows, the flesh of my arms pinched into gooseflesh.

Broom in hand, I look more closely at the plaque.

Its reads: *Let this chapel be a place for quiet meditation on how far we've come, and how far we've yet to go.*

Below the words, a dozen child-sized handprints twinkle beneath the notice: *St. Anne's Fourth Grade Class, 2014.*

God, it feels like a billion years ago. A geologic age, at least.

My phone pings—I hope it's Sonya, but no dice. It's Sandy Chase from Heidel's class.

hey u ok???

I stare at the message, wondering how long it's been since I heard from her. We used to text all the time about school stuff, but that was before Mom—before my world turned upside down. I start to type an answer, then stop. Erase it.

It just makes me sad, you know? The reminders of so much loss, of a past that can never be reclaimed.

Like kudzu, another text pops up—from Morgan, this time.

Morgan:
reishi shrooms are very healing
wanna come over? i also have
lion's mane

My classmates' concern throws me off my game. Sonya said I should try to rebuild my old friendships, but I don't have it in me today.

I sweep for another half hour before my best friend finally rings me up.

"Are you suspended?" she demands off the bat.

"How much did you hear?"

"Heard, nothing. Graham's got your walkout up on TikTok."

"How bad is it?"

"You need to watch it right now."

Quickly, I tap the app...and watch the scariest forty seconds of footage I've ever seen in my horror-loving life.

On TikTok, Layla and I stride out of Dr. Heidel's class on an eternal loop; in the corner, GIF-Oprah rolls her eyes. Layla's exactly as photogenic as I feared. Marching behind her, I look haunted, in need of rescuing. Graham made me out to be some pitiful victim, but it's not the truth.

He stole my voice, I think bitterly.

"How many people have seen this?"

"Only, like, everyone? At least Graham did some bang-up editing."

"He should've asked me before he posted it, Son. This was—" I swallow around a sudden dry spot. "This was my story to tell. Or not."

"Yeah, he should've asked. But you know his heart's in the right place."

I glance at the chapel's plaque. Graham's little-boy handprint is right there. A complicated feeling shivers through me, emotions without names.

Just this once, I suppose I can cut him some slack.

"So I ask again," Sonya says. "Did you get yourself suspended, young lady?"

"I'm suspended unless I write an apology letter to Dr. Heidel."

"Well, you're not doing *that*."

"That's what I told my dad! He doesn't get it, though."

"Can't he call the school and complain? My mom would be wilding out."

I frown, because once upon a time, Dad would've come to my rescue, too. Since Mom's death, he doesn't have the same righteous energy.

Or maybe he's just pissed that I almost got him sued by Vacation Karen.

"What do you make of Layla?" Sonya asks. "She's coming off like a big, brave ally."

I scan the comments, which indeed claim she's *so brave*, with a side of: *Great shoes!* And, *Girl, call me up!*

"Layla wants to go back to LA. And she gets that what her mom's doing is wrong. She's funny, too, and sort of—sweet? But I don't know if I can really trust her."

Sonya's quiet so long, I wonder if the connection's dropped.

"You still there?"

She sighs. "I mean... you've got to trust someone, Harriet."

"Um." I clutch the phone tighter. "She's an influencer from California. What about that screams trustworthy to you?"

"She says she wants to help, and you need a friend out there."

A migraine spears my temple, because *Sonya* was supposed to be my friend out here. Then she jetted off to Italy. And now—what's even happening? Is she sick of me? Did I finally exhaust her with my anger and grief?

"Are you trying to pawn me off?"

"We're not even in the same time zone, *Errichetta*. I'd feel better if I knew someone had your back. I'd hoped it could be Graham, or Asher, or even Sandy, but... I can tell you like this Layla girl. It's about time you liked someone."

"I like *you*, Son."

"Other than me."

It's hard to accept that I'm now in a long-distance relationship with my very best friend.

On the other end of the line, she haggles in Italian with her host mother.

"Ugh, Harriet, I have to go. Whatever you do, don't get expelled, okay?"

She hangs up without saying goodbye, leaving me all alone in this chapel.

I sweep until the last tourist rumbles out of the parking lot. Dad should be in his office by now, or app-ordering dinner. The afternoon light, streaming through the windows, is mournful, layered deep.

I sit down in a pew and ask the rage monster if she's ready to write that apology letter yet. Because really, we both know it's the mature thing to do.

You can F the F off, she growls.

"Then I guess I'm suspended," I tell the darkening walls.

But I forgot an important secret about this place at night. Even after we lock the front gates, one visitor always comes on foot.

Auntie Yates.

I watch her come through the door, a paisley kerchief tied over her hair. I'm retroactively sorry for using my cell phone in this quiet, sacred space. And I'm sure glad she didn't catch me doing it.

Every night since I was ten years old, Auntie Yates has come to the chapel to pray. So far as I know, she's never missed a single visit—except after the hurricane, when the roof caved in. She even comes on Christmas.

"Hi, Auntie."

Her eyes sharpen, focusing.

Back in the day, while Mom worked hard to restore the plantation, Auntie used to watch me. Her grandson, Dawn, was only a little older. We spent long afternoons together, zoning out to cartoons and sucking salt off ice cubes. By the time Mom's cancer showed up, Dawn was long gone—he got himself into trouble so serious, his grandma sent him to live with cousins in DC. I don't know exactly what that trouble consisted of, but I can guess. Drugs are a big problem in the poorer towns surrounding the road, and with drugs come police, prison, danger. If Dawn was selling, I hope he's doing better up North.

"If it isn't Harriet Douglass," Auntie Yates coos. "You're growing up too pretty."

I blush.

"And I know you're making me proud at that fancy school of yours."

My smile slips right off my face.

"You're not in any trouble, are you?"

"No, ma'am."

"Uh-huh. I don't like trouble, I'll tell you that."

She really doesn't. And I'm not about to tell her I just got myself suspended.

"It's just...Belle Grove, next door? It gets under my skin."

She shakes her head sorrowfully. "Can't say I didn't think of you when they broke ground today."

My chest tightens. "When they *what*?"

Auntie Yates shushes me, gesturing to the statues like they can hear.

"Those fools are digging," she says low. "Didn't assess or anything, just started ripping up earth willy-nilly. I don't like to curse, but I'm telling you it's a damn shame."

The news drops into my belly like a lit match.

Before Mom and Dad turned over a single stone, they brought an archaeological team out here. The team took aerial shots of Westwood and the surrounding land, using thermal imaging to identify anomalies in the ground. Most of the map was red and yellow natural earth, but dozens of green rectangles revealed cold spots in the ground. Those irregularities indicated possible unmarked graves. In the imaging, Westwood and Belle Grove were both riddled with them. After the archaeologists left, I had nightmares for a week.

"Didn't anybody tell them about the ground, Auntie?"

"Baby, they never asked. When I heard that earthmover, I called your daddy right away. He called the city, but no one's breaking any laws."

"How bad is it?"

Auntie Yates's chin drops to her chest—and I have my answer.

I'm so disgusted I could scream, howl until the pine walls fall down around us.

"Excuse me, baby," Auntie Yates says tiredly. "I'm gonna pray for them."

And just like that, I see red.

CHAPTER 10

THE MOMENTS WHEN I must've been running are lost in the red of my rage. When I get to Belle Grove, the sun's setting crimson over the Big House.

Not one thousand feet away are the remains of the enslaved people's village.

Victims of the slave trade lived in shacks, most of which didn't survive the centuries. Many crumbled under southern storms—or, considered eyesores, were torn down. Where they still stand, they're rare historical treasures, far more valuable than any Big House. On the whole plantation, these cabins are the only structures that tell the God's honest truth about what slavery meant.

But Claudia Hartwell didn't see it that way. The cabins didn't fit her 'gram's beige-and-tan aesthetic—and they sullied the view from her white mansion.

So she erased them.

"She doesn't know." I speak the words like a mantra. "She just doesn't know."

With my phone, I capture images of the demolished village—documenting how history was turned into so much firewood. My stomach roils. The rage monster demands to know *what these fucking amateurs think they're doing.*

Over my shoulder, I clock movement in the Big House: lights flickering, a curtain twitching.

Freshly painted, the old house gleams like new. Of course Claudia Hartwell would be respectful with the white enslavers' stories. *The real history*, Vacation Karen called it. I stare at the house so hard, it's a wonder it doesn't burst into flames.

Porch lights slam on, flooding the veranda with white.

"Hello?" The word floats across the butchered field. "Is someone out there?"

I stop breathing.

The voice sharpens. "I said, who's there?"

Mrs. Hartwell.

How could I be so stupid, coming onto this land? Black kids get shot for doing shit like this. My feet slide backward, slipping in a mud patch. I'm too scared to make a run for it. Where the hell is the rage monster when I need her?

Instinctively, I throw my arm up, shielding my face.

"Call the police!" Mrs. Hartwell shrieks—and this is it, right there. Either I'm about to die, or Dad's gonna kill me himself.

At the exact same instant, Layla's bright voice sails over her mother's: "Harriet?"

• • • • •

Inside the mansion, there's a party going on.

A dozen grown folks mingle in the salon, sipping champagne beneath an eighteenth-century chandelier. Claudia and Layla both wear sleek black shifts, though Claudia's paired hers with a vintage silk kimono.

Swirling a glass of pink champagne, Mrs. Hartwell eyes me warily.

I want to keep my cool, I really do, but what this woman did to those cabins...it's too goddamn much. I'm going in at an eleven.

"What have you *done* to this place?"

She takes a step back. "What do you mean? We're having a *house-warming.*"

"You destroyed those cabins, bulldozed them like they meant nothing! They stood for hundreds of years and you—you—"

I'm breathless with anger, my lungs working like a bellows.

"Who are you?" Mrs. Hartwell's turned a dangerous shade of red. "What are you doing here? Do I need to call the police?"

"*Mom,*" Layla hisses.

"What are *you* doing here?" I shout back. "Where did you get the balls to—"

Layla bursts into false laughter. "Aha-ha! Harriet, you're *hilarious!*"

"*Excuse me?*"

"Harriet's such a prankster." Layla grabs my arm, squeezing just a bit too hard. "She's not actually angry. She's just in character—inviting you to Westwood Plantation. We've got tickets for Saturday's tour."

In character? I think.

"In character?" Mrs. Hartwell splutters.

"Yeah. The plantation owners were rivals, right?"

Wrong. From all accounts, they were first cousins on very good terms.

Layla whispers in my ear: *"Just play along."*

The weirdness of the moment pops my rage like a balloon.

"Okay. I mean, yeah, you're...cordially invited to tour the Westwood museum. We're right next door."

"Is it a museum?" Mrs. Hartwell cocks her head. "I always thought it was a bed-and-breakfast."

Painfully, my teeth grind together.

WESTWOOD IS NOT A FUCKING BED-AND-BREAKFAST.

WESTWOOD IS NOT *A BED-AND-FUCKING-BREAKFAST!!!!*

There are too many white people in this house, nibbling tiny canapés. I cannot—repeat, *cannot*—wig out. I struggle to relax my chest. Breathe in, out.

"Mom, how many times do I have to tell you? It's *a slavery museum*."

"Enslaved *people's* museum," I mutter.

"*Fascinating*," Claudia purrs, sounding bored. "Isn't it such a blessing to own a home on the historic register? I have a passion for party planning, but I care deeply about history, too." She gestures to a twinkling chandelier, the high ceiling stamped with an intricate plaster medallion. "I like to think of myself as Belle Grove's stewardess into the future."

Can this woman hear herself? The rage monster snarls, but I hold my tongue. Education is the answer. It has to be.

"Tickets are for Saturday at noon." Layla stares hard at her mother. "I already checked your calendar, so I know you're free."

"How presumptuous. What if I have a date? A gentleman caller?"

"You said you'd make time to learn about this place."

Claudia Hartwell's frozen grimace strongly resembles the Creepy Smile filter.

"And I will, dear—after Sunny's big day. You *know* she insisted on a fall wedding. She has such terrible allergies."

Layla rolls her eyes. "God forbid she should sneeze on her *special day*—"

"Watch your tone, young lady. Sunny's been dreaming of her fairy-tale wedding since she was a little girl, and she won't let anything ruin it. Not allergies, or internet trolls, or anything."

Trolls? Is it too much to hope that Sunny Blake and Randy White are already getting dragged online?

"Those weren't trolls," Layla says heatedly. "People have every right to be mad about a movie star's plantation wedding!"

"It's a load of PC nonsense and you know it. There's no better place for love than the Old South. *I* got married on a plantation in Tennessee."

"Yeah, and how did that work out for you? Dad left when I was *four*."

Whoa. Shots fired.

Mrs. Hartwell glowers. "November thirteenth is right around the corner. I'm sorry, but your slavery tour will just have to wait."

I want to yell, maybe tear my hair out in clumps. But instead I'm frozen, my white-hot anger turned clammy and cold.

"Harriet." Layla looks pointedly at me. "Would you like a drink?"

"Help yourselves." Mrs. Hartwell waves a limp hand. "It's high time I got back to my *invited guests.*"

Layla drags me into a remodeled kitchen as someone turns the music up. White plaster dust shakes down from the fragile ceiling. The chandelier tinkles, trembling ominously. Obviously, these amateurs don't know how to treat this old house, whose walls are the original cypress, milled onsite by Belle Grove's enslaved. Those same people then insulated the house with *bousillage,* a paste made from mud and Spanish moss. When their backbreaking work was finally done, they slept in freezing cabins on cold, bare floors.

"You want champagne?" Layla gestures to a half-empty bottle. "I also have green juice. Ooh, or what about kombucha?"

"I don't want your *kombucha.*" I cross my arms. "You said you could get your mom to take our tour. That she just needed to learn the truth."

"I tried! But, like, you weren't exactly helping."

I flush.

"Not that I blame you," Layla hurries to say. "I'm starting to think Claudia's a lost cause."

Somewhere deep inside me, those words resound like a bell. Mom always said no one, no matter how ignorant, is a lost cause. So how would she get through to Claudia Hartwell?

I hear Dad whisper, *Magic. That's what your mom would do.*

But I don't have any magic. Only this useless, bottomless rage.

"Good luck with your life, Layla. I'm going home."

"Don't! I have a plan."

"Your plans—"

"Suck so far, I know. But, Harriet, if Sunny's wedding falls through, *Mom won't be able to afford this place.* Everything depends on November freaking thirteenth."

My ears prick up. "What are you saying?"

"We can sabotage this shit-storm. Drive Claudia right out of town. But I can't do it alone."

"What makes you think I want to help you?"

"Please. When you walked through those doors, you were *incandescent* with rage. And Harriet, what they did to those cabins was all Sunny's fault. Bridezilla wanted an outdoor dance floor, and she's my mom's god-daughter. Whatever she says goes."

"Sunny Blake is your mom's goddaughter?"

"Yeah, and she's the absolute worst." Layla points through the open kitchen door. "Those are her parents. They came to see the venue."

I lock on a white-haired couple holding court near the fireplace. I don't know what I expected a movie star's parents to look like, but those people look strangely normal. Their whole vibe is very Midwestern dentist.

"You have to help me. I'm not built to live like this." Layla wrinkles her nose. "In the *South.*"

"Why? The kombucha not good enough for you?"

"The kombucha is *terrible*," she moans. "And there isn't one single Pilates studio anywhere near here!"

"How exactly is any of that my problem?"

"Let me take you to lunch tomorrow. Off-campus. Maybe somewhere 'grammable? Like a waterfront café that serves alligator eggs, or whatever? My followers love that stuff."

"I can't. I'm suspended. Probably grounded, too, thanks to Dr. Heidel."

A woman walks between us, drunkenly throwing flirty eyes over her shoulder. Layla and I break apart, then snap back like magnets.

"Suspended?" A line appears between her brows. "I only had to write an apology letter."

"Me too. But I'm not sorry—so."

Layla considers this. "Let me write it for you."

I bark a laugh. "No thanks."

"Seriously. Let me be an ally."

Doubtful, I frown.

"Just give me a chance. I'm not like my mother. I swear."

Part of me wants to trust Layla Hartwell. Didn't she face off against Dr. Heidel for my sake? Isn't it possible that she's trying her best with her nightmare of a mom? And Layla's writing that letter would solve a whole hell of a lot of problems.

But...

You have to be excellent, Dad said.

"No. I can't let you write it for me."

"But you won't write it, either."

"Right."

Dad thinks I can cough up that fake apology and turn a blind eye to what's happening at Belle Grove—but he's wrong on both counts. Growing up on plantation land changes you. The earth itself is sacred to me, like it is to Auntie Yates. I'll fight at the edge of these levees until I lose my goddamn mind.

Unfortunately, I'm all out of battle plans.

Layla, on the other hand, is standing here talking about *sabotage*.

The doorbell rings, and a man's voice singsongs, "*Clau*-dia!"

She appears like magic. "Why, that's *Hugh*! Quick, Layla, where's the Veuve Clicquot? Open it, open it!"

Suddenly, I'm staring at a middle-aged man in faux-lumberjack attire. He's handsome enough to be a soap star himself, except for his chin, which is as weak as a baby's. He cradles an armful of garish white roses.

"Happy housewarming!" he calls. "Hello, one and all!"

A few people raise glasses his way, but Layla leans closer to me.

"And here's southern boyfriend number one," she murmurs. "Oh, *joy*."

Hugh frowns. "Now, now. Let's be civil."

I don't like the way Hugh stares at Layla, or the way the blood drains from her face beneath his gaze. He flashes a smile he probably thinks is charming, but I see the holes between his straight, white teeth: the menace there.

Oblivious, Mrs. Hartwell kisses him smack on the mouth.

They proceed to make out like we're not even here.

Beside me, Layla seethes.

Hugh comes up for air. "What a beautiful home. Claudia, you've outdone yourself. Now, I'd love to pick your brain about that agency...."

"Oh, Hugh, not *tonight*, it's a party!"

"Are Sunny's parents here?" Hugh cranes to see. "The least you could do is introduce me. They must have some pull in the industry, right?"

Claudia laughs uncomfortably. "Somebody turn up the music! I want them to hear us all the way in New Orleans!"

New Or-*leens*, she says, like the tourist she is.

In the next second, Stevie Wonder blasts so loud, I clap my hands over my ears. There's a shudder beneath my feet like an earthquake's coming, but that's not it. These old houses are sensitive; they weren't built for this modern noise, and old metals grow weak. Debris shakes from the ceiling, hissing like rain.

Oh, shit.

"Layla—"

In confusion, her mouth drops open.

"*Run*," I squeeze out.

And that's when a wire licks and snaps—sending the chandelier into free fall.

There was no time to run; the great glass fixture lands with a heart-stopping scream.

People clutch each other; a few champagne flutes fall. Closest to the wreck, Sunny Blake's parents look almost comically shocked, like cartoons that just dodged a falling piano. Hugh and Mrs. Hartwell barrel toward their prized guests.

"Holy shit," someone splutters. "Holy shit!"

The chandelier, crushed beneath its own weight, looks like a collapsed wedding cake; shattered glass sparkles all across the floor, sharp and dangerous.

Fucking amateurs, I think again.

"You see what I mean?" Layla cries, fanning her face with her hands. "I can't live here. *I can't.*"

She's looking at Claudia and Hugh, standing in the crush of people tending to Sunny's frightened parents. Though Layla might've been hurt, her mother doesn't glance her way once.

"Say you'll help me. We can shut my mother down. I *know* we can."

There's something very wrong with this family. If I were smart, I wouldn't get involved, but that plantation wedding's going down on November thirteenth—which is just so soon.

So, okay Home Depot: *Let's do this.*

"How hard are you willing to go, Layla Hartwell? Because I *love* this land, and *I don't play.*"

"For starters, how about we light a match and set this whole place on fire?"

My eyes widen.

"Not literally. I've just got, like, anger issues."

I mean: *same.*

"Come over to my place tomorrow. But you'd better bring your A game. If you waste my time, I'll get angry."

And you won't like us when we're angry, the rage monster chides.

Grinning triumphantly, Layla sticks out her hand.

She didn't miss my snub in Dr. Heidel's classroom, when I refused to shake with her. This is a redo. A second chance. Her post-ironic wrist tattoo continues to suggest that I *live, laugh, love.*

Our palms connect with a static shock. I feel it all the way down to my toes.

Glass crunching beneath my feet, I pick my way toward the exit.

Someone stands on a table, hyperventilating. Claudia and Hugh are still tending to their guests of honor. So far, nobody's thought to reach for a goddamn broom.

"*Thank you,*" Layla breathes at the door. "You won't be sorry."

I take one last look at the wreckage of Claudia Hartwell's housewarming.

"I mean, we'll see."

I leave wondering what I've gotten myself into... and how badly I'm bound to regret it.

CHAPTER 11

I'VE NEVER BEEN suspended before; I had no idea that it's basically just a vacation you're supposed to be ashamed of.

For one thing, I don't have to stuff myself into my stupid school uniform. For another, there's plenty of time to clean up the fast-food-cluttered kitchen and make myself a solid stack of French toast. Sun streams through the kitchen window, and I linger, fiddling with Mom's narwhal tea towel before setting it back in its rightful place.

The only thing I have to do today is feed my chickens.

If Dad weren't mad at me, and if my Brown application weren't at risk, I might even enjoy the free time.

After slipping into my muck boots, I shuffle out to feed Rosemary and her little buddies. As always, I cluck to them, letting them know I'm not Br'er Fox. These babies live in a constant state of panic—except for Rosemary, and maybe Ron Jon, the rooster. They're the cool chickens.

Wading through sawdust, I collect twelve perfect eggs.

"Good work, team. Keep ballin'."

All around me, the museum's stretching its great limbs, slowly waking.

Tour guides park their cars, then gather at the Welcome Center for the morning meeting. Dad usually gives them a pep talk before opening the floor to questions. Guides often complain about the bat-shit things tourists say, venting in the safe space.

Some evergreens:

Slavery wasn't really that bad.

Of course rape wasn't common.

They would never separate the families.

You're exaggerating.

Those cabins aren't too bad. Better than how a lot of Blacks live now!

But what about the men who built this country? Aren't they still worth celebrating?

The last one's a personal favorite of mine. If I'm not too worked up— like, if the rage monster's napping—I explain that, actually, it was *enslaved people* who built this country. Literally, from the ground up. *They* made the millions that turned the United States into a financial power. It wasn't just manual labor that they contributed, either.

When Europeans colonized this land, brutally wresting it from the Native peoples who lived here, they had no experience with the temperate climate, and no idea how to farm these fields. After they alienated the indigenous tribes, they didn't have anyone to ask, either.

But fun fact: Much of the West African coast is quite similar in climate to the American South. Enslavers didn't just buy hardworking hands; they bought an entire people's agricultural expertise. They called them heathens, but without African knowledge, the colonists never would've survived.

I live for factoids like that.

After collecting my eggs, I grab a feed bag and shake it. Clever Rosemary comes running. The other chickens aren't committed until I spill the corn kernels over the well-pecked ground. Then it's a stampede. Every chicken for herself.

"Rosemary, you're too cute to eat off the floor."

I scoop her into my lap, letting her peck at the corn in my palm. Between bites, she looks up at me with sweet, knowing eyes.

"I know," I whisper. "I can't believe I got suspended, either."

Her feathers are as soft as down. She hops from my lap, off to start her day.

Beyond the coop, a clear blue morning settles over Westwood like a hand-sewn quilt. I don't know why the sky makes me think of Mom, but in two seconds flat, grief drags me into its depths.

I decide to give Dr. Maples's mindfulness exercise another try.

Leaning against the chicken shed, I pop in my earbuds. A soothing, British voice instructs me to close my eyes, relax my shoulders, and breathe. Just breathe.

Let your thoughts come and go, the voice tells me. *Come and go.*

In my mind's eye, I picture Mom. The guide instructs me to let this thought go. To think of it as *an autumn leaf floating downstream.*

But I can't.

I keep thinking: Why can't I remember what Mom said to me, on the last day of her life? What kind of daughter am I, that I could forget something as important as that?

"Harriet?"

My eyes snap open.

Dad's here, and he's brought a young man with him. Because I look a mess, he's crazy hot. That's just science.

The stranger smiles, his lips curling in a way that's both wicked and wry.

Oh my God. I know him.

At least, I did once.

"Dawn?"

"Yeah, it's me. Been a minute."

It's been six years.

Six years since I laid eyes on Auntie Yates's grandson.

I take him in from head to toe. He's got the same smile, but he's rocking a slightly ironic fade. Back in the day, he wore baggy jeans and ratty black T-shirts—thirteen-year-old boy stuff. Now he rocks a neat gray suit. Grown, he easily clears six feet. I have to tilt my head up to look at him.

His eyes drop almost imperceptibly down my body, then flick back up. I usually hate the once-over, but I've grown, too. Can't blame him for being curious. When his eyes meet mine, I can tell I've made some kind of impression—and my heart thunders before I remember that Dawn Yates abandoned me.

We spent our whole childhood together, but he never tried to contact me after he shipped off to DC. He never called, never wrote—and he didn't come to Mom's funeral. I was too young, when he left, for social media, but I used to ask Auntie Yates how he was. She'd clam right up, telling me nothing. Still, for months, I tried to pass along updates about Rosemary, because Dawn was there when she hatched.

Actually, Dawn saved baby Rosemary's life. She couldn't crack out of her egg—that happens occasionally. Some farmers will tell you that a chicken that can't hatch isn't strong enough to live, but Dawn, with the help of YouTube, peeled back the egg's layers, ever so gently, with a toothpick.

I speak numbly. "I was starting to think I'd never see you again."

"No way." The fringes of his smile curl up, even more wicked than before. "You were my little ride or die. The baddest baby girl around."

"And you were a bully," I fire back. "Always putting bugs in my hair."

Dad clears his throat. "I need you to show Dawn around tomorrow. Say, four o'clock?"

"Show him around? Dawn knows the plantation almost as well as I do."

"I've hired this fine young man to take some photos for the brochure."

I frown. "Is he even, like, qualified?"

Dawn grips his chest. "Ouch."

"He's applying to fine arts programs," Dad says. "He'll be a professional photographer someday."

Huh.

In his middle school years, Dawn was a prototypical basketball-and-chaos boy. His hobbies included eating cereal in front of the TV, pranking me mercilessly, and clowning around with the neighborhood kids. When he was thirteen, he started getting into trouble at his public school. I don't know all the details—Dad was pretty cagey about it. Auntie Yates freaked out, though. Sent him to live with his cousins in a suburb outside Washington, DC.

What happened up North? Since when is he into *art*?

"I don't know if I should be offended," Dawn says, "considering how shocked you look right now. And hey, isn't it a school day? What are you doing home?"

"I'm suspended," I say crisply.

"Temporarily," Dad intones.

Dawn flashes a dimple. "Lucky for me, I guess."

My thoughts fully scrambled, I shake my head. "Still can't believe you came back here."

I don't want to say it around Dad, but Dawn knows what I'm talking about. He *hated* the plantation stuff. Once, he told me thinking about slavery made him feel ashamed—and in Auntie Yates's house, it was hard to escape slavery talk. She loves the history, and any story involving her ancestor Samuel.

"I came home to check on my grandmother. She's not as sharp as she used to be."

"Really? She seems pretty spry."

He shrugs, finally looking away—like he's dodging something. "Still getting on in years."

"Still baking her pies, too. Those bittersweet ones."

Dawn shudders. "Always hated those history pies. I prefer mine with sugar. But you—" He smirks. "Even as a kid, you liked them bitter."

"Yeah, well, I always valued my history. Unlike some."

Dad's looking at me like I've grown two heads.

Honestly, I don't know why I'm giving Dawn so much 'tude. I have no right to feel like he left me behind, choosing Washington over Westwood and his cousins over me. But I guess I *do* feel that way.

"Rosemary still kickin'?"

"Yeah."

"Think she remembers me?"

"Not a chance."

His laugh ties my insides up in knots.

"Head on back to the house, Harriet," Dad says sternly. "I'll meet you there."

Strangely, I don't want to leave. "I could show Dawn around now."

The boy in question blinks. Then, infuriatingly, looks smug.

"A suspension is not a vacation, Harriet, and you and I have to talk."

I swallow, knowing Dad's gonna try to break me down—convince me to write that apology letter.

But for now, at least, I'm off the hook. He ushers Dawn toward the Welcome Center, where they probably have business together.

I still can't believe that Dawn Yates is old enough to have *business*.

Watching him go, I wipe sweaty palms on my ratty sweatpants, which I would've changed out of if only I'd known.

At Auntie Yates's house, Mom once said: *Lord, that boy's gonna be a looker.*

And Auntie Yates answered, *Don't I know it.*

At the time, I couldn't figure out what they were talking about. But I sure as hell get it now. Dawn is six feet of handsome, and his legs, walking away from me, are sturdy as oak trunks. It's going to take my body some time to recover from the shock of seeing him again. When I do, I've got to make sure I don't look like such a slob. For the first time, the existence of Sephora, with its million promises of beauty, makes sense to me.

I glance at my phone's clock. Italy's seven hours ahead. I text Sonya an SOS.

ughh I think i need to learn about
makeup??

For an embarrassingly long time, I linger, waiting for her answer.

Sonya's spent years trying to get me interested in boys. Over the summer, she even tried to nudge me toward girls, in case that was the hang-up. But the year everyone started dating happened to coincide with the year Mom was dying, and then I was grieving most of the time, too distracted to feel sexy.

But Dawn's not a real romantic possibility. He's just an old friend I haven't seen since childhood. A friend who once dropped a live frog down my shirt and then ran away, knowing I'd be after him with my tiny fists.

So what if he's fine now, and grown, with a smile like Killmonger's, contemplating the taking of Wakanda's throne?

Heading back into the kitchen, I heave a big old-lady sigh. Then I fill the sink with suds, planning to take a crack at the dishes before Dad gets home. Maybe if the kitchen is really, really clean, he won't freak out at me too much.

But deep down, I know: I'm screwed.

• • • • •

Like I'm one of his pesky grad students, Dad orders me into his office.

He sits in his high-back gamer chair, which is apparently good for your posture, in front of a giant Apple flat screen. Instead of sitting across from him, I lean against the overstuffed bookshelf, sulking.

"What I'm about to say is serious." Dad steeples his fingers. "And, Harriet, I'm so very sorry."

I straighten; a pile of hardcovers flops over on their shelf.

"*You're* sorry? Why?"

Dad glowers. "Bear in mind: There *will* continue to be consequences for your ridiculous act of rebellion, but not today. I don't have the heart."

Frightened now, I grope my way to the chair across from Dad and sink bonelessly into it.

"Hey, whatever it is—"

"I've retained a lawyer to pursue a malpractice suit. They're from a very expensive, very thorough white-shoe firm."

My heart leaps into my throat.

Mom. He's talking about Mom.

After Mom died, a hospice worker confided to my father that she should've been diagnosed much sooner. That she would've had a better chance if her general practitioner had taken her seriously. The thing is, I knew her doctor: a tall southern gentleman with an office in the hospital. He stitched me up once when I took a bad fall off the tire swing. Mom always said he was *the loveliest man.*

But he didn't take her pain seriously. She visited him half a dozen times over the course of many years, outright asking for testing. He never gave it to her.

Medical neglect is common in the Black community. My grandmother's dentist once pulled her tooth without any anesthesia; Sonya's mother nearly died after giving birth because no one listened when she was stroking out.

What happened to Mom wasn't right, the hospice nurse said—and it's another reason I struggle to trust white folks these days.

"You said we could never prove that her doctor did anything wrong."

Dad twists his gold wedding band. It looks very classy, but there's a dorky inscription on the inside: *May the Force be with us. Always.*

"These sorts of cases are very hard to win. But if the proof is out there, I want to find it. Every night, I lie awake wondering." He shakes his head. "There's also the problem of money. Your mother's medical expenses were substantial, and we're very much in debt. If we don't get a cash infusion soon, we may be looking at bankruptcy."

"Substantial?" Dad never talks to me about money, and I get what a huge privilege it is that we've never really had to worry. "How substantial?"

"We owe the hospital over two hundred thousand dollars."

"What about insurance?"

"Insurance covered more than half of her care, but we're left with the balance."

Horror rises from deep inside me, sweaty and sulfurous. We paid the hospital almost *half a million dollars* to misdiagnose my mother, again and again, until it was too late to save her.

That's not the kind of thought you can float downstream on a mindfulness leaf. It's gruesome. *Atrocious.* Like a floating, human bone.

"Don't pay them, Dad. Don't give them another cent."

"It's not that simple, but I do plan to sue them. For about ten million."

"Ten *mill*—"

"Don't get excited. It's very unlikely we'll see that much money. But even a fraction of it would keep Westwood afloat, and you know how your mother felt about... well." He locks eyes with mine. "You know."

"You don't mean we'd have to sell the museum? Do you?"

If some nasty ex-soap star bought this place, I would well and truly lose my mind.

Dad speaks softly. "Worst-case scenario, we'd donate Westwood to the Louisiana State Parks Department. We would never, ever sell."

I sink back. "But we're going to win this lawsuit, right? Mom saw that doctor constantly, and he never gave her anything more than extra-strength Advil. No tests, no imaging, nothing. And then, when she started throwing up *blood*—"

Dad holds up a hand, stopping me from going any further down Bad Memory Lane.

"That doctor obviously failed her. But doctors, individually, are very hard to sue. Who's to say he didn't make an honest mistake?"

I scoff. "Yeah, right."

"But I've since learned that the hospital *also* treated her with outdated chemotherapy medication: outdated and *expired*. Holden and Joyce subpoenaed their records, and it turns out the chemo team treated your mother as an indigent."

"What does that mean?"

"People without insurance often get cheaper meds from the hospital's supply. Your mom had plenty of insurance, but perhaps assumptions were made based on her appearance."

"You mean because she's Black."

"Yes. But she was also emaciated by then. A note in her file called her a *possible addict*."

"What the hell?" I stand quickly; the chair clatters to the floor behind me. "Are you kidding me with this? Mom was on the PTA! She spoke fluent French! She binge-read YA books and collected *fancy leather handbags*!"

"Even if she were an addict, the hospital was negligent. They shouldn't offer medications of lesser quality to *anyone*."

A nauseating current jolts through me. I don't know what to do with this new horror. Don't know how to process it.

"I'm sorry to drag you into all this." Dad's face is pained. "We already suspected that something went terribly wrong with your mother's treatment. If you'd made your peace with it before now, I'm sorry."

"I'll never make peace with it. Never."

"Remember that your mother's cancer was very serious. Even if everything had been done exactly right, her illness still might've killed her."

"Possible addict?" I whisper. "*Expired* medication?"

"Our lawyers are looking into it. If the hospital was negligent, they'll be held accountable."

The heels of my palms, pressed flat against my eyes, dig into the soft, wet flesh. I want to crush this new knowledge out of me.

Isn't it enough that my mother *died*?

Despite everything she'd achieved—her Ivy League degrees, the transformation of Westwood—at the bitter end, she was still treated like a second-class citizen.

I stand there, hands over my face, chest expanding and collapsing.

A light, brushing sound; Dad's offering me a piece of Kleenex.

I take it. Loudly blow.

"The lawyers need to depose you. You must tell the truth and nothing but."

"Will you be there?"

"They've asked to speak to you alone. I'll be right here, waiting."

My new pain is jagged inside my belly, unprocessed and unabsorbed. Tears will come, lots of them, followed by the kind of empty aching that's worse than tears. By now, I know the drill.

Clutching the dirty Kleenex, I turn to leave.

"I love you, Harriet Douglass," Dad says. "I'm sorry."

The professor looks so helpless, standing beside his grand desk. All the learning in the world hasn't prepared him for me, his traumatized daughter, grieving.

"I'm sorry, too," I say.

And shut the door behind me.

CHAPTER 12

THAT AFTERNOON, LAYLA appears on my doorstep, decked out in a white felt fedora, cat-eye sunglasses, and a carpetbag the size of Texas. I consider asking her to come back another day, because after my conversation with Dad, I'm not feeling so well. After some Netflix and weeping, the rage monster's rustled up. I'm in no mood for kombucha-loving microinfluencers.

But Layla doesn't wait to be invited inside. Flashing bright-white influencer teeth, she sashays straight past me.

"The enslaved people's museum is stunning, Harriet, just stunning! The statues, the memorial wall..." She places her hand on her chest. "I would love for you to give me a tour sometime."

I frown, picturing the cabins I saw last night, and smelling, in Layla's wake, the sour, broken earth. But I said I'd give her a chance—and she gave me something, too. A taste of her own anger at Claudia—and a promise.

My gut tells me that Layla and I are on the same team. At least for now.

"What's in the bag? You moving in?"

"May I?" She pouts her lips and sort of—wiggles?—gesturing at my couch. I nod.

She sinks down onto the cushions, crossing her legs like Anne Hathaway in *The Princess Diaries*.

"So. I promised I'd come with a plan, and I have."

I raise an eyebrow. "You promised me your A game. Is that what you brought?"

With quick, prim movements, Layla starts pulling stuff out of her bag: a ring light, a tripod, a laptop, a corkboard, and, I kid you not, a potted succulent.

"What are you, California Mary Poppins?"

"Well, I *am* 'practically perfect in every way.' But seriously, I'm here in my capacity as an 'influencer.'" She does the air quotes. "To give Westwood a digital glow-up. Starting with your website." She clicks open the laptop. "I mean, what the hell even is this?"

With some trepidation, I settle down beside her.

The screen flashes a few brutal words:

ERROR. SITE NOT FOUND.

"Oh no. I didn't realize."

"Yeah. I had to get tickets for that tour at the city hall site because Westwood's was down. Whoever's in charge of your digital presence truly forgot to renew your domain name."

That was Mom.

Because she died.

"Okay, but how big a deal is a website anyway? We're in all the Louisiana travel brochures, and the tourist map at city council, and the hotels recommend us...."

Layla's eyes widen like I'm foaming at the mouth.

"How *important* is your *website*? It's the hub of your digital existence, your one-stop shop. All your social should connect back to it. Did you know that the only Westwood on Instagram is a fan-page for some elder millennial show? And did you know," she huffs, like this next bit is truly beyond the pale, "that the last time anyone tweeted from your museum account *Kim was still married to Kanye?*"

This white girl's about to clap at me. I can feel it.

"Y'all—*clap*—need to get—*clap*—your act—*clap*—together!" She shakes her hair, which appears to be made of silk and pure sunshine. "It's amazing you get any tourists here at all. Why don't you have full-time PR?"

I sigh. "Hiring staff to work for a plantation is complicated. Especially *Black* staff. My parents never wanted to make anyone feel like they were slaving. And white employees don't always get what we're trying to do here. When we first moved, Mom and Dad decided they'd do most of the work themselves."

"And where's your mom now? You don't talk about her much."

Bile rushes into my throat, thinking of how the hospital treated my mother.

"Mom, she's—" I hesitate. Start over. "Living abroad. In France."

A radiant smile lights Layla's face. "Ooh! *J'adore la France.*"

I don't know why I lied; now, I can't meet Layla's eyes.

And I'm ready to change the subject.

"So maybe we're behind on our social media," I admit. "But what does that have to do with Belle Grove?"

"I thought you'd never ask."

From her laptop, Layla launches a full-on PowerPoint display.

The Cancellation of Belle Grove, the first slide reads. *A Three-Pronged Plan.*

I'm impressed and also a little dazed.

"When did you make this?"

"English class. Now shush." The slide flickers. "Prong One: *Public Pressure.* Westwood is right next door to Belle Grove, but, like, no one planning on going to Belle Grove would know it. We need to raise your online visibility, and we also need to talk about your road sign."

"What's wrong with our sign?" I ask—though I already know.

Years ago, Dad bought a small billboard on River Road to help tourists find us. THE WESTWOOD ENSLAVED PEOPLE'S MUSEUM, NEXT RIGHT! Unfortunately, it's needed a fresh coat of paint for years. You can hardly make out the word *museum* anymore.

"It's illegible. We need to spruce it up because Sunny's publicity team is visiting soon. They should know that Westwood is next door."

"Will they even care?"

"They'll care about the optics. Sunny's already in hot water online. Does it really make sense for her to have a plantation wedding next door to a museum?"

No. No, it does not.

But I can't get my hopes up. November thirteenth, the wedding date, is speeding toward us like a bullet train.

"Is there really time to change their minds?"

"Please hold your skepticism until the end," she says prissily. "You're going to *love* the second prong of my master plan."

She taps on the next slide, and I lurch forward on the couch.

"Here's the thing, H: Technically speaking, *Belle Grove may not even belong to Claudia.*"

Document after document populates the screen, full of small print and words like *escrow* and *arrears*.

"Okay." I'm trying not to get too excited. "Break it down for me. What does this mean?"

"Mom could only afford Belle Grove because it was in foreclosure. My ex-boyfriend-slash-realtor did some digging, and it turns out that the people who owned it last were involved in some money-laundering stuff. You can see the police filing here." A very scary official document stares back at me. "I don't know how these, like—gangsters, or whatever they were—got hold of the deed, but they're not actual descendants.

"By rights, the plantation should've gone to a *Mr. Landry Heathwood.*"

I hold my breath; a giant, animated question mark takes over the next slide.

"The thing is, I couldn't find out anything about this guy. He didn't go to court when the house changed hands. He's not on social—not even the old people ones. But he's out there somewhere. And if he ever decided he wanted his family plantation back..."

My mouth drops open. "He could take the house from Claudia. Is that what you're saying?"

Layla shrugs. "I'm not a lawyer, but my ex, the one who sold me my apartment in Malibu? He says, *maybe*."

On all fronts, this is a lot to digest.

"You really own an apartment in Malibu?"

Hair flip. "Uh-huh."

"And the guy who sold it to you was . . . your *ex*?"

"Right."

"How old was this guy?"

She shrugs. "Twenty-something? You should see the apartment sometime, it really is gorgeous. My Fabletics spon-con paid for it. I just thank God for Kate Hudson every day."

I blink, sifting through layers of privilege confusingly mixed with trauma.

"It was only a few dates. Plus, I've been told that I'm an *old soul*."

Layla smiles like I'm supposed to laugh, but what she just told me isn't funny.

"Where was your mother in all this?"

Layla frowns. "Milan? No, wait—Shanghai?" She gives up. "Hard to say."

"But did she *know*?"

"Absolutely not. But." Layla hesitates.

My eyebrows rise straight into my hair. "But *what*?"

"I always worried that if she *did* find out, she just wouldn't care."

That single sentence scares me more than the entire *Conjuring* trilogy put together. Between today and the horrible housewarming, I've gotten a pretty clear picture of Layla's damage: her mom issues, her terrible aloneness. I wonder what's worse: having a bad mom, or a good one who died.

Okay, dead is always worse.

Still.

"You really think your mom wouldn't care that you were dating a grown-ass adult?"

She squirms. "I just don't know, is the thing. But like, why tempt fate?"

It's such a sad thought, I have to say something. "I'm really sorry."

"Aw, thanks." She really does look grateful. "But don't worry. I'm okay."

"Maybe it's just better to date people your own age?"

"I do sometimes, but only if they're crazy hot."

My mind wanders to a flash of smile, wicked as a falling star.

Layla speaks in singsong. "Who...are you...thinking of?"

I blush fiercely. "Literally no one."

"Mmm," she hums skeptically. "You'll have to do better than that."

"An old friend's come back, that's all. I hadn't seen him since we were kids, and then today..."

"Oh my God, friends-to-lovers, that's so romantic."

Beyond embarrassed, I roll my eyes. "Can we please get back to Belle Grove?"

"Sure." She gestures to the PowerPoint. "You ready to hear the last prong?"

"Is that a real word—'prong'? Because I don't love it."

"The next prong's the best prong." She shimmies her shoulders. *"Outreach."*

Onscreen, a spreadsheet appears, hundreds of names long.

"This is Sunny's guest list," Layla whispers conspiratorially. "I screen-grabbed it from Mom's computer, which is, like, felony theft. The names at the top are Sunny's bridesmaids, and that's where we should start."

I'm squinting at those names. "Charles Waylon the Third? *Duchess Luella Dubois?*"

"Yeah, everybody's superfamous. Singers, actresses, models, a couple of old European aristocrats. But do you know what all these people have in common? Their reputations make or break them. If we launch an email campaign explaining how wrong this wedding is...one of them just might listen."

Layla sounds excited, but my own heart sinks.

The email campaign, the optics thing, even reaching out to the descendant...all of it depends on some white person, somewhere, doing the right thing. And lately, waiting on white folks to do better feels utterly hopeless.

As if on cue, my phone blasts the theme song from John Carpenter's *Halloween*. Last night, I programmed a Google alert for *Sunny Blake + wedding*, and now, there's news. Dread curling in my belly, I click the link.

STARS GETTING HITCHED!!! a tacky headline reads above a pap photo of Sunny wearing a white maxi dress.

> **Sunny Blake & Randy White are finally tying the knot!!!**
>
> **An anonymous source dishes that Sunny couldn't be more excited for her "White" wedding, with plans to host the fete this fall at the southern plantation of her godmother, soap star Claudia Hartwell.**
>
> **"Sunny loves the antebellum aesthetic," says our tipper. "She wants old-world charm: big dresses, tuxedos, and mint juleps to celebrate their epic, timeless love."**

Enraged, I flash the phone at Layla. "She loves the antebellum aesthetic? You mean, those good old days when we were slaves?"

"Shit." Layla pulls it up on her own screen. "But look at the comments, H. People are pissed."

She's right.

I thought plantation weddings weren't okay anymore, someone writes.

I can't even, an account grumbles.

And: *The gall of posting this white nonsense on God's own Internet.*

I google: *sunny blake plantation wedding outrage*, hoping for Twitter riots or at least a few think pieces. But Google informs me that there aren't many great matches for my search.

"What the hell? Why is no one talking about this?"

Layla studies the search page. "I smell Sunny's PR. People are probably tweeting takes about the wedding, but a good publicity team can bury it in articles about her clothes, or whatever."

And in fact, one of the Google hits about the movie star is an article titled: SUNNY BLAKE STEPS OUT IN PANTS.

Now that's news you can use.

The power of wealth will never cease to amaze me…and the wedding's in just a few months.

"Um, Layla…." My voice thickens with despair.

"I know. But as Britney once said, when you really want something, *you better work, bitch*. I'll glow up your website. You start blasting emails to that wedding party. Okay?"

"Okay." I swallow. "Also, I wanted to say—" My throat squeezes tight, and I have no idea why this is so hard. "Thanks. I really didn't expect the whole, like, PowerPoint display."

She looks up from her computer, surprised. "Of course. I promised I'd bring my A game, didn't I?"

In my head, I'm already crafting my email to Sunny's wedding party. I'm looking forward to walking them through all ninety billion reasons why a plantation wedding is not okay.

But then I think of the wrecked cabins and torn-up earth. Inside my stomach, fury twists hot fingers.

"Layla, is your mom planning on breaking any more ground at Belle Grove? Building any more new structures?"

"Why?"

"Because enslaved people weren't always buried in graveyards."

Layla pales. "She's building a gazebo where those cabins were, and adding onto the second floor of the mansion…as soon as they get that chandelier cleaned up. But that's all."

"You sure?"

"I think so. Claudia's not made of money. If the venue's some big success, though…"

Helpless, I slump.

"But it won't be," Layla says. "Because we're going to cancel her."

"Right."

"We will," Layla says firmly. "And one last thing." There's an impish gleam in her baby blues. "I know you said I shouldn't, but I sort of wrote that apology letter anyway? I left it on Dr. Heidel's desk this morning."

"Excuse me, you *what*?"

"Don't be mad! If this is going to work, I need you at school with me. Mom doesn't love that I came over here, you know. Plus, it's lonely at St. Anne's without you."

Like she knows she's in trouble, Layla's already buried herself in website work. Which I do appreciate.

However.

"Not cool, Layla. Not cool, at all."

She holds up a manicured finger. "One free pass is all I ask. One free pass, for a friend."

I stare daggers at her perfect profile until she looks at me.

I'm too messed up to handle betrayal of any kind. And the rage monster, well—she's just waiting for an excuse to brandish claws and teeth. After all, Layla Hartwell's still the white girl living at Belle Grove.

"One free pass," I concede. "Just one."

Layla waggles her eyebrows. "You won't regret it, H. I swear."

And just like that, my suspension vacation is over.

Harriet Douglass is going back to school.

● ● ● ● ●

But first: some light stalking.

What Layla Hartwell revealed about her mother freaked me out so much, I'm helpless not to investigate as soon as Dad goes to sleep.

Layla's active on TikTok—she's in fact made so many *Day in the Life* videos I wonder how much time she realistically has to actually *live* her life—but Instagram is her bread and butter. She's followed mostly by millennial white women interested in purchasing face creams and beige activewear. I get the impression that Layla Hartwell is extremely busy with her collaborations, and also, extremely alone. It's the rare photo that features Layla Hartwell and an age-appropriate friend.

And, so far as I can tell, she's posted zero photos—zip, nada, zilch—of her and her mother.

She's embarrassed of her, I think at first. *No influencer wants a racist, Botoxed diva for a mother.*

Nevertheless, some instinct makes me keep scrolling.

Back. Back. *Way* back.

And there it is: the literal mother lode.

For six weeks last year, Claudia and Layla were *close*—as in #besties, #twinning, matching swimwear close.

So grateful for my amazing, glass-ceiling shattering mother!!!

Can't believe I get to go to Joshua Tree with this amazing woman!!!

Happy New Year from me and my HOT mom! Who needs champagne when you have this lady??

That last one was sponsored by White Claw.

More puzzled than before, I keep scrolling. Deeper into the past, Claudia Hartwell disappears...and then reappears.

Disappears, reappears.

I drop my phone to my chest and gaze at my ceiling. A spider's crawling around up there. I hate spiders, but Mom made sure I never killed them. *The enemy of my enemy is my friend,* she always said. *And so are bugs that eat other bugs.*

I'm not a psychologist, but if I had to guess, I'd say Layla and her mom are trapped in some kind of hot-and-cold, love-hate situation. Strong Hitchcock vibes. For six weeks at a time, they're gruesomely close. Then something happens off-stage, an argument maybe...and in a snap, Layla's back to her regularly scheduled content, living and partying and posting like she has no mother at all. Claudia Hartwell vanishes.

I'd bet money that Claudia's most recent disappearance has something to do with their moving to Louisiana—and Belle Grove.

My heart pounds, battering my ribs, and the spider falls from the ceiling. I flinch, but just in time, it catches itself on an invisible string.

Baby Anansi's not taking any risks.

So why am I?

CHAPTER 13

LIKE EVERY OTHER Catholic schoolgirl in America, I hate my stupid uniform.

I hate that grown men whistle at it; I hate the sinister black-and-green color scheme. Also, the skirts aren't made for my body. I own two different sizes, but neither of them quite fits. I'd be grumpy about it, but Mom and Auntie Yates, who never had the privilege of attending a fancy private school, both got choked up when I wore it the first time. They told me then that I'm blessed to go to a place like St. Anne's. And they're objectively right; I am.

Now, though, I'm worried about what Dawn Yates will think when he sees me later today. I'm leading him around the grounds right after school, helping him get photos for our new brochure. The knowledge that he'll be at my place when I get back sends the nerves in my stomach swerving.

To be clear, I do *not* like him.

But I wouldn't mind if I managed to trick him into thinking I'm fine.

Before Dr. Heidel's class, I'm adjusting my itchy collar in my locker mirror when Graham Lucien appears.

"Hey, Harriet," he says sheepishly.

I bristle, because I haven't forgotten that he put me up on TikTok without asking my permission. Now my history class walkout with Layla has like five hundred views and counting.

"Hey, Graham. What's up?"

"I just wondered if you wanted me to walk you to Heidel's class today. Because, you know, I've got your back." He scuffs his shoes against the linoleum. "We all do."

Now that's a straight lie.

St. Anne's kids, safe in their bubble of privilege, could care less about a history teacher's microaggressions. I'm not about to forget that when it all went down, not a single one of them stood up for me—only Layla Hartwell took a stance.

"Um, no thanks. I'm fine."

He's turning to leave when I remember again how awful it felt to watch myself slink out of class on TikTok. I didn't look like a Westwood tour guide, or a future historian. I just looked like a helpless victim.

"Graham?"

Hopeful, he turns.

"You should've asked my permission before you posted that video."

He stammers. "I—oh. I thought you'd be happy, because it captured the injustice, you know? It's like—journalism."

I slam my locker door shut. "Except not. Because you're not a journalist."

"Sorry?"

"You're a student just like the rest of us. But even if it were journalism...just remember that, like, Black trauma doesn't exist to give you more content."

"I will." His voice is low and earnest, so points for that. "Just one question."

I raise my eyebrows.

"If I'd asked your permission to post that video, would you have said yes?"

I don't know why that question gives me vertigo. "No."

"Okay. And that's totally fair. It's just that—this school's changing. People are, like, questioning their privilege. Trying to do better. Now's the time to highlight this stuff. To give people a chance?"

I open my mouth to shut him down, but I know that if I flip out, he'll run straight to Sonya. Didn't I promise her that I'd be nice to her boyfriend?

"I appreciate that you're trying to do the work, okay? I'm sorry I snapped at you."

Relief floods Graham's face. Relaxed, his precise, small features are kind of cute—I guess. For Sonya's sake, I'll try to be civil.

But I still don't trust him.

The five-minute warning bell rings. Graham flashes me a peace sign, and then lights off.

I trudge to Heidel's class like there's lead in my shoes. I even consider ditching this period, but I can't. I need this class. Whatever chance I have of getting into Brown depends on it.

Inside, I look for Layla, but she's not here yet.

Dr. Heidel starts class then: a discussion of old Confederate monuments in New Orleans and the activists who brought them down. I tense for racism, but his lecture is actually...on point? He's against the statues and monuments that cause pain to people living today; he believes in the importance of memorials for the enslaved.

My shoulders, tense from the moment the words *Confederate monuments* came out of his mouth, slowly relax. But there's still no sign of Layla, and worry gnaws me.

After class, I keep my head down. Avoiding Dr. Heidel's gaze as I stand to leave.

"Harriet Douglass? Please stay behind."

For crying out loud.

Longingly, I watch my classmates file out. They're chattering excitedly about next period, but Morgan shoots me a narrow look that I can't read.

Two years ago, Morgan was a nice kid who loved horror movies almost as much as I do, and wanted nothing more than to pet an after-rain snail. But now, who knows? We haven't really talked in years.

I figure she's just hoping for another spectacle, another show.

I break eye contact, facing Dr. Heidel. Sensing she's not wanted, Morgan shuffles out, her rain boots squeaking.

Where's Layla? Why didn't she come to class today?

"Miss Douglass." He sure as hell knows my name now. "A question."

He holds up a thick piece of letter paper—*Layla's apology*—and dread seizes me by the throat.

"Can you tell me how to spell the word 'privilege'?"

A wave of light-headedness washes over me, because this is a trap.

I don't know how exactly. But it is.

"Um."

Dr. Heidel crosses his arms. "Spell it out. Is that so hard?"

Even after his perfectly acceptable monument lecture, I hate this guy with the fire of a thousand suns.

"Spell it, or I'll mark down your participation grade."

Jesus, okay. "Privilege." I channel *Akeelah and the Bee.* "P-R-I-V-I-L-E-G-E."

"Funny how you couldn't spell that in your apology letter. You wrote, and I quote—" He consults the paper. *"Priv-ledge."*

Layla. Hard fail.

I mean, would spell-check have been too much to ask?

"What we have here is a case of plagiarism," Dr. Heidel continues. "Someone else wrote this letter, and yet you turned it in as if it were your own."

God, the man clearly hates me. Though the feeling's mutual, I'm drenched with shame. Except for math class, teachers usually *love* me.

"Prove it," I whisper. "Prove I didn't write it."

He drops the letter into the wastebasket. "Of course I can't prove it. But things will go easier for you if you admit it. Right now."

An image of Belle Grove's demolished enslaved people's village comes hurtling out of the void: history turning over in its grave.

This world is just so inside out.

It's the descendants of enslaved people who should decide what to do with an old plantation, and *I'm* the one who should be getting an apology from Dr. Heidel. Not the other way around.

"Fine. I didn't write the letter. And you know why?"

He raises one bushy eyebrow.

"Because I'm not sorry. At all."

"By turning this in, you lied to me."

"You got me *suspended*," I hiss. "But I didn't do anything wrong!"

"You wouldn't call your little outburst wrong?"

My cheeks burn, but I swear I won't cry. "You called me by the wrong name. Because *we all look the same to you*. I don't care how many donations you've made to Westwood: You're just like that dude in *Get Out*. You'd vote for Obama a third time if you could, but it's all just virtue signaling."

"You accused me, in front of a classroom full of my students, of being a racist."

"*No.* I accused you of acting racist, not *being a* racist. There's a difference. And even if I had, it's not like I called you a murderer! I was pointing out a fact supported by your behavior! I was clarifying what happened when you confused me with Sonya so I wouldn't have to torture myself, for weeks and weeks, wondering if I'm jumping at freaking shadows. And I could tell by your face that—"

"Enough," Dr. Heidel snarls.

I clamp my mouth shut.

Why do I insist on believing, time and time again, that white people care what the hell I have to say? It's like riding a sickening Ferris wheel, raging out over and over again but never being heard.

No, that's not quite right.

Layla Hartwell heard me. *Hears me.*

Dr. Heidel drums his fingers against his desk. "Out of respect for your father, I won't report this infraction to Dr. Benoit. Considering you've already been suspended, she'd have to expel you for it."

I swallow hard.

"I won't tell her. But I won't have you in my classroom, either."

"You're kicking me out."

"Drop my class or take a failing grade. Your choice. You're not welcome here."

As much as I hate being in Dr. Heidel's presence, my spirits nose-dive. Once upon a time, I'd hoped that Dr. Heidel, as a Brown alumnus, would write me a letter of recommendation. Now, I can't even take his class. Without this AP, there's no way I can raise my GPA enough to impress an Ivy League school. And how does it look for a prospective history major not to ace the hardest history class there is?

Doesn't matter. It's done.

I'm done.

"I'll drop the class."

"Wise choice."

It wasn't a choice at all, though. Not really.

Walking shamefaced out of Dr. Heidel's classroom for the last time, I firm my jaw, saying a silent, regretful goodbye to the future I might've had.

Goodbye to the Ivy League, where I'd hoped to become as charming and powerful as my clever mother.

Where I'd hoped, one day, to transform into the sort of person that people *listen* to, shedding my old helpless self like a carapace.

• • • • •

I'm not angry with Layla.

It would help if she knew how to spell the word *privilege*, but truly, I'm not mad. At this point, I'm just concerned.

Last night, I sent almost two hundred emails from a burner account to everyone on Sunny Blake's guest list, introducing myself as a tour guide at an unnamed plantation museum, beseeching them to reconsider celebrating at Belle Grove.

Today, during library block, Layla and I were supposed to comb the internet for Landry Heathwood, the Belle Grove descendant who should, by rights, have inherited it.

Why would Layla go through the trouble of getting me unsuspended if she weren't going to be in school today?

By noon, I've looked for her everywhere, but she's nowhere to be found.

Anxiety lodges in my throat. It feels like I swallowed a spider.

On my study period, I text her.

Me:
where are you?
why aren't you at school?

Layla:
sry had a rough night
mom said some pretty shit things to me when i got
back from your place

Oh no.

Me:
did she find out about the prongs?

Layla:
no but she did call me fat in front of that asset Hugh
ugh I meant *ass-hat*
stupid autocorrect

104

I truly can't picture a world in which anyone would call Layla "fat."
These white-girl standards are harsh.

Me:
that makes no sense???
if anything, you're too skinny so

Layla:
well yk what they say
u can NEVER be too rich or too skinny

Me:
so you stayed home because your
mom called you names

Layla:
she talked about my body in front of Hugh, and then
HUGH started talking about my body
and it sucked
so i had a liquid breakfast

Me:
please tell me it was influencer
green juice

Layla:
ha no but I threw up and that was green?

Okay. So Layla got drunk on a school day.

It doesn't seem like the time to mention that her letter to Dr. Heidel
backfired.

Layla:

good news tho ur website's LIVE

I open my mobile browser, and there it is, like she promised: an absolutely lovely website, filled with the copy from our brochures and city hall notices, calling Westwood *the* enslaved people's museum of the South. Frankly, I'm stunned. I want to make some changes here and there, maybe ask Dad for his advice on the wording, but all in all, Layla's done an amazing job.

She didn't have to. But she did.

Me:

thanks for this!!!

Layla:

that's just a taste
my publicist's working on some ways to drive
traffic too

Me:

i can't believe you have a publicist

Layla:

haha actually i have two
i've been an influencer since i was fourteen

I keep flipping back to Westwood's new web page.

It would've taken me months to do a refresh like this. But Layla pulled it off in a single night. Now I'm churning with renewed excitement, because, like: What if Layla's three-pronged plan actually works?

What if we *can* cancel Belle Grove, and Sunny Blake's awful wedding, too? Wouldn't Mom be proud to see me following through on her impossible dream?

I don't want to get my hopes up, but still they're rising like hot-air balloons, loosed into a festival sky.

> **Me:**
> thanks again
> i mean it

In response, Layla throws me every positive emoji in the book. Hearts and stars, party hats and popped champagne. Even, for some reason, a New York skyscraper.

Because I've learned my lesson about keeping things from Dad, I shoot him the updated website over text.

Dad:
What is this? How do I open it?

Oh my God.
There should really be a summer camp for parents who can't tech.

> **Me:**
> you're hopeless
> see you at home

But of course, I'll be seeing Dawn first.

CHAPTER 14

DAWN YATES IS waiting for me outside the Welcome Center.
Dawn goddamn Yates.

While the museum churns around him, he stares down at his phone, shoulders hunched in a way that's unreasonably hot. I can't get over it: Compared to the boy I remember, he just takes up *so much space*. I mean, his hands are like dinner plates.

Nervously, I tug my plaid skirt down.

When he spots me, Dawn's wicked smile is right on brand.

"So, you're taking photos for us. What do you want to see first?"

"I haven't seen you in six years and you're all business?"

"Sorry." I look down at my shoes. "It's good to see you."

"Harrietta, be honest." Dawn drops his voice low; surprised, I look up. "You still mad about that frog?"

I blush, because he remembered Auntie Yates's nickname for me.

No one's called me *Harrietta* in years.

"Actually, yes. I'll be pissed about that frog until the day I die."

"Well, shoot." Another smile tugs his lips. "Isn't there anything I can do?"

"You can tell me what you're really doing back here. I know you can't stand Westwood."

He shrugs. "I needed the job. Not a lot of people hiring amateur photographers these days."

I glance at the fancy camera slung over his shoulder. "When did you get into photography?"

"I took a class in school. Turns out I'm a visual genius."

I roll my eyes. "Uh-huh."

"Okay, I'm no genius, but I do love it. You know how this world is, full of lies and people with cotton in their ears. Photography is like...the antidote to all that. A way of telling the truth."

I stare at him.

"My cousins live in the suburbs outside DC, but the city is a mess of poverty. It used to choke me, all that inequality. When I started taking pictures, I could suddenly *breathe*. You know?"

Reflexively, I glance west—toward Belle Grove: the place that's choking *me*.

"And my grandma's relieved, because I'm looking into college programs now. Fine art. I wasn't always on that track."

Yeah, drug wheeling, which I assume he was doing, isn't a great extracurricular. Not that I can talk, being thin on those myself.

"Did you graduate already?"

He nods. "I'm taking a gap year." I open my mouth to tease him, but he holds up a hand. "I know that's some first-world nonsense. I just need a few months to build up my portfolio. Then I'll apply to school."

"Where?"

"Community college up in Maryland. They have a solid program."

"What about RISD?"

I bring it up because it's the best art school in the country. As it happens, it's also right down the road from Brown.

"I'm not fooling myself that I'm RISD material. You always did love that bougie, upper-crust stuff."

"What? No, I don't."

"Okay. Where are *you* applying, then? Community college? Trade school?"

I walked right into that one. "Well. I was *planning* on applying to Brown, but—"

Before I can finish, Dawn Yates throws back his head and laughs. A terrible urge comes over me to touch the strong tendons running along his throat, and that's ten kinds of wrong. Maybe Claudia Hartwell bit me the other night, turned me into a Black vampire.

"Yeah, okay, Ms. Brown. I can see you there."

I narrow my eyes. "It won't happen. At this point, it's more than a long shot."

"You were always Harrietta with the big words, even as a kid. Remember when you spent the night at my place? You must've been eight, nine." He squints, remembering. "You showed up to Grandma Yates's house with this heavy-ass suitcase. She couldn't even lift it. Had to call me in from outside."

I know where this is going. "Oh no."

"I drag that thing into the living room, and what's it full up with? Books. Like ten, twenty books! For a one-night stay!"

"But you made fun of me, remember?" Somehow my hands are on my hips, just like they always used to be when I was a girl. "Called me *Professor Baby*."

That wicked smile, oh my God.

We're standing too close beneath a live oak tree, in a patch of dappled sunshine. My cheeks burn like we're fighting, but I'm not sure we are. I forgot—or never knew—how dark Dawn's eyes were, how many angles live in his face. Every emotion he expresses is so dynamic, it's like watching a play. It always *was* like that with Dawn—and I'm kicking myself for not seeing the artist in him sooner.

Nearby, tourists meander, but they're suddenly irrelevant. Everything, except for him, is rendered in gray scale.

Hey, genius, the rage monster hisses. *He's not into you! He's just a flirt!*

As if to prove me wrong, Dawn looks suddenly serious. "When you gonna fill me in about Rosemary?"

"She's fat and happy." I can't help but smile. "A really good chicken."

"Laying any eggs?"

Forgetting myself, I punch his arm. "Yeah, weirdo, that's what chickens do." I hesitate before saying, "Want to come see her?"

A surprising tenderness floods Dawn's face. He's looking down at me like—

I don't even know.

Uncertain, my brows snap together.

"I'd love to see Rosemary."

"Come on, then."

In the chicken coop, Dawn slips on sawdust.

I snort. "Some country boy you are."

"Aw, just show me the chicken."

I pull her from her cage, where she's sleeping with her white head tucked into her chest. Her eyes brighten, looking at me. People say chickens aren't smart, but it isn't true. You can even train them, and I'm only a little embarrassed to admit that in the lonely last couple of years, I have.

"Rosemary, *high-five.*"

She bonks her head against my palm.

Dawn's thrilled. "Oh, hey!"

I let Rosemary hop down. She pecks, experimentally, at Dawn's tasty leather sneakers.

"Rosemary, *curtsy.*"

Like the sharp protodinosaur she is, Rosemary looks directly at Dawn. Courtly, with one foot in front of the other, she bows.

Dawn slings his camera behind his back and applauds. When I was little, I wanted so badly to impress Dawn Yates, the big kid down the road. Guess some things never change.

"Hey, do you remember—" he starts.

"When she was born—" I'm trying to say.

He smiles again, but this time sadness tinges the edges of it.

"We used to do everything together, didn't we?"

"I used to do things, and you used to tease me."

Bit by bit, that wicked smile's creeping back. "Ain't how I remember it."

"That's how it was, though."

"You always got me back. Remember when you tore up *Superman*?"

I blink, uncomprehending. Then the memory drops like a curtain. "Oh. No, Dawn, that was a *collage project*. I was making it for school—"

"No, ma'am, that was spite. Pure and simple."

"Spite? I was nine!"

"You were pissed! 'Cuz I spoiled *Charlotte's Web* for you, remember? Told you that cute spider dies in the end. I never saw a kid get so *mad*. Fists all balled up, *Superman* scraps flying everywhere..."

My own smile slips away now; whatever the truth at the heart of that memory, it seems terribly long ago.

And I don't like to go back in time.

Before Mom died, I could memory-walk into my past unscathed. Now, the road back burns my feet.

Dawn bends to scratch Rosemary's head, talking softly to her. Such gentleness from such a large person stuns me. For an instant, I want to hug him. Mom raised these chickens for eggs, Sonya prefers cats, and Dad's terrified of everything chicken related. But I've spent hours in here, training Rosemary and telling her my secrets. I've cried tears into her feathers, held her tight against my chest. When my life fell away, thinning like worn cloth on its way to disappearing, Rosemary was there for me.

There's only one other person on earth who cares anything about her. And he's standing right here.

But he left, the rage monster whispers. *Don't forget.*

I clear my throat. "We'd better get going. What do you want to photograph first?"

"If it's all the same to you, let's start with Anna's statue."

When we were little, Dawn *hated* Anna and her huge, bronze wings. Said she gave him nightmares.

"I still can't believe you took this job."

He shrugs. "Work is work."

I shoot him a sharp look, sensing he's leaving something out. I always could tell when he was lying.

As we walk across the grounds, the great memorial bell tolls.

In the bad old days, the master rang the bell to announce a public punishment. Whipping. Torture. A branding with the fleur-de-lis. Now, visitors ring it in honor of the spirits who died in bondage. The bell's pure iron, three feet tall and two feet deep. The sound echoes for miles. Sometimes, I hear it in my dreams.

Dawn shudders. "Never understood how you could live on this plantation."

"It's not a plantation. It's an enslaved people's museum."

"Mm-hmm. Grandma Yates was thrilled when y'all moved here," he says. "But I always hoped that someday, someone would tear this whole place down."

I suck in a breath. "But Dawn. Your great-grandpa Samuel lived here."

Dawn's ancestor worked this plantation, first as an enslaved person and then as a sharecropper, which was almost the same thing. I know from Auntie Yates that Samuel's mother bore the master's children, which is why their skin's Creole-light.

Dawn fiddles with his camera. "In the city, I put Samuel right out of my mind."

"What do you mean, you *put him out of your mind*?"

"I just put him in a box, Harrietta. Same as I did with my daddy."

I grimace. They say it's better to be dead than serve time at Angola. And Dawn's daddy is doing life.

Cooler now, I lead Dawn across the field and onto the path beyond. I can't help wondering if Dawn put me in a box, too. If that's why he never wrote, never called.

For a while, he doesn't say anything. We keep walking.

Then: "You seeing anyone right now?"

Pulse running scared, I stop in my tracks.

Because I think Dawn's working up to asking me out. A scorching terror sizzles along my spine, because *he can't know.*

Dawn Yates can't know that I didn't blossom the way he has. I didn't spend the last six years becoming a wickedly handsome visual genius—I haven't become anything but a motherless mess. He's been home such a short time, but already my reflection in his eyes is precious to me.

Shields up, Harriet.

After years of practice, they snap right into place.

"I don't see how it's your business," I say. "Who I'm seeing."

Dawn's face smooths out. "How did I already manage to piss you off, Harrietta?"

I set my jaw and start walking again. He can follow me if he wants.

After a second, he does.

In chilly silence, I lead Dawn across a small bridge, where creek water runs ice cold. At the end of it, a field opens wide—and there, glinting in the sun, is the largest statue on the plantation: the one commemorating Anna, who ran from Westwood after being separated from her children again and again.

Gazing at her, Dawn and I fall into a kind of trance, lost in separate thoughts.

Finally I sit cross-legged in the grass, preparing to stare at my phone for the duration.

The thing is, I keep peeking at Dawn.

He sets up for the shoot, going left, right, and then belly down on the ground to find the perfect angle. He settles on an army crawl position, adjusts his view, and then goes still. He's the image of a person locked in his passion, and it's mesmerizing.

Never understood how you could live on this plantation, he said.

The truth is, I didn't want to live here. Not at first.

114

Dad was born in Louisiana, but he met Mom in New York. We had a duplex in Pittsburgh, where he got tenure at the university, and until my eighth birthday I'd never been down South at all. For my present that year, Dad took Mom and me on a road tour of the South. We drove all over Louisiana and Georgia, stopping at every African American museum along the way.

At first, we had a blast eating junk food and singing along to Motown hits. Mom put her bare feet up on the dash while Dad drove. At every stop on our historical tour, Dad let his nerd flag fly. History, and especially Black history, excites him so much he can hardly contain himself, and Mom and I were just happy to be along for the ride.

Then the mood soured.

Several of the Black museums Dad plotted on his tour were closed, shuttered. He rattled doors and peered into windows, cursing under his breath. Other sites were terribly underfunded, on their way to vanishing. Dad got agitated as the trip went on, eating more junk and mumbling to himself. Mom tried to keep the mood light, but even she couldn't get through to him.

"If we don't remember our history, we're bound to forget it," Dad kept saying.

"Why don't we stop at a plantation museum?" Mom asked. "There're about a million of those."

Dad frowned. "White people run those museums, because white people inherited the plantations. They practice more willful forgetting, at those places, than remembering."

"But the sites are still standing, at least. Still getting funding."

"It's the houses," Dad said. "The big white monsters white folks find so beautiful. They attract the big crowds, the cash...but they don't center us."

"Hmm," Mom said, wiggling her toes.

Though I didn't know it then, the seeds of Dad's dream had already been planted. He'd already decided to buy one of those big white beasts, attacking the master narrative from within the master's walls.

Living here was truly awful, at first.

Mom and Dad worked so hard, trying to get funding, and then tourists, and then more funding. They bled money for years, while all around us the white-owned plantations made bank talking endlessly about the good ol' antebellum lifestyle.

So genteel. So honorable! Just look at this heirloom rose garden!

Learning to live with the past's cruelties, my family walked a hard road. But now...I gaze at Anna, bronze and beautiful.

If we'd never come to Westwood, she never would've gotten her wings.

Dawn scrambles up. "Got the shot."

He's overheated with passion. The edges of him blend with the air, blazing.

Photography brings him to life, and some deep part of me is relieved. I guess I used to worry about him: the country boy in the big city, the childhood friend neck-deep in trouble. But whatever niggling worries I had are snuffed out now. If Dawn's half as good as I'm guessing, he's gonna be a rocket ship headed straight for the stars: big career, big life, all the good things his hands can hold.

I know, because I used to be a rocket ship, too.

Screw you, Dr. Heidel, I think.

But really, I have only myself to blame.

"Hey." I gesture to the camera he cradles like a child. "This is really cool. I'm glad for you."

Shaking off his trance, Dawn strides toward me. My body stills. He's very close, and very tall—I would be intimidated, but he's too familiar. Impossibly, he still smells of denim and Tootsie Rolls.

Is it possible he still eats Tootsie Rolls?

"Come out with me tonight." It's a statement, not a question. "Burger King. No, Applebee's."

"Why?"

"What do you mean, why?" He laughs. "Because we should catch up, after all these years."

He means: after all the years he ghosted me.

"I was so sorry to hear about your mother, Harrietta."

Mom knew Dawn as a kid, but she never lived to see him grown. This disconnect is like a record scratch in my soul.

"Well, thanks." I can't resist a quick jab. "Better late than never, I guess."

"I tried to find you online. You're not on SnapChat."

"You could've called Dad, though, right? Or Auntie Yates?"

Even I'm surprised by the bitterness in my voice.

"I should've been at the funeral."

"Yeah. You should've been. I know your grandma invited you."

"I meant to get in touch with you so many times—even before your Mom passed on. Every day I didn't, I felt so guilty."

Curious now, I look up at him. "Guilty?"

"We both grew up here, on this land. We both had to live with what it all means. I always felt like...I left a soldier behind."

He flashes me that wicked smile, but I'm not having it.

"A soldier." I try on the word. "What war are we fighting?"

He cuts his eyes at me. "You know what war."

I do. It's hard to keep your dignity in the face of the history we hold. But that's what the museum is all about, and if we weren't living here, some soap star might've bought Westwood up, too.

"Okay," I admit. "Guess I do."

Then Dawn does something funny. He reaches for me, like he means to touch me—and then abruptly drops his hand.

"Go out with me," he says again.

The spine-tingling terror comes roaring back.

Dawn thinks I'm normal—the kind of girl you take on Applebee's dates. He doesn't know yet that his Harrietta is dead and gone, and all that's left is a husk of sorrow and rage.

I can't let him know how much I've shrunk. How I spend every night alone with Netflix and whatever fast food Dad happened to order. How I quit cross-country, quit achieving, quit being me.

Dawn frowns. "You're fancier than Applebee's. Is that it? Name the place and I'll take you."

"I don't date."

He cocks his head. "Okay. So think of it as...a *rendezvous*."

So close to him, I'm vibrating like a tuning fork. For an instant, I let myself imagine it.

And then, predictably, I panic. "No. Find someone else, weirdo."

I turn away, walking quickly and then jogging.

Dawn easily catches up with me. I pick up my pace, testing him, and then both of us are running while he clutches his camera, and even though I'm a rusty runner, I'm faster than he thinks. He laughs, a shocked, delighted sound, and we're moving so quickly it feels like old times, when we used to tear up these meadows like Tasmanian devils. In the summers, not a day went by that I didn't see Dawn Yates. Running with him feels so familiar I lose myself a little. One time, not far from Anna's winged statue, he chased me with his hand balled up in a fist and, the next thing I knew, something slippery and wet slid straight down my back. Stupid Dawn bolted off, yelling, *You been frogged! FROGGED!*

God, it feels like yesterday.

I glance at him, running beside me. Checking that he hasn't transformed back into the boy he once was—the cocky, cunning kid from years ago.

It's the story of my life: this past and present colliding, bending and twisting up time.

CHAPTER 15

BY NEXT WEEK, we know that our email campaign was a total, infuriating bust. Out of the two hundred guests I wrote to, only three bothered to answer—and they all said some version of *Who's this, and what's your problem?* (Duchess Luella also added a blunt "piss off.")

I'll never forget the flabbergasted look on Layla's face when I showed her my few replies.

"I just don't understand it. All these people call themselves tastemakers, but a plantation wedding's as gauche as it gets."

"Offensive, too," I clarified.

"Exactly," she said quickly. "It's extremely offensive."

I wonder if my email would've been more effective if Mom had written it. I tried to stick to the facts, but would she have been friendlier? More charming? More *something* that I can never, ever be?

Or maybe Mom would've contacted the guests by phone. She wouldn't have been intimidated by any duchess; she knew she could charm the pants off anyone.

Honestly, the more I think about it, the more I feel like Mom would've handled this whole thing differently from the start. She was always so brave. As soon as she heard about this wedding, she'd have found a way to confront Sunny Blake directly.

Kindly, but directly.

Since realizing that, I dream of meeting Sunny almost every night.

Yes, I know I'm obsessed with this damned wedding. And no, I don't want to talk to Dr. Maples about it.

In any case, it's time to let this prong go, and I'm feeling much more hopeful about our next steps.

The new website is up and running, and Layla and I just found out that Sunny's PR team is coming to town tomorrow to check out the wedding venue. Tonight we're meeting at the janitorial shed, where Dad keeps a ladder, brushes, and paint, so we can freshen up the Westwood sign before they arrive.

We're hoping the presence of a very visible enslaved people's museum (NEXT RIGHT!) will give one of those publicists a stress headache. Millions of dollars depend on people voluntarily choosing to see movies starring Sunny Blake and her groom-to-be, so maybe they'll decide to call the whole thing off.

At least, that's the hope—and it's why I'm putting on my sneakers late at night, while countless mosquitoes fling themselves into a fiery death-by-porch-light.

Technically, I'm sneaking out, but I'm not worried about waking Dad. Since Mom died, he's become a hard-core insomniac. To get any sleep at all, he basically has to casket himself in his room. He wears an eye mask and noise-canceling headphones behind an expensive set of blackout curtains.

Outside, the air's muggy, zapping with the kind of electricity that feels uniquely southern to me, made of insects and excess humidity and a lingering touch of storm. It's practically fall, but summer's really taking its sweet time.

On our porch steps, I trip on something small and green.

Eyes adjusting to the dark, I bend down. Pick it up.

It's a rubber frog.

Frowning, I flip the frog over...and get a load of the writing on its butt. In Sharpie, Dawn's penned his phone number beneath the words: *Call me.*

For a long-ass while, I just stare.

It's been over a week since I saw him last. I've been thinking about him, for sure, but I've also been busy with Layla, the email campaign, and my general perma-angst. The poor guy had to buy this bath toy from CVS or wherever just to get my attention.

And I have to admit, this play is smart.

Dawn Yates just put the frog in my court.

A mosquito whines past my ear, and I physically shake myself. I've got more important things to worry about tonight than Dawn Yates, no matter how fine he turned out to be.

Waiting on Layla at our meeting place, I worry, fleetingly, that she won't come.

Then I spot a girl-shaped shadow making its way through the dark. I exhale, more relieved than I thought I'd be.

"Hey!" I call out. "Over here!"

"Oh thank God." The shadow shivers into shape. Layla's eyes are saucer-wide. "I think I saw—well, I *thought*—"

"Statues scare you?"

She nods mutely.

"What've you got there?"

She brightens, holding out a square of cloth. "Overalls! For painting. We're going to look adorable."

"It's late. No one's going to see us."

"You're right." She frowns. "Maybe we should snap a photo real quick."

Unlocking the shed, I roll my eyes. "You're unbelievable."

"Seriously, overalls are having a moment."

In a wheelbarrow, I collect the dusty cans and old brushes. Layla, meanwhile, grabs hold of a ladder.

"Careful. It's heavy."

"It's cool, I'm certified in CrossFit."

"I don't know what that means?"

She flexes like Rosie the Riveter. "All you need to know is that I never, ever skip arm day."

I get behind the wheelbarrow while Layla hoists the ladder. Together, we strike out across the field.

Halfway to the road, Layla balks. "Okay so, I don't mean to be a jerk, but that one statue? It scared me to death."

She's looking at Louisa.

I love our Lost Children, but something does happen to them at night. The moonlight pools in their blank eyes and shadows thicken around their limbs. One time, the Domino's guy broke down crying at our front door.

"I'll introduce you to her," I say. "Then she won't seem so scary anymore."

As it happens, this particular Lost Girl is closest to the edge of the Westwood property line. Belle Grove's western field is just beyond the fence. Through wooden slats, I can see the dark of it.

"Layla, meet Louisa," I murmur, because it only feels right to speak low. "She represents a ten-year-old child who died of pneumonia in 1832. Her parents weren't with her; they'd both been sold. See how she's looking over her shoulder like that?"

Layla nods.

"Well, she's looking for her mom and dad. Hoping it was all a nightmare, and that they'll come back somehow." A familiar, elaborate pain wraps around my tongue. "And see this, how her palms face outward?"

I grip Louisa's small hand, and after a beat, Layla does, too.

"Looking back, but reaching forward. Hands still open despite the pain she's known. It represents the way she's caught between her future and the past, and the strength she needed to face it all."

"That's beautiful," Layla breathes.

Remembering how hard my mother worked to bring these bronze memories to life, not long before she lost her own, I shiver.

"Come on. We'd better get to work."

On the road, where we've dragged the ladder and wheelbarrow, I realize what an enormous job we have ahead of us.

Because the road sign is a damn mess.

Dad was so proud when we first put it up, but then, like everything else after Mom died, it fell apart.

Layla tosses me a pair of overalls. "Don't tell me you're afraid of a little hard work?"

"Me?" I scoff. "Please. I nailed down half the planks at Westwood, and dug all the rain ditches, so it's fair to say that..."

I trail off, realizing she's laughing at me. "I'm only teasing."

Grumbling, I pull on the overalls. "So, I've been thinking."

"Yeah?"

"I really appreciate all the prongs, but they're sort of...indirect?"

Layla freezes. "You don't like them?"

"No, I do. It's just that, I think we're playing it too safe."

"Safe?" A twinge of irritation crosses her face. "I mean, I stole my mother's wedding guest list. That's top secret material. A couple reality stars have already complained about your email. Now Claudia's on a rampage, trying to figure out who leaked it."

"The thing is, people don't take anonymous stuff seriously. What if we go straight to the source? Sunny Blake's your mom's goddaughter, so you must have her contact info, right?"

Layla shoots me a strange look. "Sunny *is* coming to town next week. There's an influencer conference in New Orleans."

My blood rises, bold.

"But Sunny's just like Claudia. Oblivious, privileged, high on her own farts…"

"I can get through to her. She needs to hear the truth."

Layla's silent.

"You're so smart, H," she says at last. "But I really think you're more of a background-type person. Not a front man. You know?"

"What does *that* mean?"

"Like, Sunny will only be offended by whatever you have to say."

I bristle. "Because I'm Black?"

"No!" Layla pauses. "I mean, maybe a little. But mostly, I've seen you when you're mad. I know how you react to people like Claudia. You get pissed. And you have every right to be pissed, but…" She shrugs. "It won't help us, that's all."

It never occurs to Layla that I could control my fury for the sake of the cause. It's an obnoxious assumption on her part, but I'd be lying if I said I didn't worry about it too.

The difference between my charming mother and me is the rage monster. Whatever microaggressions the world threw at her, Mom could always smile through it. But me? Even using every technique in Dr. Maples's toolbox, I still wind up raging out.

Layla and I paint for two solid hours, going over every stroke in the Westwood sign. We're using deep blues, a pale gold, and midnight black. My arms ache, outlining the lettering: THE MUSEUM OF THE ENSLAVED: HONORING OUR ANCESTORS. And then, in smaller print: WELCOME TO WESTWOOD PLANTATION.

Layla doesn't complain, but I can tell she's getting tired, CrossFit or not. Her paint arm is shaking, and she looks pale. Working side by side with her, my heart cracks open like an egg. It's well past midnight, but she's still here, breathing in fumes.

Mom would've loved her.

"Hey, Layla. Let's take a break."

She freezes mid-brushstroke, a splash of gold on her cheek. "You sure? I can keep going, if you can."

"I'm sure. Did you bring snacks?"

A grin breaks over her face. "Even better."

We climb down together, then collapse on the grass. Layla offers me a metal flask from her handbag. I take a sip, then immediately start coughing.

"You brought whiskey? *Not water?* Are you kidding me?"

Layla's affronted. "What? We're artists tonight. Whiskey's, like, a whole mood. You look adorable in those overalls, by the way."

"Did you at least bring any food?"

"It's soooo unhealthy to eat in the middle of the night."

I stare at her. "You just handed me a flask full of alcohol."

"Alcohol doesn't pooch your stomach, though."

"Okay, I need you to hold off on the diet culture stuff. It's anti-fat, and I'm just not interested."

"Diet culture is a trash fire. But people only want to see pictures of green juice if the person drinking it is a size zero, so." She barks a laugh. "I'm disordered for the 'gram."

"Maybe you should see a therapist."

"Trust me, I do." Layla smiles again, sparkling. "Have you ever read Sonya Renee Taylor?"

"No."

"She's this super intersectionist, body-positive activist, and she's the bomb. She should totally run for president."

Smelling a Strong Black Woman speech, the rage monster gives a sleepy snarl.

"Uh-huh. And is this activist Black?"

"Yes! A superstrong Black woman. You know."

Whoop, there it is.

Layla frowns. "What's wrong? You can tell me."

I sigh. "So, the whole superstrong Black woman stereotype is actually hurtful."

"How?"

"Like, my grandmother's dentist once pulled her tooth without anesthesia. And remember Serena Williams? No one took her seriously when she was having a stroke. And when she was dying, my mom had a hell of a time getting good painkillers."

In the sudden silence, I realize my mistake.

I told Layla my mom's jet-setting in France, but really, she's buried not two miles from here.

I splutter, "What I mean is—like..."

"It's okay, H." Layla scoots closer to me. "Sandy told me what happened to your mom."

"You've been talking to Sandy Chase?"

"Not really. She only wanted to talk about you." Layla touches the sleeve of my overalls. "She's worried you're not okay."

"Huh." I didn't think flimsy Sandy worried about much, to be frank.

"Yeah." Layla takes a pull of whiskey. "Your friends really care about you."

Strangely, there's an off note in her voice. Could Layla possibly be jealous of me, the *background-type person*?

"Sandy shouldn't have told you about my mom."

"It was an accident. But I'm so sorry for what you've been through." Her voice drops. "And you're right, the Strong Black Woman thing is bullshit."

"Thanks, Layla."

"You know, I'm really glad you're my friend. I don't have many. Despite my follows." She laughs; it sounds pixelated, fake. "I'm pretty sure everyone in LA already forgot about me."

"Really? Because you seem like the popular type."

"Well, when you're *almost famous*, like yours truly—" She does another one of those little shimmies. "Everyone wants something from you. And when you're gone, they forget they ever knew you."

I peer at her. "No one could ever forget you, Layla."

"That's nice of you to say." She holds my gaze for a beat. "But in LA, there's, like, a thousand of me. And half of them are way hotter."

She touches her face; for a second, I'm scared she'll cry.

Layla's not perfect, but she's clearly trying. She wants so badly to be better than people expect her to be, better than her mother and the Sunny Blakes of the world. And yet, she feels like she's not special. Like she's just one pretty face in thousands.

"Layla?"

She turns to me.

"How many of those LA hot girls would paint a plantation museum sign in the middle of the night?"

A beat. Her eyes dance. "None of them."

"Exactly."

To my own surprise, I reach for her hand. Layla holds tight, squeezing.

"I knew you were someone special," she whispers. "The moment I met you, I *knew*."

"That's funny. I thought you were the worst."

"Oh, I know." She screws up her face, mimicking me. *"You're the Belle Grove girl! You're the worst of everything!"*

I cringe. "I shouldn't have said that."

"I mean, you weren't wrong. One time I went on this diet where you only drink boiled rainwater."

I snort. "That's nothing. Last week, I yeeted a chicken at a disgruntled tourist. *A live chicken.*"

We double over, laughing. When our laughter dries up, trust blooms between us like a gorgeous night flower.

It's been such a long time since I made a new friend that at first, I don't recognize the feeling. I'd forgotten about the blissful moment when you suddenly become comfortable around someone, when you no longer care if you stink of sweat or look silly in your borrowed overalls.

I stand up, extending my hand to her again. "Let's finish this, okay?" And we do.

By the time we've emptied our paint cans, we're covered head-to-toe in splatter. Layla's retied her ponytail so many times, it's become a rat's nest; my wrist throbs from holding the wide-comb brush.

But *the sign.*

Even in the dark, it shines like a beacon.

"Sunny's publicists should get a load of this. *Museum of the Enslaved: Honoring Our Ancestors.* That's great branding."

I laugh.

"What's funny?"

"You are. Always talking about branding and shit."

"Fine. But admit I look cute in these overalls."

"Like—you look okay."

She giggles. "Liar."

We head back to Westwood to return our supplies, our ladder, and our wheelbarrow full of paint.

It's been such a strange, beautiful night.

And I think, even if the brightened sign doesn't change a thing, I wouldn't trade it for the world.

CHAPTER 16

O N A RAINY Sunday morning, for the first time in a long time, there's no sign, anywhere, of Dad's salty-sweet despair. In the eerily clean kitchen, he's set out a pot of our best coffee, laced with chicory in the New Orleans style, plus untouched beignets from a place up the road.

These are Dad's offerings to the lawyer who's coming to depose me today.

The lawyer who's suing the hospital that hurt—maybe even killed—my mother.

Last night, Dad reiterated that Mom might've died no matter what, that it's no use obsessing over what's past. But that hospital labeled Mom a *possible addict*. They robbed her of her dignity, all because of the color of her skin.

If I ever saw the doctor who misdiagnosed her again, or the chemo nurse who reached for that expired medication, I'd curse them to the grave. In a battle between the rage monster and these medical monsters, I wonder who'd win.

Dad pops in to check on me. "You okay?"

I'm perched on a stool, a mug of chicory roast in hand.

"Don't drink that." Dad points to the mug. "You've got to keep your cool."

One of the first things Dr. Maples suggested was cutting out stimulants like caffeine, nicotine (which I've never used), and even soda. But after my late-night paint session with Layla, I need a jolt of something. I mean, I'm not a superhero.

"I won't drink too much," I promise.

The doorbell rings, and Dad hurries to answer it.

The lawyer is auburn-haired and white, with the bearing of someone who's very good at what they do.

"Good morning, Mr. Douglass. Where should I set up?"

Dad gestures to coffee and beignets, but the lawyer's green eyes study me.

"Hello, Harriet. I'm Jean Calloway, and my pronouns are they/them. I'll be taking your statement today."

"Hello," I say. "Nice to meet you."

At the threshold, Dad fidgets.

"It's better if Harriet and I speak in private," they say to him. "We find that statements taken alone hold up better in court. And we want to get this right."

"Harriet, can you handle this? If not—"

"I'm fine." I'm not sure that's true, but what the hell. "Go work on your memoir."

Dad cracks his knuckles. Despite his imposing height, he looks as small and lost as a boy. Finally, he shuffles off, leaving us alone.

The lawyer snaps open a briefcase full of paperwork, withdrawing a yellow legal pad, a fountain pen, and a small black recording device.

"Everything you say will be on the record, do you understand? It's very important that your statements are as true to your memory as possible."

Interesting they didn't say that my statements should be true—only *true to my memory*. Historians talk a lot about how truth is relative to the speaker, and their putting it that way makes a lot of sense.

"If I make a mistake, will I get in trouble?"

"It's not a criminal case. Just try your best. Okay?"

"Can I ask you something?"

They uncap their fountain pen. "Of course."

"Do we have a chance of winning this thing?"

Jean Calloway considers this. "I believe so. Yes."

I blow out a breath.

"Ready to get started?"

Not waiting for my answer, they switch on the recording device. "I'm speaking with Harriet Douglass, daughter of Renee and Myron Douglass. The date is Sunday, September 18, 2022." They level patient eyes at me. "Can you tell me what you remember about your mother's illness, in the months before she was diagnosed?"

I launch into it. Jean Calloway is very thorough; we work month-by-month from Mom's first symptoms all the way to diagnosis. It's detailed and painstaking, and by the end, I want to throw up.

Then they ask, "Can you tell me where you were on the night of May 21, 2021?"

That was the last night I saw Mom alive. "I was at the hospice."

"They're affiliated with the hospital that treated your mother. Isn't that right?"

"Yeah. They're on the ninth floor."

Jean Calloway makes a note. "Now, Harriet, these questions might feel a little uncomfortable. We're trying to understand how the hospital treated your mother in her last year of life. You're not in any trouble; we're just leaving no stone unturned."

My neck is so damn tense, it's difficult to nod yes.

"In your own words, tell me what happened on the night in question."

"I drove to the hospital to visit Mom."

"Any particular reason?"

"Because my mother was dying, and I hadn't seen her in a while." I hesitate. "At the end, she didn't want me to see her so sick."

"Did you go alone?"

"Dad was trying to get some sleep. He visited her earlier."

"Did you sign in upon arrival?"

The questions force me to remember facts that are better off buried: the hospice, which reminded me of every dark institution I've seen in a horror movie, no matter how many flowers tried to brighten the place; the sound of soft nurse shoes scuffing linoleum; the front desk with its sign-in sheet, its dish of hard candies; the way I always felt like I was breathing fire, not air.

"I signed in."

"And then?"

"There's a hand-washing station." The water hot as lava. "I scrubbed my hands."

"And your mother was in Room 30. Was it a single?" Mom slept in a mechanical bed by a small, grated window. I picture her thin face, her swollen eyelids, and the stupid television they always left tuned to the most inane possible thing: reruns of daytime soaps.

Hell, now that I think about it, Claudia Hartwell might've starred in some of those reruns.

"Yes. She was alone."

"According to the sign-in sheet, you only stayed for thirty minutes. What happened during that time?"

Oh, God. This is the part I don't remember. The space in my mind so blank it scares me.

"I don't know."

Calloway's pen is poised over paper. "Try."

I close my eyes and see it clear: Mom lurching in bed, grasping for the kidney-shaped bowl they kept on her lap. Doubled over, she vomited, and vomited more, her too-thin shoulder blades contracting under the thin medical gown. There was no marijuana in the hospice to keep her nausea at bay. I held back her hair, and a thick piece of it came away in my hand.

Peeled straight off her skull. It disgusted me, that patch of hair. Mom's cancer didn't care that a daughter should never see her mom like that; her cancer didn't care, either, what a vibrant person she'd been before.

"She threw up. I tried to help. But after that...I can't remember. I guess I blocked it out. Does it really matter? To the case?"

Reluctant now, Jean Calloway taps their pen on the table. "I ask because the staff said they heard shouting. Fighting. A bedpan was thrown."

My cheeks flame. "*Fighting?* Why would we—"

The memory flings itself at me, baring vicious teeth. On her dying day, my mother *did* shout at me—fury smoldering behind her brown eyes.

Oh my God.

I'd forgotten until just now: On her dying day, my mother transformed into the rage monster.

"Harriet? We can take a break, if you want."

I grip the table, reminding myself that I'm not at the hospice. I'm here, in my kitchen, with a lawyer. But all I see is Mom's face, riven with disgust. All I hear is the thunder of my heart, trying desperately to escape.

Why was Mom mad at me? What could I have done that was so wrong? And what did she say to me, the last time I ever saw her?

Recollection tickles the back of my throat, but I can't catch hold of it.

That last day, Mom looked up from her bowl of vomit and said—

"Can I get you something?" Jean Calloway sounds alarmed. "A glass of water?"

Their voice jolts me back to the present. Rudely, I shush them. Then I press my fingers to my temples, trying to get back to that memory place.

Mom held the bowl of her own vomit. She looked up, and said—

"I'm sorry." Tears, salty and warm, stream down my face. "Maybe we were fighting. Maybe she yelled at me. But I can't remember why. Or how. She never—*we* never—"

Jean Calloway hands me a pocket-sized pack of tissues. I struggle to get an individual tissue out, and then blow my stinging nose.

With a firm *click*, the lawyer stops the recording.

My stomach drops, because I've failed.

I couldn't tell the lawyer what they needed to know. I couldn't tell them because I don't remember the last, most important words my mother ever spoke to me.

What's wrong with me?

From far across the fields, a jackhammer drones.

That'll be Claudia Hartwell, building gazebos and shit for a plantation wedding.

"Can I ask, are you in therapy?"

I snap back into the room. "Yeah, I am."

"Okay. Don't worry about the deposition. You did just fine."

Jean Calloway's a busy person—they're already standing, packing up their briefcase. Watching, I feel bereft.

"If I think of anything else, should I call you?"

"If you like."

"It's just that—I can't understand why Mom and I would fight." Disgraced, sweat trickles down my back. "What did the hospice staff think?"

"Don't worry about them. Emotions run high at the end of life; it's nothing they haven't seen before." They smooth their hair. "Would you like me to fetch your father?"

"No, thanks."

Jean Calloway seems to understand. Low heels clicking, they exit the kitchen, leaving me with nothing but a lonesome ache and the endless growling of construction at Belle Grove.

I rise, headed for the high cabinet above the sink. Mom's narwhal linen is up there, along with the tombstone Dad made.

Tea towels, c. 2010, it reads. *Crosshatch fibers. Fanciful narwhal design. Representative of a mother's love.*

My hand wrinkles the fabric, clenching. My chest swells, filling up with fear and grief.

For a blessed instant, the jackhammer halts.

Then starts again.

Maybe it's the coffee, but suddenly, my pulse is pounding against my jugular. I run from the house, letting the porch door slam behind me, ignoring Dad's shouting, "Harriet, wait!"

But I don't want Dad.

I want *Layla*.

A long oak corridor runs between Westwood and Belle Grove like an artery. Spanish moss shelters a faint trail, because no one comes this way anymore.

Long ago, master enslavers traveled this path in order to meet or exchange goods; enslaved people, meanwhile, bore messages between the plantations—we have the handwritten "pass" notes to prove it. According to our archives, a white Westwood daughter once married a Belle Grove owner. Enslaved people also intermarried, but those records are as scarce as leaves in winter.

From here, I can make out the outline of Belle Grove's Big House.

Since I last faced those grounds, Claudia's begun work on a white gazebo, readying the plantation to become a wedding venue. All the ugly feelings the deposition brought up in me tangle into one ugly storm front. At the eye of it all is fucking Belle Grove.

Sunny Blake's wedding is on November thirteenth, less than two months away, and so far, Layla and I have been helpless to stop it. The email campaign did nothing, we haven't been able to find the descendant, and it feels naive to think that Sunny's PR will give a flying shit about our freshly painted sign. Staring at that awful Big House, my fury climbs scale after scale, finally reaching a kettle's boiling pitch.

When I call, Layla answers on the first ring.

"Harriet?"

My words come in a rush. "I want to talk to Sunny Blake."

Silence.

Then, "Like I said, she won't listen to you. I wish she would."

"I know you have enough influence to get me a meeting."

Layla sighs. "I never promised I'd use my influence."

"You promised me your A game."

"And I've tried my best! You know I have."

I remember our laughter beneath the newly painted sign, and the feel of her hand in mine.

"Maybe, but the wedding's so close." I'm grinding my teeth, thinking of it. "It's time to go all out."

"I hate to say it, H, but confronting Sunny won't change anything."

Tears sting my eyes. "We have to try."

"Harriet, what's going on? You sound—I don't know. Kind of obsessed?"

Obsessed.

I squeeze my eyes shut.

My mom's last words are lost to me, possibly forever, and the last hour I spent with her we wasted fighting—something we never did when she was well. Now, time draws short again, the blasted wedding hanging over me like an ax. I can't waste these hours. Can't squander this time. I need to do something ferocious to protect my mother's dream. I need to do what she would've done, if she were still alive.

"All this time we've been dancing around Sunny, but it isn't working." I try to keep my voice steady. "Your mom will never listen to us, but Sunny's not that much older than we are. If we tell her the truth, maybe she'll listen."

I shouldn't be shocked when my voice breaks. Strains of music time-travel back to me from ages ago, from the days when Mom would pour herself a glass of wine after a long day, when she'd drink and hum about dreaming *the impossible dream.*

"What makes you so sure?"

"Mom changed minds all the time. Even hardened, racist ones. She

136

once led a seminar for the Louisiana State Police. By the end of it, they were all in tears. Every day that she was alive, every last *day*, Mom tried—"

"Please don't cry," Layla says. "Let me think."

Over the phone, I can practically hear the gears turning in her head. Meanwhile, my pulse pounds double time.

"Sunny's already put down her wedding deposit," she muses. "But it was only fifty thousand."

"*Only* fifty K??"

"Trust me, that's nothing to her. Do you remember that time she flashed her boobs at those Mayan ruins? She got so much flak on social media, she donated half a million to their cultural center like *that*."

Now that Layla mentions it, I do remember. The entire internet called Sunny out on her blatant disrespect. At first, she wouldn't back down. Then there was an op-ed, I think, and a boycott of her newest rom-com.

To shut it all down, Sunny shelled out.

Hope shimmers through me. Sunny Blake's changed her mind before; she could change it again.

"I'm gonna make some calls. I bet I can get us tickets for Sunny's event in New Orleans. Want me to try?"

"That's all I want. Please try."

I plant myself beneath a live oak tree, its mossy hangings swaying in the breeze. In the space between two plantations, I think about what Mom would say to Sunny if she met her face-to-face.

The half-memory bubbles up again: Mom bent over a kidney-shaped bowl, looking up to say—

What?

What did Mom say in the end, and why was she so angry with me?

Why can't I remember—and how, Jesus God, did I ever forget?

CHAPTER 17

I ALMOST REMEMBERED," I tell Dr. Maples that afternoon, twitchy while I wait to find out if Layla has any luck getting those tickets. "I almost remembered my last day with Mom."

My therapist sits bolt upright. "What did you remember?"

I recall the smell of vomit, unmistakable and pungent. Remember the chatter of daytime TV.

"I was at her bedside." My eyes trace the kaleidoscopic colors of the Klimt. "She vomited into a bedpan. Mom hated throwing up, and before she went into hospice care she smoked weed, like, all the time. But in the facility, it wasn't allowed. So she vomited, and looked up at me. Then her face twisted like she—"

Like she hated me. Was furious with me. Like I'd broken her heart.

My sinuses burn. For once, I wish the rage monster would step in, to keep my tears from spilling. But she's walking in circles inside my rib cage, tail between her legs. Freaking useless, that monster.

"Go on."

"She was mad at me. Madder than I've ever seen her. A different person, almost."

"And then what happened?"

"She said something, but I don't know what. Talking to the lawyer, I almost remembered. But I could only get so far."

"So the deposition triggered the memory."

"Yeah. Hit me like a ton of bricks, too."

"That's a sign of trauma. Sudden, clear memories."

For a long time, I couldn't even accept that Mom's death *was* a trauma, because plenty of people—alive and dead—have been through so much worse than me. After all, it's not like I went to war. But Dr. Maples taught me that trauma is defined not by its cause, but by its effect. And my symptoms are pretty clear. I have trouble sleeping, trouble concentrating, chronic nightmares. There are gaping holes in my memory, and of course I struggle with "executive function"—the simple ability to control myself.

Who says I'm not learning anything in therapy?

"I don't understand why I can't remember her last words." Frustration sets my tongue on fire. "I just don't understand."

Dr. Maples looks steadily at me. "Memories are tricky beasts, Harriet. Many people lose time, whole days, when they're angry or terrified. Do you remember why?"

"Because extreme emotion cancels out memory."

"Correct. Memories literally cannot be encoded when your emotional temperature runs high, because those feelings overwhelm your brain.

"Whatever your mother said, it must have threatened you in some way. Your brain was—and is—trying to protect you."

"How could *she* threaten me? I loved her more than anything."

"The people we love also have the power to hurt us the most," Dr. Maples says.

"But Mom wouldn't hurt me. Not knowing she had so little time."

"After you spoke with her, you drove away from the hospice, yes? Do you remember how you felt behind the wheel?"

The memory sears me. "Awful. I was skidding all over the place. And at every red light, I just wanted to scream."

Dr. Maples holds my gaze.

On the crest of a breakthrough, my eyes widen. "This is why I can't drive, isn't it? This is why I always freak out in the driver's seat. It reminds me of a traumatic moment. Something my brain's still trying to run away from."

I'm sure I'll get a smile for this, but nope.

Dr. Maples is digging for something bigger. "When you drove away from the hospice, were you angry *with* your mother? Do you remember?"

I shudder. "More like angry with the whole stupid world. But Dr. Maples, I can't keep going like this, always wondering what she said. Can't you, like, hypnotize me or something?"

"I don't think that would be productive. You'll remember your mother's last words when you're ready. Not a moment before."

Panic clutches at my throat.

Because what if Dr. Maples is wrong? What if I never remember?

What if I'm doomed?

Outside, an ambulance wails down the street; I startle, cringing.

"The memory will come, Harriet. Right now, you need to focus on moving forward.

"What do you say we try something new to help with your anger?"

"Don't we always?"

Dr. Maples still doesn't smile—but is that a twitch? "It'll sound silly at first. I need you to trust me." She eases back in her chair. "Next time you feel angry, I want you to address that feeling as if she were an honored guest."

"Excuse me?"

"Welcome the emotion. Thank your anger for visiting. Then, gently but firmly, tell her she cannot stay. Ask her where she's going next. Wish her well on her journey."

In her chest cave, the rage monster rolls her eyes.

FFS, I'm not going anywhere, she says. *I'll be on you like white on rice until the day you die. Put* that *in your pipe and smoke it.*

"This technique worked wonders for me as child," Dr. Maples says.

Since I learned she's a childhood cancer survivor, I'm sorry for every rude thing I've ever thought about my therapist. And I really want her to see how hard I'm trying, that I don't take this opportunity for granted.

I peer at her. "When you were sick—you got angry?"

"Not angry. Sad. An oncologist taught me to greet my sadness as I would a guest. Let the feeling visit for a while, before suggesting she move on."

"Did you think you were going to die?"

She doesn't flinch. "They told me it was more likely than not."

"Was your mother very scared?"

"It's every parent's worst nightmare."

From across the room, I can feel Dr. Maples willing me to speak. To try.

"Anger's different from sadness, is the thing," I say. "Being sad doesn't hurt anything. It doesn't destroy your life."

"Depression is quite destructive, actually."

I flash on an image of Dad, shoveling fries into his mouth like he's trying to smother his pain. Is it possible that *he's* depressed?

"Some say anger is only sadness by another name," Dr. Maples goes on. "You, Harriet, were born with an acute sense of justice. Your mother's death collides with that sense, because it's never fair when a loved one dies."

"So I was always destined for the rage monster?"

"Think of your mental health like a hurricane. Multiple factors determine whether or not a storm becomes something more: there's wind chill, sea temperature, humidity, and electrical activity. Alone, no single factor would result in a serious storm. That's all your 'rage monster' really is: a great mental storm."

"I don't see how talking to the rage monster will help, though."

"Isn't it worth a shot?"

I mean, I guess. So far, the rage monster's cost me my ability to drive, Dad's trust, and the Westwood tours.

Maybe, just maybe, she's lost me my last memory of Mom, too.

Heat floods my skin like a fast-moving rash. I roll up my sleeves as sweat drips down my back. I'm ready to get mad—like, really mad—at the rage monster, who's stolen so much from me. But it's like an Escher painting: How can I get mad at my own anger, without losing my mind?

"I'll try it. But what if—" I hesitate, obscurely frightened. "What if she talks back to me? What if she has something nasty to say?"

"Let her say whatever she wants. Then remind her that while you welcome her visits, she can't stay long."

Our session's nearly over. While Dr. Maples makes her last notes, I peek at my phone.

Layla's texted.

i got tix for sunny's thing

u sure u want to go through with this?

In Dr. Maples's waiting room, I text her back.

i'm ready let me at her

142

CHAPTER 18

AN HOUR LATER, I'm standing in Mom's closet, slipping into her green velvet fundraising dress (which doesn't quite fit me around the bust) and questioning all my life choices. Despite fighting so hard for this chance, I don't actually want to meet Sunny Blake tonight. What I want is to watch *The Walking Dead* spin-off for ten to fifteen hours until I fall asleep.

Instead, I'll be attending the Women in Fashion and Media Con at the Morial Center in New Orleans—and it's way too late to back out now.

i only got these because i volunteered to schmooze, Layla explained.

i'll need to spend a couple hours chatting with baby influencers and pretending i understand the clock app algorithm haha

will u be okay on your own?

I texted that I'd be fine, but now, I'm not so sure.

If Mom were standing in front of this mirror, wearing this green dress, she'd see a woman full of confidence and charisma. A woman like a Siren, who made magic every time she spoke in her Ivy League English (or her fluent, study-abroad French). But I only see a powerless, grieving girl with an anger problem, wearing an expensive dress that doesn't quite fit.

If Mom were here, what advice would she give?

What did she say to me on the day she died?

My black flats are in my room; I pad across the hallway to retrieve them.

On the way, my eye snags on a certain rubber frog.

While Dawn Yates lives rent-free in my head, that bath toy's been chilling on my nightstand, looking very pleased with himself.

One hand holding up my dress, I flip the frog over.

Call me, it says.

I hold bronze-statue still, weighing pros and cons.

Pro: I don't know anything about fancy influencer parties, and I'd love some backup from River Road.

Also pro: Dawn's very good-looking backup.

Con: There's a solid chance that I'll rage out on Sunny Blake, and I don't want Dawn to see what's become of me—how mentally ill my trauma's made me.

Truthfully, I don't want *anyone* to see how sick I am. That's a big reason why I withdrew from my St. Anne's friends and avoid them to this day. Dr. Maples says I shouldn't be ashamed of what's happened to me, but I am. Now, I have no idea if contacting Dawn is my best idea, or my all-time worst.

In the end, my fingers decide for me, flying across my smartphone screen.

Me:

hey you busy tonight?

My stomach flips when he answers.

Dawn:

nope just playing CALL OF DUTY

but surely YOU don't want to see me harrietta

I bite my lip—and swallow my pride.

> **Me:**
> it isn't for a date
> i just need a friend lol

Dawn:
i've been here for weeks
how come you suddenly need me now?

I feel guilty for not visiting him at Auntie Yates's place, but that guilt quickly snowballs into indignation. I mean, Dawn doesn't know what I've been up to. How hard I'm working to cancel Belle Grove.

> **Me:**
> you know what FORGET IT

I'm tucking my phone away when it buzzes angrily.

Dawn:
hold up i didn't say no
i'm just surprised
what exactly are you up to, miss trouble?

Picturing his wicked grin, the tips of my ears burn.

> **Me:**
> i'm headed to the Morial Center
> in NOLA
> Layla's taking me to some influencer thing
> but I don't want to go alone

My shoulders tighten, waiting for his reply.

Dawn:
ngl that sounds like a date

                                             Me:
think outside the box Yates

Dawn:
dress code?

I glance into the mirror. In sumptuous velvet, I barely recognize me.

                                             Me:
fancy
like black tie?

Dawn:
dead rn you killed me

                                             Me:
yeah but you owe me

Dawn:
for what exactly???

                                             Me:
for the frog you put down my shirt obv

Dawn:
amphibian reparations got it
you driving?

I don't want Dawn to know that I'm too broken to drive. Too prone to rage blackouts and temper tantrums.

> **Me:**
> layla and i are taking an Uber
> so just meet me at the Morial maybe
> around 8?

Dawn:
got it see you there

My breath hitches.
Oh my God.
I think I have a date.
Despite my unpleasant business with Sunny Blake, a not-unpleasant chill runs swiftly down my spine.

• • • • •

On the steps of the Morial Center, I'm still fighting this damn dress, which wants nothing more than to slip off my chest. Even with the safety pin holding it tight in back, I'm constantly adjusting the bust while Layla chats with her influencer connections.

Approximately one million teenaged-looking girls (though I'm fairly sure some of them are older—their eyes tell me they've seen some shit) congregate outside the center. There's a pop-up sign advertising the party's caterers, some hipster restaurant called GRITS, and a selfie-bait lightning bolt painted on a brick wall, declaring YOU'RE STRAIGHT UP MAGIC!

After a long drive in an Uber Lux, I'm salty as hell. Lonely, too, because Layla knows everyone and Dawn's nowhere to be seen.

I text Sonya: bet you can't guess where i am

No answer. Of course. It's the middle of the night in Italy.

When Layla makes her way back to me, I'm decidedly surly. "Where's Sunny Blake?"

"She'll be fashionably late, of course. Then she'll give a speech, take some selfies, and bounce."

"Not before she talks to us."

Layla takes my hand. "That's the spirit."

Name tags wait for us on a table in the lobby. Layla even called one in for Dawn. His name's been misspelled: *Yeats* (like the poet) instead of *Yates*.

Right now, he's stuck in traffic.

Come on, Dawn. Hurry up.

The lady behind the name-tag desk takes one look at Layla and loses it.

"Layla Hartwell!!!!! Are you Layla Hartwell? I was just telling my friend that you're, like, a PIONEER in the lower-belly shapewear space, and that's my dream niche. Kayleigh's, too! Kayleigh, come *over* here, I want you to meet—"

Layla turns on her heel, coolly cutting off her fan.

"What was that?" I whisper on the way to the ballroom's double doors.

"If she'd stopped at 'lower-belly shapewear space,' I would've smiled and signed her iPhone case, but it's like I said: When you're famous, everyone wants something. Ten bucks says Kayleigh's sponsor-fishing Spanx."

Like in a dream, Layla's words are fully meaningless to me.

If Spanx are not a fish in a hell dimension, they absolutely should be. But I'll never know for sure, because Layla's already peeling off.

"I need to step-and-repeat," she says wearily.

"What's that, a TikTok thing?"

"It's where you stand on a red carpet and get your picture taken. Total snooze, but mandatory for the drink tickets. Meet you in an hour, okay? Oh, and can you order me a G and T? Or a julep?" She pauses. "Wait, are juleps racist?"

Mint juleps, while tasty, are indeed a symbol of old-school "southern charm." They're not racist, exactly, but they're not *not* racist, if that makes sense?

"Maybe stick with the G and T."

Layla snaps her fingers. "Got it."

Alone, I stumble through the ballroom's double doors and instantly wish I'd shrunk like Black Alice in Wonderland. Next to the tiny, pretty girls in here, I feel like a giant. Also, *super* Black. Even though New Orleans is one of the most diverse cities on the planet, the crowd in this ballroom is so monochromatic, it's wild.

Servers in GRITS polos press through the crowd. I take one look at the trays and find my worst suspicions confirmed: They're serving white soul food, which is always a bummer. People wander across a parquet floor, eating little balls of fried mac and cheese and impossibly fancy cups of red beans and rice. (Like, why?)

They're also drinking—a lot.

I meander over to the bar, but I order Layla a seltzer instead of that gin and tonic, fully planning to tell her I forgot. I don't want to confront her, when it comes to her constant drinking, but I don't want to encourage her, either.

At the bar, dozens of bright eyes slide over me, baring perfect teeth before deciding I'm nobody important. But I'm not here to make friends. Like a superspy in a Blaxploitation flick, I'm infiltrating this party.

Memories rush in of Belle Grove's bulldozed cabins—all that priceless history beaten into the heartless soil, and for what? A gazebo. An open-air pavilion where Sunny can kiss her groom before she lives happily ever after.

On my phone, I check the Notes folder I use for therapy.

Next time you feel angry, welcome the feeling, thank the rage monster for visiting, and tell her she can't stay.

I gear up for the moment when I'm face-to-face with Sunny. Preparing to feel that anger rise, and to welcome it. The rage monster's strong as a riptide, anyway: It's no use swimming against that current. Every time I try to fight her, she feeds on it, growing stronger. But accepting her, welcoming her? Maybe that'll feel different.

The bartender hands me my two seltzers, and right on cue, my dress up and slips.

Shame spiraling, I tug it back into place.

Hey, dummy, the rage monster snarls. *This is gonna be a shit show. You know that, right?*

Thanks for coming, Miss Rage Monster, I think back.

Any damn time, she sneers.

Hawk-eyed, I watch the doors. My palms won't stop sweating. I'm wiping them on a napkin when I spot another Black girl huddled in a group of haughty-looking YouTuber types. She's gorgeous, her eyes a striking green. Her group's heatedly discussing thumbnail design, but I'm still happy to see her.

It's unbelievable that there're so few of us here.

When I was still in middle school, Mom took our family to an Easter breakfast at the New Orleans Ritz. She was so excited, dressed in her Sunday best. We were headed to the buffet for seconds when an older white man stopped us.

Smiling at Mom, he asked, "Are you here to sing?"

The blow reverberated through my every bone. Mom was so proud, taking her family to the Ritz. But according to the southern gentleman, she could only be *the help.*

I wanted to shout at him. Call him names. But Mom didn't so much as blink. She nodded graciously to the racist old man and steered me forcefully toward the food. No big thing.

Once again, I adjust my stupid dress.

The outer doors open, and everyone turns—looking for Sunny Blake.

But the late arrival is Dawn.

He appears on the carpet, looking like he wandered into the wrong fairy tale. He's completely, ridiculously overdressed in a white tuxedo,

150

ill-fitting, with ruffles across the chest. Not to mention a cummerbund and matching bow tie.

Titters sweep the room.

I clock the moment when he realizes his mistake, self-consciously snapping his cuffs. And I wince, because I didn't mean to do him dirty when I told him the event was fancy. The influencers *are* dressed up, but it's a cool kind of fashion they're sporting, with everyone showing lots of skin. Dawn Yates, meanwhile, looks like he's arriving for prom in the 1970s. The amount of effort he put into this disaster makes me want to cry.

His eyes roam the room. When he spots me, all his nervousness evaporates. He pops his starched white collar and breaks out that wicked smile.

Suddenly, I don't feel sorry for him anymore. If these stupid influencers don't know a Black James Bond when they see one, that's their loss.

Never taking his eyes off me, Dawn carves a path to the bar. I get a whiff of cologne—masculine and mossy—that makes my knees weak.

"Hey, Harrietta." His voice falls somewhere between a purr and a growl. "Dope party. What're we drinking?"

"Water. Because we're underage."

He leans over the bar. "Hey, man. Can I get a Coke?"

The room laughed at Dawn as he walked in, but the girl standing on the other side of him pulls a double take. With those strong cheekbones, he's actually kind of a heart-stopper.

He daps the bartender before taking his drink.

"You having fun?" His eyes catch mine. "Like, is this fun for you?"

"Nope. It's way worse than I thought."

"Yeah." He steals a look over his shoulder. "This influence game seems hella vapid all around."

"Are you one of those rebels who hates social?"

"I just think it's gross the way people sell stuff. Regular Tok, I don't mind. Actually—and you may already know this—I went viral once myself."

"Oh, really? For what?"

"Okay, technically, my boy went viral. I directed the video, though. You're looking at a writer-director right here."

"And what did your boy go viral for?"

Dawn looks like he regrets opening his mouth. "Aw, the details don't matter."

Now a smile's spreading over my face. "I won't judge."

"He ate a worm."

"He—"

"But it wasn't, like, some stupid prank. It was about climate change. If people ate insects for protein, see, we wouldn't be destroying the planet. It was even a cooked worm. But he made this face, and the internet ran with it."

"Ew, Dawn."

"I admit it didn't have the impact we hoped, and also, that we were super high."

A laugh rips out of me. "That's the most ridiculous thing I've ever heard!"

"That's just the tip of the iceberg, Harrietta. Hang around some more, and you'll see how ridiculous I can be."

My bust slips—I yank it up. "I hate this dress. Keeps falling down."

Dawn hoists an eyebrow. "Oh, I get it now. This is a dream. I'll be playing ball with LeBron in a minute."

Is Dawn just flirting? Or is he really crushing?

Nah, there's no way. He's probably got girlfriends all over this city. Not to mention in DC.

We're gazing at each other when we realize that a small circle of influencers, complete with the green-eyed Black girl, are chattering about us.

"The thing with most of these country people is that they're sloppy," the Black girl says. "They can try to dress like us and talk like us...but they'll always forget to tailor their clothes, you know? That's how you can tell."

She means my dress, which *does* look sloppy.

The white girls laugh; I want to crawl into a hole and die.

"She's fronting," Dawn murmurs, stepping close. "Doesn't want her white friends to think she's like us. You know the game."

"And that *tux*," titters another girl.

The rage monster has heard enough.

Give these vapid a-holes a taste of their own medicine.

"Hey, Becky, *love* the new nose," I say loudly—pitching my voice toward the brunette in the middle.

The white girl's hand rises to her face. Her friends lean back, scrutinizing her.

"No hey, it's not—I never—" she protests.

Dawn takes my hand, steering me away from the trash fire I just lit. It's probably for the best, considering the rage monster's got choice words for all of them.

Most of the influencers are staging photos, but a couple of the drunkest ones have taken to the dance floor. Dawn leads me that way and places my hands on his shoulders. Like we're gonna slow dance to this TikTok viral hit.

His hands, his face, his body close to mine...it's like a goddamn drug.

"You're beautiful when you get mad. Did I ever tell you that?"

"Don't say that. It's, like, my worst quality."

"Hard disagree. I love seeing you righteous."

No one's ever had a nice word to say about the rage monster—not Dad, not Sonya, not Dr. Maples. From her rib-bone cage, the monster preens.

Up close, Dawn looks tired, with heavy bags beneath his eyes.

I frown. "You okay?"

"Yeah. Sure."

"You weren't really playing *Call of Duty*, right? You were out with your friends? That's why you look so exhausted."

Dawn grabs my wrists, cinching me closer. "I'm sorry to report that I was, in fact, playing *Call of Duty*. Alone."

I hate the idea that Dawn's been lonely. "But you still have friends out here."

He shrugs. "Lots of the old River Road families have moved on, looking for something better. Auntie Yates is heartbroken, because she misses throwing her big BBQs. Remember those?"

I do. But because Mom always helped with the cooking, the memories set me to aching.

"My grandma misses the old community," Dawn says. "So do I."

"I know some of your friends are still here."

"They're not the same, though. Don't want much to do with a city boy like me." His eyes tease me. "I studied too hard for those damn SATs, and now I don't talk right."

"What about—" Despite myself, my throat convulses. "Girls?"

"No girls, Harrietta."

My heart pulls some kind of death-defying stunt. Bungee jumping or parachuting.

Rude.

"You had people in DC, though. Seems like you managed to stay out of trouble, anyway."

Dawn laughs. "Grandma acts like I was on my way to becoming a kingpin, but I just got caught smoking at school. Not even weed. A cigarette."

I can't believe we haven't talked about this yet.

"Auntie sent you away from home for *smoking a cigarette*?"

Dawn tugs his ear—a childhood tic that pierces me like a knife.

"The way Grandma tells it, my daddy was bound for Angola since he was twelve years old. She thought I was on the same path. She panicked."

"I didn't know."

Dawn shrugs. "It's okay. DC *was* good for me. Got my camera, didn't I?"

A thrill runs through me, remembering how he looked in that army crawl, every inch of him laser-focused on photographing Anna. My eyes travel over his chin, his jaw—stubbled with five o'clock shadow. I stumble closer to him and he catches me, tightening his arm around my waist.

"Well." I'm breathless. "At least you got to get away from Westwood. I know you never liked it."

"I don't dislike it. I told you. It makes me feel ashamed."

From the bar, an excited screech.

Dawn and I both turn, but it's just an influencer fangirling over someone I don't recognize. Maybe another superstar in the lower-belly shapewear space.

"Dawn." I speak carefully, telling him exactly what I tell Black kids on my tour. "There's no reason to be ashamed of our past. Because we were nation builders. The backbone of the United States, even if the books don't say so. The founding fathers get the credit, but our ancestors did the work."

A muscle in his jaw pops. "They did it because they were forced to. How can I be proud of that?"

"It's not just the work they did in the past. Look how far we've come."

"Not that far, Harrietta. They still kill us when they feel like it."

I sigh. "I still don't get why you took the Westwood job."

He grins. "And I don't get why you're at this party."

If I wanted to, I could rest my cheek on his chest. "I'm waiting for Sunny Blake."

"Never took you for a Blake fan."

"She's getting married at Belle Grove. I'm trying to stop her."

I stiffen, waiting for Dawn to tell me that I've lost my damn mind. Finally, he whistles. "You're *wild*, you know that?"

I tip my chin up, daring him to say more. Then the front door swings open and the crowd stills. Dancing stops, and drinking, too.

In the next instant, everyone's snapping pictures of Sunny Blake.

She prances into the room, trailed by a coterie of phone-twiddling assistants and hangers-on, like the guest of honor she is. On her way to the dais, she brushes right past Dawn and me.

I've never seen a movie star in real life, but I get what people mean, now, when they call someone a star. Gorgeous and golden-haired, Sunny Blake exerts an almost gravitational pull. There's no arguing with her sheer power IRL.

"Hello, Women in Fashion and Media!" Sunny rasps in a southern-fried baby voice. "I'm so honored to be here, in a room with so much talent. Before you ask, yes, I'm looking to collab." The crowd laughs politely. "But please send your portfolios to my PR, okay? Tonight, I'm here to par-*tay*!"

The crowd swallows her up, cameras flashing. Sunny smugly gives out selfies, smiling her million-dollar smile.

My eyes scrape the room, searching for Layla.

From the crush, she shouts, "Harriet!"

I break away from Dawn. "Be right back."

As soon as I reach her, Layla grabs my arm. "Okay, so here's the plan. We corner her on the way out, and then you tell her how the Black community really feels about her wedding plans."

This is it.

This is my moment.

"Wait, is that the childhood-friend-slash-love-interest?" Layla asks.

"Yeah, in the tux. His name's Dawn."

Layla beckons to him. He plays a little game with her where he pretends to not know who she's pointing at, ducking his head and cheesing. Finally, he lopes over, slow and cool as can be.

A quick whiff of his cologne, and my stomach flips all over again.

"Stand—not there, no—here." Layla stage-manages us. "Perfect."

Waiting beside me, Dawn tugs his ear, clearly nervous about what's going down.

For a fleeting, bright-hot second, I hate Layla Hartwell.

She abandoned me at this party, and now she's making some kind of token out of Dawn. Like, *Look! I've got not one, but TWO Black people on my side!*

But I can't unpack all that right now, because Sunny Blake's already saying her goodbyes...and heading straight for us.

My name is Harriet Douglass, I'll say. *I live next door to Belle Grove. Please don't get married there. It isn't right.*

Only, how much does she really care about what's right?

At Westwood, Mom once led a couple of white women—both vacationing accountants—on a tour. From the jump, they argued with her, insisting that slavery wasn't that bad, that she was exaggerating.

Finally, Mom asked them to wait in the chapel while she ran to the archives. Dad and I were there, covering old documents in wax paper.

"I need records with lots of numbers," she said. "These women are accountants. They'll believe the data, if nothing else. And children. They're soft for them."

Dad found her a spreadsheet breaking down the life expectancy of Black children under five. Over the course of five Westwood generations, enslaved women each gave birth to an average of ten children.

Fully 75 percent of them died before their fifth birthday.

I trailed Mom back into the chapel. Looking at those cold, hard numbers, the lady accountants looked suddenly ill. One of them began to cry.

So what does Sunny care about most?

Fans and followers, right?

My name is Harriet Douglass, I'll say. *And if you get married at Belle Grove, you'll break the heart of every Black fan you have. Of every little Black kid who wants to grow up to be you.*

Now mere feet away, Sunny notices Layla. "Hey, girl, DM me, you hear?"

Sunny's assistants are already herding her toward the door.

Layla hollers, "Sunny, I want you to meet Harriet."

The movie star's eyes meet mine. "Ooh, Harriet. Such a pretty name—like Harriet Tubman?"

That shocks the air from my chest.

LIKE HARRIET TUBMAN??? the rage monster shrieks, before exploding into a mist of blood and gore.

Just like Dr. Heidel, all Sunny sees, looking at me, is the Black.

Where America's sweetheart is concerned, I'm utterly invisible.

"And who's this tall drink of water?" Sunny smirks at Dawn. "I *love* the tux."

A movie star is eye flirting with my childhood friend, and until this moment, I didn't know I could actually vibrate with jealousy.

One of Sunny's assistants flicks his eyes up from his phone just long enough to smile cruelly. "Yes, the tux is *very* John Travolta, 1977."

The shade is crystal clear, but Dawn doesn't flinch.

"I wore it for Harriet Tubman," he says, smooth as butter.

Then Dawn winks at me, and air rushes back into my lungs. But I don't have time to find my voice. Before I know it, Sunny Blake's out the door. Gone in a hiss of fine fabric before I had a chance to say a word.

No, no, no.

The hard fact of it hits me like an 18-wheeler: In the moment of truth, I did what Mom never would.

I choked.

CHAPTER 19

ET'S GET OUT of here," Layla mutters.

"Worst date ever," Dawn whispers in my ear.

"Not a date," I snap—but if it were (WHICH IT'S NOT), he'd be absolutely right. All night long, we've been Black, bored, and insulted from the get.

Layla offers to call an Uber Lux, but Dawn's happy to drive us in his old Pontiac.

"I don't want to go home yet," Layla says. "I think we should go...to whatever the opposite of this whole situation is."

"Black Burger King," Dawn suggests.

I laugh. He's thinking of the ratty one a half mile from home. I've only ever seen Black folks in there. The white Burger King, on the other hand, is catty-corner to the Black one. It's nicer looking, but there's no hot sauce on the tables. No vibe.

"There's a Black Burger King?"

"Oh yeah," Dawn deadpans. "They've got a secret menu and everything."

"Seriously?"

"Naw, I'm just messing with you."

In fact, they *do* have a secret menu. You can get canned oyster dunked in the fryer, if you're so inclined.

In the parking lot, night has fully fallen. Layla sprawls across the back seat while I sit in the passenger bucket. My brain wants to go over what happened with Sunny, running through every painful second again and again. But Dawn's cologne is scrambling the few brain cells I have left. Eventually, I give up.

"Where'd you get the tux?"

"It was my dad's. He got married in it."

"You miss him."

"Hardly knew him. But yeah. And I know you miss your mom."

My mood plummets. "Mom always knew...exactly how to handle things. She'd have made Sunny listen to her. Unlike me."

As he navigates the Quarter, the lights of New Orleans flicker over Dawn's face. Every now and then, he risks a glance my way. "You can't know that."

I finger the velvet sleeve of my dress. "It was her superpower, making people listen. Helping them understand."

"She was a lot older than you."

I shake my head, knowing there was more to it than that.

"You were brave to confront Sunny," Dawn says. "Even if it didn't go how you wanted. When I saw you step up to her, I thought, *Yeah. That's the girl I knew.* Courageous as hell."

His words touch something old inside me. Something deep.

At a stoplight, I lean toward him. He leans toward me, too...and though I can't be 100 percent sure, I think he plants a kiss in my hair.

Then the light turns green.

Memories cascade around me, a waterfall. I see Mom, bent over the kidney bowl, as mad as I've ever seen her. Snarling her lost, last words to me. The hospice scene plays on an eternal loop. Over and over again, I let her down.

"Harrietta." Dawn jostles me. "You're snoring. Also, we're here."

I tumble onto the sidewalk. My legs are stiff, and my velvet dress is still cursed. I tap on the back-seat window to wake Layla. Together, we file into Burger King.

The medicinal lights of the fast-food place revive me, as does the relief of finally being out of the convention hall. I didn't realize, until now, how my muscles had tightened, bracing in that unfamiliar space. Though I'm well and truly sick of fast food of any kind, I order a fish sandwich from the kid behind the counter ("Risky. I like it," Dawn says), and all of us collapse into a slippery, red pleather booth.

After the traumatic influencer con, our dining experience feels oddly intimate.

"We got nowhere with Sunny," I grouse. *"Nowhere."*

"I told you," Layla says. "Sunny never listens."

"I didn't even have a chance to talk. She called me Harriet Tubman, and I just couldn't come back from that."

"She didn't see us, really," Dawn says. "Famous people are like that sometimes."

"And who do *you* know that's famous?" I tease.

"Sunny's a bitch," Layla says suddenly—and way too loud.

A fry halfway to his mouth, Dawn freezes.

"I hate that she was rude to you, H. And you know what? She and Claudia deserve whatever happens. They should be publicly shamed. They should be canceled for real."

What does Layla think we've been trying to do this whole time?

"I wasn't straight with you earlier." Glowering, Layla picks unconvincingly at her salad. "There's an easy way to hold their feet to the fire. It's the nuclear option. I wasn't sure it was worth it before. Now I am."

Clearly enjoying the drama, Dawn dunks his fry in ketchup.

"What's the nuclear option?" I ask.

Layla sweeps her hair over her shoulder, stroking it like a pet. "So, you know I'm pretty famous."

"I mean, someone once told me you're a pioneer in the lower-belly shapewear space. So…"

"Yeah. My followers really get swept up in the whole Team Layla thing, probably because I've gamified my online friendships. They compete for giveaways, for attention, for audio messages from me…."

Layla makes a face, like her own specialness bewilders her. Like she isn't the least bit responsible for the situation she's in.

Which, *please*.

"What I'm saying is, I have an army. Not an *army* army, like the Swifties, but same idea. I can guarantee that whatever I choose to hate, twenty thousand other people will hate it just because I do. Frankly, they'll hate it *more* than I do. The magic of the internet, amirite?"

I chew that over. "You're talking about a slam video. Right?"

"I'll call out Claudia and Sunny. Point out everything wrong with plantation weddings, their whole worldview. If my followers dogpile them, if they really *drag* them through the worst of internet hell…well, Sunny's publicists will have to pay attention to that. And Mom will fold like a cheap suit."

"Your followers are white women, though," Dawn says. "I mean, I'm guessing."

"Sure, but it doesn't matter. Everyone on the internet's just waiting for a reason to be pissed. The algorithms that run the place are such nasty little rage vipers."

Layla says *rage vipers*, but what I hear is *rage monsters*.

I shudder.

"You'd drag your own mother?" Dawn says. "That's ice cold."

Layla shrugs. "She deserves it. Because of Claudia, I've had an eating disorder since I was ten. Then she tore my whole life out from under me, all for a stupid, racist dream." Layla knocks over a tiny saltshaker, flicking it like a losing king on a chessboard. "You call it cold, I call it payback."

I think again of Claudia and Layla Hartwell's unholy Instagram cycle. The way they're the best of friends until suddenly, they're not.

"Okay," I say. "If you think a video would help, you should make one."

"I can't do it alone. I need you to be my executive producer. Help me with the script, the facts. You're the expert."

Dawn's nodding. "She's right, Harrietta. You know more about plantations than most people ever will. And you know, for the right price, you could get yourself a cameraman, too."

"What cameraman?" Layla asks.

"What *price?*" I say.

Dawn winks at me; my body reacts like I've been struck by lightning. Somehow, I already know what he's going to say.

"I'll take the video if Harriet promises to go out with me again."

I narrow my eyes.

Dawn points to his chest. "Come on, Harrietta, I wore a *tux.*"

Layla looks at me, mouthing, *Oh my God.*

I scowl, but inside, I'm gooey as ice cream. "Fine. One date."

"What was that now?"

"I said yes, okay?"

He grins. "For the record, I also think Harriet should be starring in this video, not you, Layla. No offense."

Layla's so startled, I feel slightly insulted.

"*Harriet?* Oh, no. She's not front-man material."

I steal a glance at Dawn, whose expression's turned watchful. "In what way is she not 'front-man material'?"

"I just mean, most of my followers *are* white women, you know? And Harriet has a tendency to get—" Layla's eyes flick to me. "*Exercised.* About the plantation stuff. It might rub them the wrong way."

Dawn's jaw tightens. "Harriet doesn't need your followers, is the thing. She's got the wisdom and the message. BlackTok will eat her right up."

"Well..." Layla screws up her face. "After tonight, I just think it's too much pressure."

"How? You'll be making this video on plantation land, where Harriet's been leading tours for years. She'll be amazing on camera."

"And what are you, her agent?"

He shrugs. "Could be."

"No, hold up. I don't *want* to star in any video," I say.

But Dawn and Layla, locked in some invisible battle, ignore me.

"I'll be slamming Claudia." Layla can't keep the frustration out of her voice. "That's where the drama is, the draw: 'Daughter reveals mother is morally bankrupt.' It's not about..."

Wisely, Layla doesn't finish that sentence.

"It's not about what?" I say quietly. "*Westwood and Belle Grove?*"

"No, of course it is." Her cheeks pink. "And I really don't mean to be like...centering whiteness."

"No?" Dawn asks—too softly for Layla to hear.

"It's just that I know what sells."

Layla's eyes touch mine, and I soften. From Dawn's perspective, Layla's behaving insufferably, making Sunny Blake's plantation wedding all about her toxic relationship with her mom. But it's way more complicated than that. *Layla's* more complicated than that.

In fact, she's quickly becoming one of the best friends I've ever had—despite our Romeo-and-Juliet setup, or maybe because of it. Sure, she makes mistakes. But the bottom line is that she's on my team, and has been from the beginning.

"Of course you should star in the video," I say. "My dad wouldn't like it if it were me. It'd reflect poorly on Westwood, and I need to stay on his good side to get my tours back."

"Is that really what you want?" Dawn angles himself toward me. "For *Layla* to make a video about how wrong plantation weddings are?"

"She'll do a great job."

Layla smiles, relieved. She's the star; I'm clearly the background person. It's the way of the world.

Dawn's phone buzzes. "That's my grandma. She thinks I'm up to no good."

Layla laughs. "What's wrong with being up to no good?"

164

Dawn and I exchange a glance. Layla's clearly never met a shell-shocked Black grandma before. If she had, she wouldn't joke.

Dawn hunches over the phone. "Yeah, I'm coming home ASAP. No, I'm with Harrietta." His eyes run over me, setting my skin on fire. "She wore a green dress. It's velvet, maybe?"

I bury my face in my hands.

Layla shouts at his phone: "It's an emerald velvet plunge cut with lace detailing."

"Did you get that, Grandma?" He pauses. "No, don't touch the smoke alarm. I'll fix it when I get home."

Dawn hangs up. "I'm sorry. Are you two okay taking an Uber home? Auntie Yates thinks the smoke alarm is giving her the evil eye. She's never trusted it."

"I get it. No problem."

When he stands, brushing crumbs from his blinding white tuxedo, yearning weaves between my ribs like yarn. I remember how it felt to dance with him, swaying. How he showed up at that party, so gallantly, just for me.

"Thanks for coming, Dawn."

"I had a great time," he lies.

I wince. "No, you didn't."

"Regardless." Dawn bows from the waist, his arm around his cummerbund. "I'm gonna hold you to our *rendezvous*."

As Dawn heads out, Layla looks wonderingly at me.

"So that's getting serious," she says.

"Nope."

"It is. And I like him. He's got this sort of...white knight vibe."

"Black knight, you mean."

She giggles. "He's a snack. And damn, the way he *looks* at you..."

I feel a little sad, realizing this is girl talk. Like I'm betraying Sonya, somehow. I check my phone again, hoping she found time to text me back.

It's crickets.

When I glance up again, Layla wears a look so melancholy it scares me.

"Hey. You worried about slamming your mom?"

Her mouth twists. "Like I said, she deserves it. Especially now."

"Okay, then what's going on with you?"

"Nothing."

"Just tell me."

She bites her lip. "You remember that guy, Hugh?"

I *do* remember Hugh: his smarmy smile, his entitled attitude on the night of Claudia Hartwell's disastrous housewarming. And of course I remember the way he looked at Layla. Like he wanted to eat her alive.

"Okay, so. He maybe, *possibly*, hit on me. Mom sent him to give me a ride home from school, and he tried to take me back to his place."

My blood spikes with rage. "He *what*?"

"Maybe I overreacted, but I got scared. I had to call my own car. And tonight, he's staying at Belle Grove." She furrows her brow. "I really don't want to go home, H."

Jesus. That Hugh's a real piece of shit.

I'm way out of my depth here, but I *do* want to help Layla. She doesn't have a white knight to call. Or even a real mother.

"Come home with me," I say impulsively. "We'll have a good old-fashioned sleepover."

"Really?"

"Sure. We can watch a movie."

"Okay." Layla's trademark sparkle slowly returns. "But if it's a horror movie, I won't sleep. Can we compromise on sci-fi?"

"You like science fiction? I figured you for strictly rom-coms and mumble-core."

"I used to watch *Star Trek* as a kid. Mom had a walk-on role, and after that, I just kept watching. Actually, it used to babysit me."

I love *Star Trek*. Especially since Starfleet got 50 percent Blacker.

I stick my hand out. "Layla Hartwell, you have a deal."

We cross Westwood's grounds together, passing the memorial bell, the chapel, and the Big House. She lingers at the thin point between our plantations, the long oak corridor leading to Belle Grove.

"Mom and Hugh will be back by now."

"Will Claudia worry about you?"

"She probably won't even notice. Hey. Do you have anything to drink? Maybe tequila? Oh, it's a perfect night for tequila."

Ridiculous. "Sorry. I'm fresh out of liquor."

"Oh well."

In my living room, we eat microwave popcorn and watch *Star Trek: Discovery*. Dad drops off a pair of musty-smelling sleeping bags, warning us not to bother him. In his insomnia cave, he won't hear a thing.

"I really like your dad," Layla says.

"He's a good one." I frown, thinking of his fast-food lifestyle. "I worry about him sometimes."

"I worry about Claudia sometimes, too."

Layla and Claudia have an awful relationship, but they're still mother and daughter. It feels important to remember that.

As the night wears on, Layla gets sillier, opening up. She tells me what a big crush she has on all the Vulcans, with their goofy winged eyebrows. We snuggle down into our separate sleeping bags, and though Layla doesn't say so, I know we both feel it: Right now, there's no such thing as a plantation wedding. No such thing, even, as warring Westwood and Belle Grove.

In this moment, the only thing that's real is *us*.

"Hey, H?"

"Yeah?"

"Do you think Claudia would care? If I told her about Hugh, I mean?"
Poor Layla.

I elbow myself up, squinting in the dark. "Of course she'd care. She's your mother. You have to tell her."

"But what if she doesn't believe me?" I hear Layla swallow. "I mean, what do you do if you find out...that no one's ever really loved you?"

In the silence, Layla's words expand like a black hole.

I remember when the chandelier fell at Belle Grove—how Claudia rushed straight to Sunny's parents, never sparing a glance for her daughter.

"I'm sure your mother loves you. She's just, maybe—terrible at it."

Really, this is the only scenario that makes sense to me.

Layla's quiet so long, I wonder if she's fallen asleep.

"Hey, H?"

"Yeah?"

She separates her fingers, flashing the Vulcan peace sign. "Live long and prosper."

"Nerd." Relived we're not talking about Claudia anymore, I chuck a pillow at her.

Onscreen, credits roll, music swells, and the auto-play kicks in, trapping us in an endless space-time loop.

With Layla fast asleep, I get a text from Dawn.

Dawn:
hey be careful with Layla
even her issues have issues

Heat floods my body. Where does Dawn Yates get off warning me about my own friends?

Me:
don't you dare big brother me
you don't know her like i do

Dawn:
you're right
sorry

But I'm all fired up now.

Me:
she says some ignorant stuff but
she's never double-crossed me
i KNOW she has issues
but her heart's in the right place

Dawn:
forget I said anything

I barely read his words; I'm too busy staring at mine.
Her heart's in the right place, I wrote.

It's exactly what Sonya said about Graham when he posted that video without asking my permission. At the time, it annoyed me. Now I finally understand the excuses we're willing to make for people outside the community, when we love them.

Layla Hartwell snores a foot away. I gaze at her in astonishment.

Back in August, when those awful jackhammers were giving me headaches and filling me with molten dread, who would've ever thought that I'd come to trust—let alone love—the girl from Belle Grove?

CHAPTER 20

THE NEXT MORNING, I expect Layla to catch the bus to school with me, but since she has to run home for her uniform, she decides to drive herself instead.

Alone on the 27 Bus, while the cypress trees whiz past in a green-black blur, I tap out a script for the slam video we're planning to make. After school, Dawn's coming over with some sound equipment, and obviously Layla's bringing her pretty, socially acceptable, front man's face.

As the bus pulls up in Metairie, Layla texts me.

Layla:
guess what??

Me:
?

Layla:
HUGH IS GONE FOR GOOD

so long farewell auf wiedersehen goodbye
bish!!!!

Me:
what happened??

Layla:
mom and i got into this EPIC argument after he left
this a.m.
it just slipped out what Hugh tried with me
and GET THIS MOM BELIEVED ME

Me:
she broke up with him?

Layla:
YES!
i was sure she'd say i imagined it but she called
him up right there in front of me and tore him a
new one
then she made us morning margaritas

Me:
so happy for you!

"Morning margaritas" aside, this is great news. For once, Claudia Hartwell acted like a mother.

Layla:
ikr?
mom's making me dinner tonight and she never
cooks for any reason ever

I imagine Layla and Claudia Hartwell, sharing a warm and loving meal at the cruel heart of a plantation. As happy as I am for Layla, I don't love what I'm picturing. I swipe past quick.

All in all, this is *good*.

Me:
we're still on for today, right?
the video?

Layla:
totally
mom's not off the hook for Belle Grove
dollars to donuts, she'll cancel Sunny's wedding
then blow this Popsicle stand

Me:
that's a lot of food metaphors

Layla:
yeah i'm pretty hungry rn

Me:
my advice is to eat

Layla:
funny!!!
ok mom's calling
live long and prosper h-queen

It occurs to me that Layla might change her mind about the slam video. As her friend, I'll try not to show my disappointment. Her safety has to be what matters most. And anyway, it's not just us in this war anymore.

Last night, I saw it in his eyes: Dawn Yates cares about Belle Grove, too.

* * * * *

On Monday mornings, St. Anne's forces us to attend long, boring assemblies. Sometimes I skip it. Sometimes I nap.

In the crowded state-of-the-art theater, I take my seat. Sandy and Asher sit just ahead of me. Asher's wearing his good sneakers—he's probably going for a run later today. Sandy's bopping to the music playing through her earbuds. Graham comes bustling in late, and takes the aisle of my row.

I make a point of smiling at Graham for Sonya's sake, but he doesn't smile back.

He's as white as a sheet.

My first thought is: *OMG they broke up.*

I'd text Sonya right now to ask, but using a phone in assembly can land you in detention, and I don't have time for that.

Suddenly Sandy pulls her earbuds free, whirling to look at me. Her features compress into a frown.

"I quit the prom committee," she says tightly. "Just wanted you to know."

My face twitches, searching for the right expression. What does it matter to me if she quit the prom committee? And why does she look like she might cry?

A microphone squeals; Dr. Benoit takes the stage.

The assembled students hush.

"Happy Friday, everyone! We have a lot to do today, so I'll jump right in. First up: I'm thrilled to announce we've found a location for this year's senior prom! We know y'all were no fans of last year's zoo venue—" The student body groans, unanimous in its disapproval. "So this year, we've partnered with Claudia Hartwell, star of *California Hearts*. She'll be hosting senior prom at the historic Belle Grove plantation."

Blood rushes in my ears, silencing the auditorium. I feel like a spider, trapped in an overturned glass. My mind races from thought to thought, looking for an escape.

A plantation *prom*?

Surely this is a nightmare, a sickening stress dream.

Surely Dr. Benoit's not serious.

But Sandy's turned to look at me again, mouthing something that looks like *Sorry*. Finally, the brutal shock lands.

St. Anne's has forged an unholy alliance with Claudia and Belle Grove. Come prom night, half the kids in this auditorium will be dancing and drinking and making out in that house, that goddamn *Big House*.

Somehow, it's even *worse* than a celebrity wedding. Mom always said this generation was special, different. But these kids who were supposed to *be the change*, who witnessed BLM's great rise, are being miseducated all over again. When they grow up, they'll fondly remember their plantation prom, and if there ever comes a time when they're asked to question their silence, their passive violence, they'll be on the defensive.

After all, slavery wasn't really that bad.

And what about the men who built this country?

There were good owners, too.

Hands fisted at my sides, I stand.

"This is BULLSHIT."

Onstage, Dr. Benoit clutches her pearls.

Yes, southerners really do that in real life.

"Who said that?" Dr. Benoit visors her hand over her eyes. "Who—"

I'm already up and moving, heading for the double doors.

Asher calls: "Harriet, wait!"

But it's Graham Lucien who chases me up the steps and into the empty hall. "Hang on, just wait, we have a *plan*," he says.

But his words couldn't be more poorly chosen. Right this second, I'm sick to death of plans. The muscles of my chest are tight, holding in a dreadful scream.

I whirl. "Excuse me, you have *a plan*? There's nothing you can do, *Graham*. Clearly nothing will ever, ever change."

Scraps of lyrics glow neon in my mind: *To dream the impossible dream . . .*

But I'm no match for hundreds of years of rewritten history. Even Mom's precious love was no match for good old-fashioned southern hate.

"We're planning a collective action," Graham insists. "There's a group of us who want to fight this—Sandy, Asher, even Chase. I'm going to document every minute of our work, maybe even send the footage to my mom at NPR."

Of course his mom works at NPR.

"But we need your help. We need to hear a Black perspective—"

"Enough!" I explode. "I'm not your tool. So what if we do a collective action? What then? It won't help, but you'll get a great college essay out of it—maybe even an NPR piece! Well, screw that. You're part of the problem, Graham Lucien."

Stunned, he gapes. "I'm trying to be an ally."

Fury sizzles, jumping like water in a hot pan.

I know I'm about to say something awful—I can see it coming like a car crash—but I can't stop myself. Can't find the brakes.

"Oh, I've met allies like you before," I snarl. "I bet you tell everyone that you're down for the cause, that you can't be racist because you have a BLM bumper sticker and a Black girlfriend. I bet you're *endlessly* proud of yourself."

Graham looks stricken, and I know I've crossed a line.

I don't know what's between my friend and this boy, but I do know that Sonya would never let anyone tokenize her. The words that just flew from my mouth were cruel, petty, and monstrously unfair.

I could blame the rage monster, but for once, it's not her fault.

It's me.

It's always been me.

With tears clouding my vision, I flee the hallway.

"Harriet, wait!" Asher's finally caught up to us.

But I don't wait, and I don't turn, because I don't want Asher or Graham or anybody else from St. Anne's. Only Layla understands all the nuances that are so exhausting to explain. After our weeks together, she knows *exactly* why a plantation prom is not okay.

And I have to get to her—before I lose my damned mind.

CHAPTER 21

THERE'S A GOOD chance I'll be expelled for shouting *bullshit* in Dr. Benoit's precious assembly. I have no idea what'll happen to me after that, but I do know that I'll never have the balls to apply to Brown with an expulsion on my record.

And all this, on top of what happened with Sunny Blake? It's too much. Part of me wants to hide in my room and cry forever, but here's the thing: Characters who survive a horror movie don't make it to the final round by dwelling on horrors past. They keep running, staying one step ahead of death and trauma and feelings. I've got to keep running, or I'll lose my last chance to save Belle Grove.

Mom and I once watched an interview with an Olympic ski jumper whose coach jet-lagged her before her competitions. The theory was that if she'd just stepped off a plane from Australia and hadn't slept in days, she wouldn't hesitate when it came time to jump.

"Life really is like that," Mom said. "There's no room for hesitation. You've got to act certain, even when you're not."

That's how you fight the unbeatable foe: You don't think about how slim your chances really are. Not ever.

Layla and I are supposed to meet on the path between our plantations at 4:30 sharp, because Dawn wants to use the light at magic hour, which hits between five and six. I walk in circles around the museum until then, feet pounding dirt. Every now and then a scrap of my conversation with Graham floats by in my psychic wind, but I snatch it and tear it up. I can't think about St. Anne's right now; so far as I'm concerned, that whole school betrayed me.

Honestly, I just want to see Layla.

At 4:30 p.m., I stand in the corridor between our plantations.

But Layla's not here.

I jump at the ping of a text.

Sandy:
i'm so sorry today was the g/d worst
want leftovers from the Bake Sale for
a Better Uganda?
i have carrot muffins

Oof, problematic international aid muffins? No, thank you.

What I want is to live in a world where plantation proms are not okay.

At 4:35, I launch into jumping jacks, burpees, and high knees, like we always did before cross-country practice. Two years off my game, I'm weak as a kitten.

At 4:45, my spirits sink, tumbling me into darkness.

Did something happen to Layla?

Oh my God, did *Hugh* happen to Layla?

I should've told Dad about that creep. Should've watched out for her better.

Finally, I spot her coming down the path, hands stuffed into the pockets of the white overalls I recognize from painting the Westwood sign.

"Hey!" I'm so relieved to see her, but Layla doesn't look right. "Wait, did something happen? You seem—"

"I need to talk to you, H." Her expression's grim. "I can't drag Claudia online. I've thought about it a lot...and I just can't. You get that, right?"

Well, I'm not exactly surprised. It was a big ask for Layla to drag her own mother on the ever-loving internet. But there're other ways to cancel Belle Grove, and right now, I'm more interested in talking about that infuriating plantation prom.

"It's fine." I quirk a smile. "I mean, there're plenty of other prongs in the sea."

For some reason, she's still acting like I'm about to stab her.

"Mom's got her problems, and what she's doing at Belle Grove isn't right." Pain streaks her words. "But this morning, with Hugh, *Mom chose me.* For the very first time, she put me first. See?"

"Yeah," I say carefully. "But you said that didn't cancel out—"

"She's my *mother*," Layla whispers.

"Honestly, the video's not a big deal. You've already helped me so much. Done so much. There're no hard feelings. We have to focus on St. Anne's now. On the plantation—"

She interrupts before I can say the word *prom.*

"No hard feelings, really?" She's coming in hot. "Because I know how you feel about Belle Grove. You're just *so angry.* All the time."

My fingertips go numb. I don't appreciate her tone.

One free pass, she said. *Just one.*

I offer up another—even though, if I really think about it, she might be on her third or fourth.

I take a breath. "We can keep reaching out to the descendant. We can ask around at city hall."

"Harriet, I'm not allowed to hang out with you anymore."

What the hell?

"You're not *allowed?*"

"Mom asked me to stay away from you. She thinks you're a bad influence."

I narrow my eyes. "What did Claudia say *exactly*?"

She sighs heavily. "She found out about the emails, H."

"What emails?"

"The ones you wrote to Sunny's wedding guests."

I bark a nervous laugh. "Um, you gave me that spreadsheet. The email campaign was all your idea."

Layla squirms, and in an awful, plunging instant, I know exactly what she's done.

"So...I may've told Claudia that *you* stole that guest list. While you were over for the housewarming."

"You *what*?" I explode.

"It just slipped out, okay? She kept saying someone leaked her guest list, that someone, like, stole it. She was so angry she threatened to hire a private investigator! I couldn't let her find out that it was me, not after everything she did for me with Hugh...so I told a teensy, tiny white lie."

"Oh, it was white, all right. You threw me under the goddamn bus!"

"I know it seems that way," Layla says, pleading. "But you have to understand, when Mom and I are fighting, it's like everything's painful, like *everything* hurts. Now, after Hugh, I think we're finally healing."

Except they're not.

Layla and Claudia are just entering the clingy phase of their weird cycle. In the next few weeks, I expect Layla will post about Claudia approximately a thousand times, blissed out on her love-bombing...and a few weeks after that, Claudia will disappear from her life, and her page, all over again.

"You didn't really lie about me like that," I say, still hoping. "You wouldn't."

Layla scuffs her ballet flat against the loamy soil. I can't help but think of who worked that soil, but I'd bet my life Layla isn't thinking the same. She's thinking of her mother, herself. Her mind free to roam.

When Layla finally meets my eyes, my chest's filled up with bitter ire.

"Will Claudia tell my dad I stole that guest list, Layla? Am I about to be in trouble?"

She flinches. "I don't think so. I mean, I hope not."

Damn it, Layla.

My mind struggles to understand what's happened to Layla Hartwell and me, but actually, it's pretty simple, isn't it? She chose her mom over what's right. She chose Claudia.

The trouble is, Claudia Hartwell can never be anything more than the illusion of a mother, a ghost. Despite everything, my heart pangs for her daughter. After all, I certainly know a thing or two about loving ghosts.

So I try, one last time, to give Layla an out. "You could still tell Claudia the truth. It's not too late."

She gnaws hard on her lip, answering me with stony silence.

Rusty gears turn behind my eyes; I'm on the verge of tears. Layla played ally for a while, but she's still the white girl from Belle Grove. That means she can quit anytime.

Unlike me, she can walk away.

"I'm so sorry, H," Layla murmurs. "Really."

My disappointment welters like a vicious burn. Soon enough, I know, it'll become like the others: just another white scar.

"They're throwing my senior prom at your plantation," I say acidly. "Did you know about that?"

Her face twists. "Mom reached out to the principal months ago. But I never thought it would happen. St. Anne's is your school, so I was sure they'd never go through with it." Her brow furrows. "Are they really going through with it?"

Miserable, I close my eyes.

I've been a student at St. Anne's since the fourth grade. The teachers, administrators, and students all know that I live at the enslaved people's museum. Dad's given speeches at assemblies, Mom invited kids to the chapel's dedication…but in the end, none of that mattered.

What the hell did you expect from this world, you little dolt? The rage monster seethes. *WE TRUST NO ONE. PERIODT!*

More broken than before, I storm away from the girl from Belle Grove.

I think she calls after me, *Harriet.*

But maybe that was just a wish, the wind.

CHAPTER 22

IN THE WELCOME Center, where Dawn's set up to film our stupid video, I throw my backpack to the floor and sit on it, arms wrapped tightly around my knees.

I'm shaking. If we were in a murder show, somebody would surely shout, *Shock! She's in shock!* Then I'd get an ambulance ride and maybe some of the good drugs. And frankly, I'd rather be in a murder show. It sure beats being stabbed in the back by someone you thought was your friend.

"Shit, Harrietta." Dawn rushes over to me. "What's wrong?"

"Layla *bailed*. Not just on the video—on me."

The set of his lips tells me Dawn's not surprised.

"Oh, Harriet." He squats down, gently touching my hair. "I'm so sorry."

"I trusted her."

His face is close, studying mine. "Yeah. I know."

"You warned me, though. Said even her issues have issues." I dash a renegade tear from my cheek. "Should've listened."

"I won't say I told you so. Sure, she had a bad case of main character syndrome, but I liked her still."

I take in the floodlights Dawn's set up, the electrical cords and wiring.

"Sorry to waste your time in here," I say. "Let's be real, though: Her followers weren't going to give a damn about Sunny Blake's plantation wedding."

"Yeah, you're right. That's why we've got to start you up, instead. It's your voice we need to hear, not hers."

My thoughts pulse slowly, like swamp sludge. "You're not still thinking we should make a video."

"I am." The wicked grin flashes. "And so are you. You just haven't caught up with me yet."

He rises, slinging an extension cord over his shoulder.

"Dawn, I'm exhausted. I need to get home."

"Hear me out. We can make a difference for Westwood right here, right now. All you have to do is tell the interwebs how you really feel."

"Uh-huh. Because the internet just *loves* angry Black girls."

"Hey, it's a brave new world on that clock app. And I, as your humble director, would be honored to introduce you to it."

"Why? No one follows me. I'll be screaming into the void."

"You let me take care of that. Told you my boy went viral."

"Your boy ate a live worm."

Dawn shrugs. "I still manifested that shit."

"What's your end game, Dawn Yates? What do you care?"

"Oh, you know." He drops his eyes, and when he raises them, the fire is real. "Mostly, I want to impress this one girl. I'm kind of hoping she'll fall head over heels in love with me."

Oh, Lord. I can't process any of that right now. If I do, my cheese will slide right off my cracker.

"No one wants me to express myself, is the thing."

"Why not?"

"I've got a little anger problem. Actually, a big one."

"It's cute you think I don't already know that."

I barrel on, needing him to understand. "I call it the rage monster. She showed up after Mom died. I'm supposed to get rid of her."

"I don't think your rage monster's anything new. You always were a terror. Even as a kid."

"That's not helpful." I throw up my hands. "It's not even true!"

"Remember that time I didn't pick you for Wiffle ball? You were the only girl hanging with us, so obviously you got picked last. You took me to *task*, Harrietta."

I wince. "I just told you how I felt."

"You wagged your little finger in my face, told me I'd *broken the social contract of our friendship*. What kid even talks like that?"

"I was a brat."

Kneeling again, Dawn pries my hands from my eyes. "I *loved* that brat. And I still think you shouldn't change a thing about yourself. Get mad when you want to. Lord knows there's enough to be mad about."

He's close enough, now, to kiss; my skin heats.

"Your rage is beautiful. A light comes on inside, a fire blazing. I've never seen anything like it."

"What do you care about these plantations, Dawn?" I'm whispering now. "Why did you even take the photo job? What are you even doing here, with me?"

He's still holding my hands, warming them.

"I told you I came home to take care of my grandmother," he says quietly. "But honestly, I took the Westwood job to see you."

I suck in a breath. *"Me?"*

"Ain't that what I said?"

It's suddenly hard to breathe. "If you know what's good for you, Dawn, you won't have anything to do with me. I mean, I'm about to be *expelled*."

He rocks back on his heels, chuckling. "Oh, Harrietta. What'd you do this time?"

For some reason, a laugh tickles my throat. "I yelled *bullshit* in a crowded theater."

"So you were truth-telling like always. No shame in that game. And, Harrietta?" Dawn ducks his head, the better to look into my eyes. "Golden hour's waning. If we want to make this video today, we need to get down to it."

Outside the windows, the world is softening, its edges blurring. From somewhere, Ron Jon the rooster crows sleepily.

We're eight weeks out from Sunny's plantation wedding. And maybe this video's just a message in a bottle, a hopeless final play. But like Dawn says: This *is* the golden hour. Our very best, last chance.

When he stands tall, there's a challenge in his eyes.

I never could resist a dare.

"What do you say, Harrietta? Are you ready for your close-up?"

"Okay." I nod once. "Let's do this."

Dawn scrabbles up, heading for his camera.

"Should I fix my face?"

"Nothing to fix," Dawn says. "You're perfect just the way you are."

I frown, thinking how untrue that is. I take one look at the camera's haunted black eye and fold like a deck of cards.

"Oh, no. I can't talk to a camera."

"Don't. Just talk to me."

The camera whirs to life, but I'm still torn. "I mean it. I'm not good on video. I'm not a front man. Layla was right about that."

"You want to cancel Belle Grove, don't you?"

"I did. But maybe I need to let this go."

Dawn spears me with a look. "Is that what you want to do?"

I gnaw a hangnail. "No."

The camera's on now, its red eye blinking.

"Don't think about the camera." Dawn's as patient as the Mississippi. "Just look at me. Tell me the most ignorant-ass thing a white tourist ever said to you. Remember it—get good and mad. Then ease into Belle Grove, Sunny Blake, that wedding. Tell us what it means to you."

What it means.

Thinking of Mom, my shoulders slump. "I'm so tired, Dawn."

Dawn studies me like I'm a puzzle. It reminds me, somehow, of the way he studied Rosemary's eggshell, toothpick in hand, before he carefully pried her out of it.

"Harrietta, did I ever tell you about Angola? Where Dad's at?"

I shake my head.

"So, like, I visited Dad when I first got home. Shot the shit with him. You know." He clears his throat. "After, on the shuttle out—the place is huge—I rode through these sunlit fields. Do you know what they were growing?"

My hands clench in anticipation. "No."

"Angola was a cotton plantation before it became a prison. It's still a plantation, even today. And you know who was out there picking?"

"No," I say, but this time it's like, *No, God.*

"Prisoners, Harriet. Prisoners work the fields."

The floodlight casts shape-shifting shadows. The afternoon heat presses against the window, cocooning us together.

"So I asked the bus driver, how much do they pay these dudes to pick that cotton?"

Dawn's not looking at me anymore, lost inside his own mind, his own memories.

"The driver says to me, *twelve cents an hour.*"

"Shit," I breathe.

"It's almost one hundred percent brothers up in that prison. I didn't see a white inmate the whole time I was there.

"My great-grandfather Samuel, up there on your wall..." Dawn points to the sepia photo on display. "He was a slave. And you know what? Hundreds of years later, my daddy is, too. You told me that's nothing to be ashamed of, that we built this country. But my daddy's not building anything but pain."

"Oh, Dawn, I'm so—"

"Don't be sorry." He murmurs. "Be *mad.*"

And just like that, his wicked grin slots back into place.

Fire floods my fingers, my hands—and for once, I don't fight it. I breathe, letting my fury grow strong. Uncaged.

"Atta girl."

It's intense, having Dawn call up this heat.

He gets behind the camera, long fingers working. "The craziest thing a white tourist's ever said to you. On three."

I whiplash back to one of those final days of summer, when Vacation Karen walked through the door.

"One..."

This isn't a plantation tour, it's an ambush!

"Two..."

Don't you know *slavery used to be normal? There were such a thing as good owners, too!*

Nodding to me, Dawn holds up three fingers.

Looking at Dawn, I've got tunnel vision, my heart pounding too hard. Claws sink fast into my voice box—and when I speak, the voice isn't exactly mine.

It's fiercer. Stronger. *Powerful.*

"Okay, listen up y'all, I'm Harriet Douglass, a tour guide at Westwood plantation, one of the few enslaved people's museums in the country, and what I'm about to tell you is gonna blow your mind...."

Dawn's nodding, vibing while the rage monster retells the whole encounter with Vacation Karen and her white fragility. All around us, the room tinges red.

I segue into Belle Grove, jamming about the pure ugly entitlement that would motivate a star like Sunny Blake to throw her wedding on plantation land, dancing on people's graves. I'm telling true facts, but they flow like a river of lava.

I am not careful; I do not tread lightly. I'm not leaving room for differences of opinion. With the rage monster on the loose, I'm the opposite of Harriet Douglass, the tour guide, who must not get mad and must not mess up, because in this world, a Black girl can't be anything less than excellent.

Except, furious, what if—I'm *more*?

I run out of breath, and it's a good thing, because the walls are bleeding. Everything's red, blazing. Aflame.

"That's a wrap," Dawn says.

And then he's setting the camera down and making his way to me. As rageful as I allowed myself to be, smoke surely still curls from my lips. My face is twisted, un-prettily, with wrath.

But Dawn doesn't stop at the desk; he bounds over it. There's no space between us, and that feels right.

The red behind my eyes blazes on.

My arms reach up.

He kisses me, and fans the flames.

CHAPTER 23

OVER A TACO Bell dinner (*blerg*), I watch my father closely.

He can't know about my trouble at St. Anne's. If he did, I'd be grounded by now. Not to mention lectured to a bloody pulp.

I don't know why Dr. Benoit didn't call him right away, but it's only a matter of time before they expel me. Maybe they're gathering evidence, putting together an ironclad anti-Harriet dossier. It doesn't help that Dr. Heidel runs the disciplinary committee, either. Surely, he'll be all too pleased to see the last of me.

Waiting for the call, my shoulders creep toward my ears. I pick at my greasy burrito. Dad, meanwhile, robotically tosses back chips and salsa. In the last couple of years, he's sprouted more wrinkles than I remember, and the hair at his temples is silver. The dorky T-shirt he's chosen today reads: REAL GOTHS DON'T MOPE. THEY'RE TOO BUSY SACKING ROME.

His phone buzzes loudly, and I think, *This is it.*

"Hello?"

Gut-punched by shame, I drop my head into my hands.

Nothing on God's green earth is more important to my father than education. Decades ago, he became the first member of his family to go to college—Harvard for undergrad. Mom was also a first-gen student at Yale. Dad dreamed of two generations of excellence, and the truth is, we almost had it. Before Mom's death, I was on track to follow them into the Ivy League. It's astonishing how quickly everything fell apart.

"Yes, I heard you," Dad says into his phone. "And there's nothing we can do?"

Oh no.

I've gotten myself expelled, and of course it had to happen the day I got my first kiss. I mean, how unfair is that?

"Of course. I'll call you tomorrow."

Dad turns haunted eyes on me. I want to tell him I'm sorry—that I couldn't help myself. That I wish I were the daughter he dreamed of. But my throat's so thick, I can't speak at all.

"Harriet."

I tense. "Yeah?"

"Our lawsuit's been thrown out."

The lawsuit!

It wasn't Dr. Benoit on the phone, after all. It was Jean Calloway.

"Your mother won't see a penny's worth of justice. Neither will I."

We look at each other, my dad and me, our eyes wide.

A year and a half ago, Mom's hospice called to tell us that she'd died in the night. Then, as now, neither of us knew what was supposed to come next.

Dad looses an awful, grating sob. Like a lightning-struck tree, he doubles over, crumpling.

I clap my hands over my ears, like I could protect myself from the sonic boom of my father's grief.

It's breaking him, I think.

The medical racism suit on top of Mom's death...it's too much.

Like every Black father in the country, Dad has one mantra for raising his family: to protect and provide. He couldn't protect Mom from her cancer. And as in debt as Westwood is now, with the money he's sunk into hospitals and lawyers, his ability to provide's in jeopardy, too.

"What happened? Didn't they believe us?"

Slowly, he straightens. Drags a hand down his long face. Something inside me quivers, afraid.

"Our suit didn't meet the burden of proof. That's a fancy way of saying they didn't believe us, I guess."

"But it was racism that hurt Mom. Wasn't it?"

I ask the question as much for myself as for him. In this world where I never know who or what to trust, I must know this one thing for certain.

"Yes. We just can't prove it."

He doubles over again, and I feel like I'm losing him.

"Everything will be okay, Dad."

"You're not supposed to say that. I am." There's the ghost of a laugh. "Those are the lies parents tell their children: that everything will be okay."

I flash back to my mother bent over a kidney-shaped bowl. Face twisted in anger, she looks up at me to say—I don't know what. I remember the chatter of daytime television, the pungent smell of vomit. It's all so vivid, clear as a video recording... but then, the recording cuts out.

"Put everything in your memoir. Maybe we can't get the lawsuit money, but we can tell the world. Right?"

He doesn't answer. I want to see his face, his eyes, but he's clenched shut.

His heart broke when Mom died. It'd just started to heal, scabbing lightly over... and then, he opened the lawsuit. It wouldn't have made things right to hear, in a court of law, that Mom was wronged, but it would've set the record straight. And Dad's a historian. The record matters to him—and to me. In the end, when our quick lives are over, the record is all we'll ever have.

Abruptly, I stand, heading for the kitchen speaker. Since Mom's death, it's covered in a thick film of dust. I hook my phone into the jack, swipe through my music, and press play on *Brian Stokes Mitchell at the Martin Beck Theatre, 2003.*

"Listen to this Black man's voice, soaring," Mom would say. "Five years before Barack Obama was elected president."

It begins with a snatch of dialogue, a woman's voice asking what it means to have a quest.

And Mitchell, playing Don Quixote, answers haltingly that it's the mission of every true knight, his duty and his privilege.

Then he sings about the dream.

The impossible, unbearable, unreachable pursuit of what's right in a world that's long since stopped caring, stopped questing, stopped dreaming at all. But we don't have to achieve our great dreams to make our lives matter. According to Don Quixote, there's nobility in reaching, in stubbornly trying, even when we're doomed to fail.

As Mom was doomed in her quest to live.

As Dad was doomed in his quest for justice.

As Layla and I were doomed, too.

I'll never tell anyone how my father cried when that song crescendoed to its heights. His cries, like gusts of grief straight from heaven, shaking the foundation of the house we built.

All the broken pieces fall into place: Dad's junk-food diet, his obsession with the lawsuit, the way he's stopped asking me about my college future...

My father, Myron Douglass, is depressed.

Cries knife through him, again and again.

And I know now, as I knew then, that so long as my arms don't grow too weary, I'll carry the sound of my father's twice-broken heart to the grave.

• • • • •

Grief doesn't stop time.

Doesn't erase consequences, either.

When I'm alone in my room, I find half a dozen texts from Sonya.

She's livid.

Sonya:

where the HELL do u get off shouting at Graham like
he's the problem
what did he ever do to u?

Sonya:

accusing him of only wanting to fight that
plantation prom so he could write his college essay
about it???

Sonya:

and THEN you accuse him of having a token Black
girlfriend, but u don't speak for me!
u hardly even KNOW me anymore! all u do is sit
around and watch gory shit on your laptop and
ignore calls from the people who actually freaking
care about you

Sonya:

u know what, Harriet on a High Horse?
i'm done
i can't do this anymore
i can't even with you

Stunned, I collapse onto my bed.

Above me, the ceiling fan spins, twisting shadows around its blades. These words from Sonya would feel like the end of the world if my life weren't so apocalyptic already. I see myself in one of those zombie horrors about the end times, wearing nothing but rags and a backpack full of supplies, dust and death as far as the eye can see. Maybe I started out as Harriet on a High Horse, but I'm going to wind up Harriet, All Alone.

Except I know she doesn't mean it. Not my best friend. Not *Sonya*.

I tap out an apology, erase it.

I need to speak to her. If she won't take my calls, I'll leave a voice message. But first, I text Graham.

> **Me:**
> i'm so sorry
> i was out of line yelling at you
> i never should've flung your
> relationship with Sonya in your face
> if there's anything I can do to make it
> up to you tell me
> please

Graham gets back to me so fast, I brace for trouble.

Graham:
Apology accepted. Just hope you're feeling better.

Does he have to be such a nice kid? If he could just cuss me out a little bit, I wouldn't feel so guilty. But no. He's Mr. Southern Manners. He even punctuates his texts.

Graham:
Also, about today? No one told on you.

I blink, not following.

> **Me:**
> told about what?

Graham:
Dr. Benoit wanted to know who shouted bullsh*t.

Ever polite, Graham Lucien stars out the cussword; my mouth twitches, but I can't quite bring myself to smile.

Graham:
She grilled everyone in the row. Sandy, Chase,
Asher, Morgan, Cody, and Molly G. She kept calling
it "hate speech."

Oh, I see how it is: Dr. Benoit okayed a plantation prom, and I'm the one engaging in hate speech?

Graham:
Everyone knew it was you. But no one said anything.
Some of the teachers probably suspect but the
auditorium was so dark, I think you're in the clear.

I rub my forehead.

Me:
there's no way i'm in the clear
other kids must've seen me walk out

Graham:
Actually a bunch of people walked out. You know
Lilah Singer? And Mandy B.? They started it, but
others followed. I think the whole entire glee club
wound up leaving, but they might've just been
confused?

I know what he means. This year's batch of glee kids have hearts of gold, but God help them, they're not the brightest.

Graham:

Anyway, no one wants to get you into trouble.
The story of Dr. Heidel and his bullcrap really
got around. The whole student body is outraged
for you. We talk about it all the time.

I let that roll around in my brain, thoughts clicking together like marbles.

I quit the prom committee, Sandy Chase told me, tear-soaked anger in her eyes. *Just wanted you to know.*

Me:
thanks graham
really

Graham:
Anytime.

I hesitate over my next text, wondering if it's even fair to ask him about Sonya at this point. But I can't bear not to—so.

Me:
sonya's pretty mad at me
she told you that right?

Thoughtful ellipses appear and disappear.

Graham:
Sonya loves you. I'm sure y'all will
patch things up. Just give her some
space. Okay?

Though Graham can't see me, I'm nodding vehemently. To comfort myself, I touch my lower lip, still swollen from Dawn's kisses.

Me:
okay i'll do that
thanks

CHAPTER 24

WHAT GRAHAM TOLD me about the St. Anne's kids standing up for me?

It blew my socks off.

Standing outside St. Anne's spear-tipped gates, I'm more conflicted than ever about my fancy private school. On the one hand, there're people inside this building who truly think a plantation prom is okay. On the other, half a dozen kids refused to give up my name in Dr. Benoit's interrogation room...and that thought fills me with fresh, clean hope. Dawn hasn't finished editing our TikTok yet, but I'm eager to drop it ASAP. Knowing what really happened at that assembly, St. Anne's is starting to feel, strangely enough, like a place on the verge of change.

That's a dream, sis, the rage monster hisses. *Half these kids' parents own AT LEAST one Confederate flag.*

Sure, but these kids aren't their parents. They're more keyed into the culture. More online. And Mom always said education is the answer.

Yeah, and look how that turned out with Layla and Claudia Hartwell.

God, I hate this timeline.

Shouldering my backpack, I buck up—and head inside.

●　●　●　●　●

All morning, I'm braced to run into Layla.

After our epic fight, I expect epic awkwardness—or maybe even a repeat battle, complete with the rage monster yeeting cafeteria trays.

But Layla Hartwell's not at school.

Though I know I shouldn't, I obsessively check her stories between classes.

There's Layla and her mom, sipping Bloody Marys in the French Quarter.

And there they are again, heading into the Voodoo Museum. The caption on that one reads: *Got my fortune told today! Looks like the universe wants me to play hooky this week . . .* 😜

Around noon, she posts a pic of her and Claudia boarding a small plane, headed for a two-week "detox retreat" in the Barrier Islands.

Why doesn't Layla's mom care that she's missing too much school? What kind of future is she supposed to have if she doesn't graduate?

"Not my monkeys, not my circus," I murmur to myself outside the lockers. Layla Hartwell can't be my problem anymore.

"Hey, Harriet," Morgan whispers by my elbow.

I jump, because she came out of nowhere.

"I'm wearing my moccasins." Morgan nods to the leather slippers on her feet. "They're silent, for sneaking around squirrels and such."

O-kay.

A week ago, I'd have hustled away from Morgan if she came up to me like this. But Morgan was in my row at Benoit's assembly. She knew exactly who called *bullshit*, and she didn't snitch.

That means I owe her.

Frankly, I owe a lot of people.

"So." I shift my weight from foot to foot. "How's the foraging?"

"Amazing. I'm making this chart of different types of animal scat..."

Seeing the stricken look on my face, Morgan trails off.

"Anyway. I just stopped by to say sorry about prom and everything. Administration's a bag of dicks."

"You can say that again."

"Okay." Her eyes dart around. *"Administration's a bag of dicks!"*

I laugh, defenses crumbling. "Hey, can I ask you something?"

Morgan's smile brightens. "For sure."

"You got into goblincore because of TikTok, right?"

"TikTok, Reddit...some other places, too."

"Do you think a video could ever change things? For the better, I mean?"

Morgan cocks her head. "Actually...I think TikTok saved my life."

"Really?"

"Yeah. Before I found my aesthetic, I felt so lost. Now, it's like I can really be myself. And it was all because of the Black Forager."

I blink. "The who?"

"You've never heard of her?"

"Um. No?"

"Okay, you need to see this." Morgan texts me a video. "Some people think goblincore is, like, an all-white thing, but it isn't true. The Black Forager covers all the basics, which is how I got hooked. But she also talks about the history of foraging, which goes all the way back to plantation life. Enslaved people needed to forage to supplement their diets. There's a whole art to it."

I stare at Morgan's open, innocent face, looking for the racism here.

Because *of course* she'd connect me with the Black Forager.

And yet...the rage monster's apparently off-duty today, because I can't get worked up about this. I actually *do* want to watch this video. In my head, I'm already wondering if foraging might warrant its own exhibit at Westwood.

From behind her ear, Morgan pulls out a sprig of something—rosemary?

"Wild thyme." She presses it into my palm. "Supposed to be good luck."

After Morgan walks away, I stand there for a long time, staring at this random bit of plant matter. It's such a kind gesture, it physically hurts.

Hope physically hurts.

Because Morgan said: *TikTok saved my life.*

In math block, I puzzle over the St. Anne's kids, wondering what they'll make of my plantation video. Watching them laugh and talk and joke, I feel like it could do good here. Even if the video doesn't go viral enough to shut down Sunny Blake's wedding, it could still make a difference right here at St. Anne's—and that's not nothing.

Mom would say it's *everything*, because every heart matters.

I'm genuinely happy that quirky Morgan found a place to belong. But the feeling's bittersweet, because her evolution is just another thing I missed out on, living so long inside my grief shell.

For the rest of the day, I twirl Morgan's bit of thyme…and, amazingly, I don't think about Layla Hartwell once.

CHAPTER 25

Aᴏfter talking with Morgan, I'm more anxious than ever to post. There's a restless feeling under my skin, itchy and uncomfortable. I won't rest easy until I've said my piece.

Unfortunately, Dawn Yates is taking his sweet time with the editing.

"When will it be ready, though?" I ask in the Welcome Center after school. "How long does cutting a video seriously take?"

Dawn's eyes widen. "Whoa."

"Sorry." I shake out my hands. "I'm just a little keyed up."

We're at the Welcome Center's main desk, next to the comment box and the till. Two tours are still in the field, and I've booted up the register so people can buy books and drinks. Dad doesn't show any signs of ever giving me my tours back, but he always needs help with the gift shop.

"I told you, it's not just one Tok, Harrietta. If you want reach, we need to post segments at least once a day for a couple weeks, *bam, bam, bam,* one after the other. That's your best chance of going viral. It takes a while to slice up the footage."

"Yeah, okay."

"I'm breaking it into fourteen parts. By the time the last video uploads, you'll have a serious following."

"How long are these videos?"

"Short and sweet. I think you'll be really happy."

It's hard to imagine being happy while the plantation prom's still on St. Anne's digital calendar, and while Sunny Blake's wedding draws closer every day. So I hover over Dawn's shoulder, watching him work.

"Harrietta, you're stressing me. Why don't you go work on your college applications or something?"

I actually do have to work on my college apps.

Reluctantly, I turn to the gift shop computer, where I'm keeping the list of colleges that might reasonably accept me. Having set my heart on Brown long ago, I'm less than jazzed about my options.

Trying to picture myself at one of these safeties, I think of Dad.

Last night, he ordered in a bunch of unnecessary Mickey D's, and this morning, he wouldn't get out of bed. When I was hustling to catch the bus to school, he was still tucked under the covers yelling at the History Channel.

What will happen to him when I leave for college? Will he survive being stranded on this plantation, full of tombstones and memories he can't escape?

Brown was always a long shot, but I assumed I'd go to some college somewhere. How selfish am I that I never stopped to wonder what would happen to Dad when I left?

"Dawn," I say, tormented now. "I don't think I should go to college next year."

"What?"

"Dad's not okay. He needs me here. Maybe I should just take a gap year."

"No." Dawn puts his phone facedown on the desk. "Absolutely not."

"*You* took a gap year. Like, you're sitting right here."

"I literally came back here to make sure you wouldn't pull any stupid shit like this. Taking a gap year, staying at Westwood..." Dawn shakes his head. "Nope. Not on my watch."

I'd never have guessed that Dawn had a horse in this race. "But why?"

"Is that a serious question?" Dawn frowns. "The plantation isn't good for you. No, don't stare those daggers at me. *You* are very good for *the plantation*, but the reverse just isn't true. Look at the situation with Layla, with Sunny Blake and that wedding. You need to get free of this place. Take a nice deep breath of faraway air. And college? It's perfect for you. You freaking love school."

That's true. But—

"You don't understand what Dad's been like."

He rolls his office chair closer, bringing his huge knees in line with mine. "So tell me."

"I hate going into the kitchen every morning. There's always a ton of rotting fast food from these binges Dad goes on."

Dawn listens intently. "He's got a food addiction, huh?"

"I'm not a psychiatrist. But yeah, maybe."

"For my grandma, it's the television. She plays it all day long. She even needs it to sleep."

"You're worried about Auntie Yates?" I ask. "She seems so...put together."

"She's careful about looking right. Always irons her dresses. But she's had a hard road. All the old folks have."

I sigh. "They all thought respectability politics was the way to get free. But it takes so much effort to present this respectable outside that..."

"They don't always take good care of themselves inside. Yeah."

As he finishes my sentence, I marvel at Dawn Yates. It's amazing how well we understand each other.

"But that's *them*, Harrietta. Our future's a whole other thing. You need to focus on yours. Get your ass to college."

"I mean, I will." I pause. "After a gap year."

His brows knit. "Weren't you excited to go to Brown?"

I flinch, thinking of how things have changed for me in the last couple years. But I don't want to get into that with Dawn.

"They only take the best of the best," I say.

"From where I'm sitting, that's you."

I smile sadly. "The college game is crazier than you think."

"Oh, I get it. You think I don't understand because I'm a public school kid?"

Shit. "I didn't mean it like—"

"Public school's not the moon." He's irritated now. "Trust me, I do know how competitive the college rat race is. And I still say you should apply to Brown. In fact..." His wicked smile makes a heart-stopping appearance.

"Oh, no, Dawn, don't."

"I dare you to apply to Brown. Right now. Today."

I scowl. "They'll just reject me."

"Then you can take your gap year. Hell, you can still take it even if you get in! But the one thing you can't do, Harrietta, is stay at Westwood for another twelve months."

"Uh-huh. And what would I do instead?"

Gripping my chair, he rolls me closer; my heart flutters. "Come to DC with me."

"Have you lost your mind? We've been dating for ten seconds."

"You know time's not the same for us."

It's true. Raised on this strange land, Dawn and I were wrapped together in some timeless cocoon, the silk strands of it woven into our bones. Time *isn't* the same for us. It feels like I've known him for hundreds of years.

But does he really know *me* as well as he thinks he does?

He might've met the rage monster the night we made our TikTok, but that's very different from encountering her in the wild. Right now,

Dawn's the only person on planet Earth who likes me just the way I am. Losing that would hurt like dying.

I'm wringing my hands when the door swings open, and the last tours of the day wander into the Welcome Center. They spread out around the gift shop, looking at the merch on our shelves.

A little girl marches right up to Dawn, a children's novel clutched in her hand.

"Excuse me, mister. I want to buy this."

We stock books that tell the stories of enslaved people on sugar plantations like Westwood, both fictional and real. She's picked up a copy of *Sugar* by Jewell Parker Rhodes.

"That's a good book," I say. "I'll ring you up."

She hands me her mom's credit card.

"What did the tour mean to you?" I ask.

"It made me proud of where we come from," she says with piercing certainty. "Because they tried their best to keep us down and they couldn't. Also, people shouldn't sugarcoat history. It's stupid and wrong."

Dawn laughs, delighted, and the little girl's parents—her father white, her mother Black—come to collect her.

"Thank you so much," the mother says. "What a powerful experience."

My throat tightens, thinking of how hard my family worked to build this place, and how much we lost along the way.

"Thanks for coming."

When the last of the tourists have gone, I level a meaningful look at Dawn.

"See? Westwood's a good place. An important place."

"Let's table that. Because your first video's ready to post."

Then, at last, I watch myself explain, in a twenty-second segment, why a plantation wedding is tacky as hell. It's a little embarrassing to watch yourself speechify, but the video looks gorgeous. Dawn really does know his way around a camera.

"This is amazing," I whisper.

"Yeah. And that's just part one."

"What if we get trolls?"

"I'll handle them. No big."

I gaze at him. "You don't have to do this, you know. It's a lot of work, and I'd go out with you no matter what."

Dawn slides his hands to my waist, cutting off my cognitive function.

"First of all, I enjoy this stuff. I'm a photographer, remember? Second, I missed your mom's funeral—I wasn't here when you really needed me. Think of the TikTok series as, like, my version of bringing you casserole."

I snort. "Hashtags, *yum*."

"Hashtags don't matter anymore. It's concerning to me that you're this offline."

"It just doesn't seem fair, all you're doing."

He kisses me quickly; I see stars.

"If you want to do something for me, promise you won't stay too long at Westwood. I'd never forgive myself if you wound up trapped here, somehow."

I arch away from him. "Westwood's not a trap."

"It is," he insists. "Because it's not your dream, Harrietta. It's your *mother's*."

My arms break out in goose bumps.

I'd never planned to stay here for the rest of my life, and I can see how taking a gap year to look out for Dad might become a kind of trap. What if he doesn't get better? What if I never do apply to any reachable schools, either by accident or inertia? What if I end up swapping my life for my mother's?

"Okay, I'm gonna post this now," Dawn says. "Buckle up."

One thumb tap brings up a loading bar. The 'for you' page rushes at us in a great wave, and somewhere, my video joins the digital current. Belly knotting, I whip out my own phone.

The first person I send the video to is Morgan. Then Asher, Sandy, and Graham Lucien. I'm still giving Sonya some space right now.

this is amazing OMG, Sandy texts back.

Asher and Graham both send clapping hands.

Eventually, Morgan texts me a photo of a dirt-encrusted crystal.

"Now what?" I ask breathlessly.

"Now," Dawn says. "We wait."

I want to keep checking the video, watching the view count climb, but Dawn tells me to ease off.

"Ignore the numbers. We need to give this at least two weeks to gain traction. Be patient, okay?"

"I can't believe you asked me to stay with you in DC. Like we're grown-ups or something."

Dawn gives me a funny look. "We are grown-ups, Harrietta. The future is now."

Maybe because I don't quite believe it, or don't *want* to believe it, I don't do the thing I definitely should: apply to *all* the schools, right this second, so there's no chance of my getting trapped here, losing my chance to forge my own path.

But that evening, while Dawn wraps up his work on Dad's new brochure, I *do* apply to Brown.

After all, a dare's a dare.

CHAPTER 26

THE NEXT MORNING, Dawn and Auntie Yates show up at my door. I'm still wearing pj's and Mom's pink bunny slippers. The kitchen is a Taco Bell graveyard, and I'm so embarrassed by the mess, I only open the door a crack.

"What's the matter, Auntie? It's early."

"I'm coming in, child," she says tightly.

I panic. "Oh no. You can't—"

But Auntie Yates pushes right past me, spies the mess, and gasps.

"Lord have mercy. Dawn, baby, hand me those gloves."

Dawn's toting a blue bucket full of cleaning supplies and a smug smile.

"You can't clean for us, Auntie. Not with your arthritis."

"I'm not cleaning, I'm supervising," Auntie huffs. "This is for the dust check."

Ah yes, the dust-check: a southern woman's best friend.

She runs a gloved finger over the kitchen counter, the windowsill, the table. It comes away just about as gross as I expected.

"Where's your father?"

"He's still sleeping."

"He sure did let this place get filthy."

"Auntie, I think he's depressed."

Coming out of my mouth, the D word shocks even me.

"'Course he's depressed." Auntie Yates scowls. "It's the lack of community, the emptiness 'round this old road. He should be going to church, potlucks, BBQs. Good company and good food satisfies the spirit of grief, you see? It ought to eat its fill and then be gone. But you can't satisfy anything with this fast-food nonsense."

Auntie Yates talks about grief like Dr. Maples talked about my rage. Like strong emotion is a visitor, a wandering spirit.

"Dawn, start those dishes, honey," she says. "Harrietta, you get ready for school now. I know you've got to be on the bus in half an hour."

I hurry upstairs for a quick shower. When I'm through, a text comes in from Dawn: a gif of Brandy playing *Cinderella*, sweeping the kitchen and singing about her own little corner, her own little chair. I hustle downstairs, but Auntie Yates and her grandson are already gone.

So is the fast-food mess.

In its place is breakfast: Auntie Yates's homemade rolls and fatback bacon. I'm nibbling at the bacon when Dawn texts me a video preview.

here's the next TikTok installment
what do you think?

In this segment, I tackle plantation proms. The work Dawn's doing, the way he teases out my voice, turning the rage monster into an activist, blows me away. As usual, I don't love staring at myself, but the message, at least, is coming across.

Me:
let's post

Dawn:
aye aye captain

Then Dad stumbles downstairs, bleary-eyed in a T-shirt with Abe Lincoln's face on it. The joke reads: THAT WAS SOOO FOUR SCORE AND SEVEN YEARS AGO. Mom got it for him for his forty-fifth birthday, because she's an enabler.

"What's all this? Did you cook?"

"Auntie Yates came by. She says you've got to eat better if you want the grief demon to go away."

"That what she said?"

"I'm paraphrasing."

But Dad's no longer listening. He tucks into this homemade breakfast—a very southern, *Mom*-style breakfast—like he's eating for the first time in years.

• • • • •

Over the next two weeks, Dawn and Auntie Yates bring breakfast every morning—a blessed relief after years of fast-food pancakes.

But the best part comes later, when Dawn sends me the day's new video to preview. Sometimes I Ping-Pong those previews to Morgan and Graham, who help make the captions quippier. When the video's up, the whole gang forwards it around St. Anne's. People message me all the time now, asking questions about prom, like whether I'm planning a protest. Once, in the cafeteria, I startled at the sound of my own voice. A table full of juniors was watching one of my videos and vigorously debating the issues. Graham's even writing an op-ed series in the school paper entitled: *Just Say NO to Plantation Prom.*

So far, though, the coolest thing about being almost-famous is what's happening to the rage monster.

One day, the tall, imposing lacrosse captain stopped me in the locker hall.

"You're that girl who thinks proms are racist, right? What's your deal?"

Old Harriet would've lit into him like a honey badger into a hive, but the new and improved TikTok Harriet kept her cool.

"You should watch part five of my series. It really digs into all the problems with plantation proms."

"It just seems dumb to call proms racist when they're just, like, a *dance*."

Whoo, boy. "What's your username? I'll message you right now."

"But what I'm saying is—"

"This one's set to Doja Cat. But maybe that track's too racy for you? Do your parents, like, monitor your account?"

"No, man, that song's obviously *extremely* dope. And my parents don't even know about this app." He looked surprised and vaguely irritated by this conversation's new direction. "I'm @ballsandsticks87 if you want to, like, throw me a follow."

Yeah: @ballsandsticks87 stans me now.

But even if he hadn't, it'd be okay.

Since I got my message online, I don't have to battle every garden-variety racist asteroid that comes hurtling my way anymore. I can just refer them to my body of work—to my and Dawn's work—and go about my business. Even the rage monster seems to realize that I no longer need her services. At least for the time being, she's departed from the house of my brain.

The relief is enormous, and it's all thanks to Dawn. He encouraged me to channel my fury into something else, something *useful*.

I swear to God, it's better than therapy.

Also, with real breakfast in his belly, Dad seems to be doing...better?

One afternoon, I catch him whistling around the house. It's such a surprise, I put my homework down and just listen. No one's whistled in this house since Mom died.

Now, in a celebratory mood, I head to the kitchen to heat up some of Auntie's leftover cornbread. There's a calendar on the fridge, where I've discreetly circled the date of Sunny Blake's plantation wedding. It's going down just a week from now, on November thirteenth, but I'm not crushed. TikTok's been the best possible distraction—and so has Dawn.

What's your end game? I asked him on the day we made the long-form video. *What do you care?*

Oh, you know. Mostly, I want to impress this one girl. I'm kind of hoping she'll fall head over heels in love with me.

213

While the yellow square turns circles inside the microwave, I realize with a shock that I've fallen hard in love with Dawn Yates.

It comes out of nowhere. Like the ocean wave you never see coming. I mean it just *swamps* me: this feeling like I couldn't go a day without him.

The microwave beeps, but I've lost my appetite.

Realizing I'm in too deep, I proceed to flip the fuck out.

Me:
you gotta stop bringing breakfast D
you and auntie have done enough

Dawn:
lemme think about it . . . no
someone's got to take care of y'all

Me:
seriously you've done more than
enough!

Dawn:
you're buggin but it's all good
you should see grandma bustling
around now all full of purpose
she hasn't been this excited since the
reverend came over for thanksgiving
dinner
and that was back in like 2008

Me:
but you're editing videos all day
aren't you sick of it yet?

What I mean is: Aren't you sick of me?

Dawn:

i could never get sick of anything about you h-etta
shit I thought you knew

Warmth fills me from head to toe; in pure relief, I house my square of cornbread, barely even chewing.

Then the doorbell rings, and I answer it. Dad's right behind me.

Outside, there's a group of men with an armful of red carpet—*long* carpet, like the kind they unfurl at the Oscars. It takes four of them to hold it up.

"Where do y'all want your carpet?" a surly young Black dude demands. "It's the premium burgundy. Plus, there's canvas for the step-and-repeat."

Shit. I know what this is about.

Belle Grove.

Lately, I've started to think of the rage monster as being on vacation. After all, Layla and her mom jetted off to a "detox retreat" in the Barrier Islands; who says rage monsters can't do the same?

But now I realize, with a twitch of fear, that she was only napping.

Somewhere inside my rib cage, she's already scrambling to get her clothes on.

"What on earth is a step-and-repeat?" Dad asks.

"Celebrity thing," I explain through gritted teeth. "It's where they get their pictures taken, like at a movie premiere? I think it's meant for that plantation wedding."

Dad narrows his eyes. "This is an enslaved people's museum, not a movie theater. If that's for the Hartwells, they're right next door."

"Our mistake." The deliveryman gestures to his compatriots, readying to leave.

I curl my hands into fists, willing myself to stay cool. I've been doing so well. Honestly, I'm like a brand-new Harriet.

But the rage monster's wide awake now, and ready to *ROCK AND ROLL*.

Where the hell does Claudia Hartwell get off throwing this tacky-ass wedding? Does Layla know there'll be a red carpet, like it's the freaking Golden Globes? How many photos of preening celebrities will we be subjected to after this disaster? And again I ask: How the hell do people still think a plantation wedding is somehow okay?

Desperate to get hold of myself, I try addressing my rage: *Hello there, Ms. Rage Monster, I really need you to leave.*

Hello there, Harriet Monster, she claps back. *You're not the boss of me.*

Honestly, talking to that manifestation is like trying to pick a fight with a mean girl who's way hotter than you.

"Hey," I call after the delivery guys.

Awkwardly, with arms full of premium burgundy, they turn.

"I'll pay you a hundred dollars to dump that carpet in the Mississippi. Belle Grove's a plantation too, you know. This shit ain't right."

The young man looks around him, noticing the statues, the serious cast of the land. Understanding settles over his features.

"I'll ditch it for two hundred."

"Deal."

"No, no deal," Dad hollers. "Harriet, inside, *right now.*"

One of the deliverymen laughs; Dad slams the door. "What was that?"

"You know that movie star wedding's just a week away?"

"You've been doing so well. I'd hate to see that change."

I roll my eyes, even though I know he's right.

"You have. Maybe it's the therapy?"

"That must be it." I risk a sidelong look at him. "Maybe it's time I got my tours back?"

"Nice try. But I did see the road sign, you know. I assume you repainted it?"

Dad must be feeling better, if he's finally noticing that. Or maybe he just never felt like mentioning it until now.

"Yeah. It was actually Layla who—" I snap my jaw shut, cutting the words clean off. I try not to think of Layla if I can help it. What happened between us is too tragic.

"Well, I think it's the nicest thing you've ever done for me. Try to keep on this track, okay? And understand: You're not to get involved with that wedding in any way."

"I get it."

Dad looks skeptical. "Swear on your mother."

I hesitate. "That's not fair."

Thunderclouds gather in Dad's eyes. "Harriet..."

"Okay, I swear on Mom. Jeez."

But the sight of that red carpet's shattered my hopeful mood. Like the pilot of a crashing plane, I can't pull up.

Worse, the rage monster's back and ready to punch things.

How crazy was I to think a series of teenaged TikTok videos would change a damned thing in this racist world? Like, how deluded can you get?

That night, I stream a zombie movie and try to shut off my brain. When that doesn't work, I clean up my desktop, enjoying the satisfying crumpled paper sound effect when I drop a file in the trash. That's when I stumble on a copy of Layla's PowerPoint. Masochistically, I open it.

Back when we were a team, we tried all the prongs—emailing the wedding guests, freshening up the sign, sprucing up Westwood's website— to no avail. I even called every Landry Heathwood in the phone book, trying to track down a descendant. The people who got back to me didn't know what I was talking about. Most never bothered to call me back at all.

But there's one name that still has my history sense tingling: *Landry Heathwood Esq.* in Savannah, Georgia.

It's really the *esquire*, for me. A law degree speaks of wealth and privilege, and the urge to write it by your name feels very old-fashioned.

It's all a long shot at this point...but my gut says this is the guy.

Though I've already left a message, I dial this particular Landry Heathwood on the phone again, aiming for one last shot.

He doesn't pick up; a polite robot asks me to leave a message at the tone.

"Hi, Mr. Heathwood, this is Harriet Douglass again," I say. "Just wanted to see if you got my message before. About Belle Grove plantation?"

This is a waste of time, the rage monster snarls. *If he wanted to talk to you, he'd have called you back already.*

"I'm not sure that you're a Belle Grove descendant, but if you are, can you please call me back? Because something awful's happening there. A soap star's turning it into a wedding venue. She's making a mockery of history, of everything." Feeling awkward as hell, I swallow. "So this is an SOS, I guess. I live here on River Road. We could really use some help. Let me know—"

A second tone cuts me off, and I hang up thinking, *stupid.*

The whole descendant idea was always a shot in the dark, and now I'm just flailing, falling into the abyss.

I tuck myself into bed early that night, grief nipping at my heels.

Things were really looking up...until they weren't.

Now I'm not sure what scares me more: the return of the rage monster, or the return of despair.

That night, Graham texts me a draft of his anti-prom op-ed, but I don't bother reading it. I stare at the cracks in my ceiling instead, hyperaware of all my failures—and of the foul wind blowing at the plantation next door.

CHAPTER 27

F I WERE braver than I am, I'd visit Mom's grave the day before the plantation wedding. I'd kneel before the stone and confess my failures, maybe even tell her about the gorgeous surprise that is Dawn Yates. But with the rage monster back in business, there's a non-zero chance she'll eat me there, then wear me like a skin suit while she rampages across the city.

As Dr. Maples pointed out: *Some say anger is only sadness by another name.*

On this plantation, mossed with tragedy, there's no sadder stretch of ground for me than the grassy foot of Mom's grave.

So, on November twelfth, I find myself in Mom and Dad's old bedroom instead. It's at the end of the hall, past the guest room where Dad now sleeps. Since Mom went into hospice care, we never enter her old bedroom except to grieve.

Or, in my case, to confess.

"No surprise, I couldn't stop the wedding," I tell the neatly made bed, the nightstand we left just the same. "I did try, but it was honestly such a clusterfuck."

I give Mom's ghost a beat to swat me for cursing; unfortunately, she doesn't take the bait.

"They bulldozed the enslaved people's cabins to build a new gazebo, and there's nothing to be done now." I pause. "Except, I guess, to hope it freaking rains."

Alone in Mom's room, my heart beats hard against my chest, pumping my veins with acid misery. An aggressive push notification informs me that Layla's posted for the first time in a while. Without looking at it, I crawl under Mom's soft green comforter, curl into a ball, and cry.

I lie there for a long time, waiting for my breath to even out. When I finally open my eyes, I take in the wealth of tombstones that have proliferated in this room. Some are mine, some are Dad's. He comes often, treating the primary bedroom like his own personal shrine. Everything in here feels precious simply for being so near to her. But I marked the really important things with index-card tombstones, just in case.

On the wall shelf: *Red Makeup Bag, referred to as "My Armor," c. 2016. Leather with an alligator print. "For a professional woman, makeup is armor."*

Stuck on the mirror: *Post-it Note c. 2020. FRAGILE ARCHIVAL MATERIAL. A reminder to call the dentist for Harriet. Evidence of an organized life, and a slight obsession with her daughter's teeth, brought about because teeth are a class marker and hers were never right.*

On the bookshelf: *Special edition young adult novels, 2004–2017. Text works. Collected by a woman who wished her daughter liked YA books as much as she did.*

Dad's scattered other tombstones around the room, but a glance at the label on the nightstand—*Bedroom Furnishings, Memories of Love*—tells me that these are private.

Stale air presses against me, baleful because it's slowly aging every item in this room. I know from Westwood what toll time takes on historical objects, and on textiles and natural materials in particular. My imagination hits the fast-forward button, and in living color, I see how the paper objects will yellow, how the canvas will tighten and shrink, how the Post-it will shrivel, how the furniture will soften and warp. A depressing future as certain as global warming.

My phone rings, startling me in this quiet, tomblike space. Irritated, I thumb the screen. I don't recognize the number, and if this is a telemarketer, I swear to God...

"Harriet Douglass? Do I have the right number?" The deep, throaty voice isn't Louisiana southern—it sounds upper-class Atlantan. Every vowel lazes expansively in the sun, so that "number" sounds like *numbah*.

"This is she." Mom always answered the phone like that.

"I'm returning your call." *Call* sounds like *caw-la*. "You are correct that I am in fact a descendant of the original owners of Belle Grove, lately foreclosed."

It's Landry Heathwood.

Landry freaking Heathwood, the (possible) rightful inheritor of Belle Grove.

In my mother's bed, I straighten my skirt, even though he can't see me.

"Thanks for getting back to me, Mr. Heathwood." My voice only trembles a little. "I had some questions about the line of inheritance, because the property was willed to you. Wasn't it?"

"How old are you?" *Hah old ahhh you?* "What business is this of yours?"

If I ever reached him, I'd planned to tell him that I was grown, working for Westwood's historical society. But Mom wouldn't've approved of that lie.

"I'm young," I admit. "But I live at Westwood Plantation. All of us here—" I clear my throat, still clogged with sorrow. "We hate to see what Belle Grove's owner has done to the place. It's a celebrity wedding venue now. Among other things. Claudia Hartwell is not a good steward of the past, the *real* past. Do you understand?"

I can't see this man, but I imagine him in a wood-paneled library, luxuriously smoking a cigar. That's probably not fair, but the descendants of plantation owners often remain filthy rich to this day. It's hard for us to grasp, now, just how ludicrously wealthy these enslavers were. Think Rockefeller wealthy, Romanov rich. Or better yet, think of all the decadence of France before the revolution.

"Now listen here." *Lissen he-ah.* "As it happens I do know what you mean, and I sympathize with y'all on principle."

Whenever anyone says *on principle*, all I hear is the sound of red flags waving.

"What I don't understand is what you think my part in this is. I do not own the land in question."

"You could contest Belle Grove's current ownership. Couldn't you?"

"Perhaps so, but I never will." *Nevah weel.* "If you knew the whole story, you'd understand."

I grip the phone, knuckles whitening. "Why don't you enlighten me, then?" Belatedly, I add, "Sir."

He makes a disgruntled sound, and I fully expect him to hang up.

But he doesn't.

"My long-dead ancestors owned and operated three plantations across the Deep South. I was raised on what remained of Heathwood Plantation outside Savannah, before they tore the rotten place down."

He pauses for a good long time. It takes everything in me not to interrupt.

"The Belle Grove will came to my attention, but I have no wish to take on the land. I do not expect you to understand how weighty it is to inherit these shameful crimes against humanity."

Shameful crimes. "I'm glad you feel that way. I mean, not glad. But it's refreshing."

Silence.

"With all due respect, though, what good does your shame do? Shouldn't you take some responsibility? If you contested Claudia Hartwell's ownership, those plantations could become museums. Or you could gift them to a social justice nonprofit. Isn't that more useful, and more noble, than idle shame?"

"Ah, nobility." He chuckles, inhales. Now I'm certain he's smoking something. "My ancestors believed themselves noble, once, and they were wrong. For this very reason, I do not involve myself in acts of nobility. Who's to say, in a hundred years, what we'll call right and wrong?"

Oh, God. A philosopher.

I pinch the bridge of my nose. "What's happening at Belle Grove seems dead wrong to me."

"Perhaps so. But a memorial would not necessarily be better. I'm of the opinion these plantations should be let to crumble. They should be bulldozed from the face of the earth."

"But a memorial is educational. There's a war on, you know. A battle over which version of history America plans to remember."

"You know nothing of war."

I wonder how old this descendant is. Could he have served in Afghanistan, or even Vietnam?

"Sorry," I murmur. "I just meant—"

"Have you ever heard of the Shoes on the Danube Bank?"

It sounds familiar. Like something Mom mentioned once.

"Along the European promenade, there are dozens of bronze shoes on display, representing thousands of lives lost when the Arrow Cross slaughtered the Jews. If I were ever to support a southern memorial, it would not come in the form of a grand old house. It would be small and plentiful and public, like those shoes."

Yes, I remember now. Mom referenced the Shoes on the Danube with her bronze sculptures of Westwood's Lost Children.

"We commissioned statues," I tell him. "Representing the enslaved."

He pauses. "You're at Westwood, you say?"

"Yes. The plantation next door."

"Interesting." He pauses again. "But no, I will never contest the deed of Belle Grove. I want nothing to do with the awful place. Surely I have borne enough dishonor for one lifetime."

I'm irritated now. "So basically, it triggers you."

He laughs, full and loud. "I suppose it's true. I am, indeed, a very wealthy, old—and dare I admit conservative—snowflake."

This, I know, is where Mom would make the hard sell. Where she'd dazzle him with her pure humanity, her intelligence, her loving kindness. She'd soothe his shame and bring him around to her way of thinking. And at dinner time, while *Man of La Mancha* played and her hands gracefully prepped every healthy vegetable under the sun, she'd regale Dad and me with the tale of her righteous conquest.

You only have to open your mouth, and everything comes right, Dad used to say wonderingly. *Your superpower is* talking.

But for me, no powerful words come to mind.

Like with Sunny Blake before, I choke.

"Good day to you, Miss Douglass. This has been highly entertaining. But I would greatly appreciate it if you never called again."

My vision clouds with tears of frustration. The wedding's tomorrow, and Claudia's about to make a mint from it. After, she'll have all the money she needs to turn Belle Grove into a museum of pure lies, like the Miller place. She'll symbolically annihilate the enslaved people who lived and suffered there, possibly even tearing up more sacred ground—and she'll face no consequences. For years, even decades, she'll sell the very lies that keep hate alive.

When the line goes dead, I bury my face in my mother's cotton pillowcase. It muffles a cry, a scream.

But that's the end of it.

There's nothing more that I, Harriet Douglass, can do.

CHAPTER 28

ON THE MORNING of the wedding, there's no hint of rain in the baby-blue sky—not one goddamn cloud.

River Road's crammed with honking, belching vehicles: the catering service, the DJ, and who knows what else. This is not a cheap affair.

It's also, like Dad said, not my business.

I go about my morning chores, but I can't help noticing that the plantation's not exactly bustling.

Coffee mug in hand, I head toward the employee parking lot. Naima and some older docents cluster there, rubbernecking at the road. Auntie Yates has showed up, too.

"Hi, baby," she says to me.

Naima's vaping, which technically isn't allowed on the grounds, but she's clearly stressed. Who could blame her?

She gestures with the pen toward Belle Grove's iron gate. "See those fools over there? The ones with the cameras?"

I spot them, but can't figure them out. They're too shabbily dressed to be wedding photographers.

"They're paparazzi."

I suck in a breath.

"Mmhmm," says Auntie Yates. "Swarming like vultures."

"As for the rest of the cars, that'll be the caterers," Naima continues. "I heard a rumor they only hired Black servers. Now how do you like that?"

"Awful," Auntie Yates intones.

I think of her watching television in her little shotgun house all day long. Auntie Yates grew up with the truth of this road: the sad history, the hard poverty. What an insult to her that these movie stars, with their circus in tow, have chosen this neighborhood to play make believe.

Something uncurls in my belly.

Not today, rage monster. Not today.

"You need any help getting home, Auntie?"

Mrs. Yates blinks tired eyes at me. "A shame your daddy couldn't stop this."

"I know. I'm sorry."

"You don't have to apologize to me."

But she's a direct descendant of Westwood's enslaved people, so actually, I feel like I do.

"And I ought to thank you, Harrietta, for taking care of my boy. Dawn's been so happy since he's come home. Matter of fact, I owe you a pie. A real sweet one." She chuckles. "I told your mother that you and my grandson were bound to get together one day. She laughed at me, but Auntie's always right."

Naima waggles her brows; I ignore her.

"Thanks for making him clean our kitchen, Auntie."

"Now, that he was less excited about," she says.

Then her gaze swivels back to the road, where an employee unloads an ugly flowered arch. Wearily, Naima pulls at her vape pen. There's something deeply unsettling about seeing these older Black women—my mentors, in their own ways—looking so damned defeated.

Mom wouldn't have let it come to this. Not in a million years.

On my way home, I scoop Rosemary from her coop. She's not allowed inside the house, because of Dad's irrational fear of chickens, but I make an exception today.

In my room, I scroll aimlessly around the internet, trying to numb myself out.

In the online world, CGI Muppet Babies are twerking, some dude's preaching about "miracle tones," a CEO's gatekeeping and girl-bossing, a blogger's writing from the POV of a homeless Sim, and a TikTokker's shouting about how the Chuck E. Cheese mouse is hella problematic. I don't feel a whole lot better...but there's comfort in knowing that way down deep, everyone feels bad.

Also, those Muppet Babies are sending me.

Then—

Dawn:
hey beautiful how you holding up

He called me beautiful, which is a damn lie but I'll take it.

Me:
okay i guess
trying to figure out what to do with
my life today

Dawn:
i'm coming over with grandma's oyster rice so you
don't have to figure a thing
you're not into weed tho, right?

Me:
horror is my weed

Dawn:

okay weirdo be there in an hour

I'm about to switch my phone off when, miracle of miracles, Sonya reaches out at last. At the sight of her name, excitement zips through my circulatory system.

Sonya:

graham told me u apologized
thanks for that

Oh, thank God. *Thank God.*
And thank Graham, because he didn't have to tell her that we talked.

Me:

i'm so so sorry
i would've called but Graham said you
needed space?

Sonya:

ya thanks for respecting that
u know i'm coming back this week?

Me:

should dad and i pick you up at the
airport?
like we planned?

Sonya:

graham's picking me up

Damn. I close my eyes, trying to figure out how broken the two of us really are—and how long it'll take to fix us.

Sonya:
but that's not like a punishment
we just buddy-watched all these rom-coms while
i was in bella Italia and airport scenes are a whole
trope

                                             Me:
i get it
but yeah just wanted to say i'm the
asshole
i lost my mind and it's okay if you
don't forgive me
i miss you so so much

Sonya:
YES YOU ARE THE ASSHOLE

A joyful laugh rips from my throat, because this is the Sonya I know. The tough-loving best friend I've been missing for so long.

                                             Me:
i don't know what came over me
that prom business just freaked me
out

Sonya:
yeah but u played dirty with graham
i never thought you'd do that

A sharp pain rips up my side.

Me:

i'll do anything to make it up to you

Sonya:

oh really? anything?
because i had two anxiety attacks this month
about my final exams and didn't even want to
call you

I've always been Sonya's go-to person for academic panic attacks.

I don't know which option is more terrible: that she had to weather those attacks alone, or that she called someone else. Probably Graham.

Me:

did you get through it okay?

Sonya:

graham talked me down it was kinda cute

Me:

i'll do anything to make things right
just tell me what to do

Sonya:

i DO have some demands

My lips curl in a tentative smile.

In fifth grade, Sonya and I used to watch *America's Next Top Model* in our living room, throwing pork rinds at the screen when drama went down. Mom would check in occasionally, making sure the show wasn't giving us an eating disorder.

"You know that's not a typical human waist, right?" she said. "That girl right there is a darn unicorn."

"Don't worry about me, Mrs. Douglass," baby Sonya answered. "I don't care what I look like, as long as I'm making three hundred thousand dollars a year."

Mom cracked up, hugged her, and watched the rest of the episode with us.

"You stick with Sonya," she told me. "She's got a core of steel."

Mom could see through people, all the way to their innermost hearts. She was telling me then that Sonya was a survivor, but the core of steel has a flip side, too. When you cross her, you'd better brace yourself.

Sonya:
so I'm gonna need you to call me ebony queen from
now until forever
and i want those peach gummy snacks dropped off
in my locker on fridays
and yes bish we WILL be watching Italian movies
with subtitles every saturday for the rest of your life
also you have to hang out with me and graham
non-negotiable

Relief floods my veins like the best drug on earth, because Sonya's finally forgiven me. Petting Rosemary's silky feathers, I float on an ocean of peace.

Me:
i'm not calling you ebony queen!

Sonya:
k but all the other stuff tho

Then my phone rings.

"Hey," Sonya says softly. "Just wanted to hear your voice."

Rosemary hops off the bed, and I don't try to stop her.

"I'm so glad," I say. "For a while I thought...maybe we wouldn't talk again."

Sonya sighs. "Of course we were gonna talk again. I just had to work out some feelings. Anyway, I know Sunny's getting married today. It's today, right?"

Outside, voices ride the air—caterers and staff—while trucks crunch gravel. Plantations are wide but flat. These sounds carry.

"It's today."

"How's the rage meter?"

"Honestly, I'm trying not to think about it."

"That's good."

"You were right about the St. Anne's kids. They're not so bad. A bunch of them walked out when Dr. Benoit announced the plantation prom."

"Glad you finally noticed! They're not perfect, but they are trying. We all wanted to support you after your mom died. Sandy organized this meeting, and we brainstormed about, like, what we could do. It wasn't much, but we always tried our best for you."

"I don't deserve you, Son. Like you should get the hell away from me."

"Why do you think I went to Italy?" She laughs. "Seriously, though. Your mom told me to stick by you, because we're peanut butter and jelly. I'm the jelly, obvi."

This is news to me. "Mom said that?"

"Uh-huh. When she was dying. Made me promise to stay in touch with you, even after college or having kids or whatever."

I need a chicken to hug, but I have no idea where she went.

"When was this?"

Sonya takes a while answering, and my eyes find the photo of Mom on my desk. Then suddenly her ghost is everywhere. She's picking out the color of my walls ("luminous ecru"), and fixing my desk chair when one of the legs broke, and adding an Octavia Butler novel to my bookshelf (she and Dad love the one called *Kindred*, about a plantation), and then she's right here, beside me, kissing me good night.

Normal mom stuff that, due to historical events, has become acutely painful.

Why was she mad at me, on her last day?

What could I possibly have done? What did she say?

"She invited me to visit her at the hospice. I don't know why I didn't tell you before," Sonya says. "Except after the funeral..."

After the funeral, I was a hot mess. Still driving and having rage blackouts. An accident waiting to happen.

On the phone with my best friend, I break down and cry.

"Hey," she says, alarmed. "It's all right."

"I'm sorry."

"It's cool."

"I need to hug a chicken."

"First of all, gross. But you do you."

I have so much to tell her, but now's not the time. We need to let things rest for a minute, now the storm's passed. Let the choppy waters calm.

We hang up, and I clutch the phone to my chest, feeling grateful and blessed because Sonya forgave me.

I look for Rosemary in my closet and under the bed, but she's nowhere to be found. I've just started to worry when, from down the hall, Dad lets out a high-pitched scream.

"Goddamn it, Harriet!"

I leap up. Somehow, Rosemary's escaped into the stairwell, where my dad's looking rumpled and aghast. He's backed against the wall, like the chicken's a velociraptor who escaped from *Jurassic Park*.

I pick Rosemary up, tucking her under my arm like the warm little bundle she is.

"Oh my God, she's just a chicken."

"She has pointy leathery feet with claws, and I don't like her beady little eyes. Don't bring her up here again."

Properly offended, Dad brushes past us on his way downstairs.

At the bottom of the steps, he pauses. "Mrs. Yates says Dawn is coming over today. Do we need to go over any ground rules?"

Oof, yikes.

Me and Dad have never had "the talk," and frankly my nerves can't handle it now.

"We're just watching movies. No big."

Dad sighs. "That's what they all say. Your mom and I were 'watching a movie' the night you were conceived."

I plug my ears with my fingers. "This is completely unnecessary."

"I should hope so. Excellence, Harriet. Remember that."

He retreats into the kitchen; I roll my eyes, but I'm more pleased than mad. It's good to hear Dad sounding like a parent again. I'd started to worry that the lawsuit had broken him.

I should've known better, though: Dad's got his own core of steel.

We need it, living here on River Road.

CHAPTER 29

DAWN SHOWS UP with Auntie Yates's oyster rice and chicken wings. He looks cute in his white sneakers and jeans. I answer the door with Rosemary in my arms.

"Hey there, chickie," he says, carefully petting her head.

Rosemary preens.

"So, uh, is it okay for us to eat chicken in front of her?" Dawn asks.

"She knows she's special, it's cool."

We eat off napkins, too lazy even to set out plates. It's a miracle, eating real food. After a year of near-constant McNuggets, you don't realize how much grease you're consuming; how heavy and gross you feel. At this point, I don't think I'll be able to stomach fast food ever again.

Dawn doesn't say much, but his brow's furrowed. He's got something to tell me. Something he's worried I won't want to hear.

When I'm done eating, I nudge him. "What's up with you?"

"I don't know how you feel about this, but Grandma Yates went to Baton Rouge this afternoon. She's got a doctor's appointment, and she's gonna stay with a friend. So her house is empty."

Dawn holds my eyes, and I flush. "You mean, like, you want to...?"

Have sex. Those are the words I somehow can't force my tongue to say.

"No—I mean, like, yes, maybe someday." He looks like the chicken's not sitting well. "I thought it'd do you good to get away. Grandma Yates's place isn't far, but the river drowns most everything out. You won't have to hear the wedding. Or see it."

A rush of love floods my veins, because Dawn's trying to take care of me.

Getting away from Belle Grove is exactly what I should do...but there's one problem.

"It would feel like abandoning ship, Dawn. I belong at Westwood for now. Even when it isn't easy."

"I can respect that."

I stroke Rosemary's small head. "We can still hang out here, though? Watch a movie?"

He's quiet for a second too long.

"Dawn?"

"Okay so, I know you like horror, but you should know: I'm more chicken than Rosemary when it comes to that stuff. Maybe we can do a rom-com?"

"Let me think about it...." I tap my lip. "No."

Dawn groans but lets me grab his hand, tugging him toward the living room. On our old leather couch, we lean into each other. He rests his chin on top of my head. But then he shifts, and we're kissing. A pool of golden warmth fills my belly, and I tell myself this is enough. I don't need anything else. Certainly not a perfect world where plantation weddings never happen, where that deep-track racism isn't even a thing.

Then Dawn pulls away, smiling wickedly. "Congratulations by the way."

I frown. "On what?"

"Part twelve of your video series just hit thirty thousand views."

It's been a few days since I checked the app. I fumble for my phone, tapping madly. "Holy crap. This is incredible."

"It's not viral, but it's not bad, either."

He must see the conflict in my face, because he asks, "What's wrong?"

"I just wish I'd been able to do more about Belle Grove."

Dawn brandishes his phone. "This, right here? It's bigger than Belle Grove. You're telling your story, your truth. And people are loving it."

Relieved, I smile back at him. For so long, *nothing* has been bigger than Belle Grove. Dawn plays the video again, and I realize he's right. This video's about memory, and history, too. It's about how we can learn from the past, and how we respect those who came before. It's about fury, but there's a note in my voice that sounds like prayer.

Dawn's wicked smile is close enough to kiss.

My phone—thankfully ensconced in a plastic case—clatters to the floor. Time folds in on itself, slowing or maybe stopping altogether.

I could kiss him forever, feeling this pride, this satisfaction at what we've made.

And in some dimension somewhere, maybe I do.

But in this timeline, I draw back. Strains of music, stringed and crystalline, float through the open window.

They're playing the "Wedding March" at Belle Grove.

My blood runs cold.

"Movie," Dawn says. "Quick."

Remote in hand, I flick through the streaming options. "If you don't watch horror, you may not know that we're currently in the midst of a Black Horror Renaissance. Consider this your education."

"Rosemary, save me."

The chicken, cleaning herself on the rug, ignores him.

I cue up the Jordan Peele collection. *Get Out. Us. Candyman. Nope.*

I'll start with *Us*. I crank the volume almost as high as it'll go.

Dawn pulls me into him, settling in to watch.

When my phone pings, I almost ignore it. Sensation wise, there's a lot going on, what with Dawn and the way Dawn smells...but it might be Sonya, and her texts are too precious to ignore.

Onscreen, a girl wanders into a hall of fun-house mirrors.

Layla:
i'm so sorry H
for everything

I stop breathing. Where's Layla right now? At the wedding? Out drinking? Hiding in her room?

Out of nowhere, sorrow blinds me.

I still want Layla to be happy, and she still reminds me, with all of her effervescent ease, of Mom.

The thing is, there's more to Layla than what the rest of the world sees. But also, there's less?

No. I refuse to get trapped in the Layla spiral tonight.

I'm here with a boy, my chicken, and my trusty remote control. The curtains are drawn, and Belle Grove and its atrocities, past and present, might as well be a thousand miles away. Dawn yelps as the movie gets creepier, and then I'm laughing so hard, I forget everything else, too. I settle my head on Dawn's chest. When my eyes close, I don't try to stop them.

Before I'm fully sleeping, Dawn adjusts, discreetly turning down the volume. The wedding music's stopped, and I think—well, that's the end of it. The end of the Battle of Belle Grove, in which I fought nobly, though I never stood a chance.

At least I can say I fought. Like the Man of La Mancha, who hopelessly tilted at windmills.

I wish the idea gave me some consolation, like it did Mom. But in my belly, that comfort's as cold as a bronze statue. As hollow as an un-rung memory bell.

CHAPTER 30

I'M WOKEN BY a skull-splitting crash.

A shattering sound, like glass breaking against metal.

I push away from a sleeping Dawn.

"Ow," he moans—but he's heard it, too. "What was that?"

We wait, feeling into the night's silence. It's dark in the living room, except for the screen's flickering, and dark outside, too.

A deep, southern dark with teeth.

Even though I wasn't born here, I've inherited some ancestral memory when it comes to nights like this. There aren't many streetlamps on plantation land. Only the smell of river water, thick and tumid, and a tumble of stars that feel terribly far away. Anything could happen out here. Klan could come, and in the past, have. We are very far from reason, and farther still from what passes for justice.

Like a gunshot, the crashing, scattering sound raises the hair on my arms.

And then, distant but unmistakable, the roar of male laughter.

While I rub crusted sleep from my eyes, Dawn's fixated on the living room window.

"Harrietta? Stay here."

He gets up slowly, his long legs carrying him. He moves like he's braced for violence. He flicks the porch light on.

"Shit."

"What is it?"

"No, don't—"

I rush over, pressing my face against the glass.

Our little Lost Girl, Louisa, is *bleeding*. The bronze statue dressed in rivulets of gleaming blood.

I'm out the door before Dawn can stop me, stamping the ground with bare feet. On the porch I pick up a splinter, but don't stop. Then I'm careering across grass, picking up my knees like I'm in the last quarter mile of a cross-country meet. I'm racing toward Louisa like she's a living, breathing girl.

Face-to-face with her, I cup her cheeks.

They're wet, but not bleeding. The broken glass at my feet is green, and the sticky liquid reeks of champagne.

Dawn's caught up to me.

I whirl. "Someone threw this. Over the gate!"

I bend to pick up the glass—jagged as disrespect—but Dawn's hand on my arm stays me.

"Wait until morning."

Callous male laughter ripples like so many thoughtless stones across a pond.

I approach the iron gate separating Westwood from Belle Grove. It's late—the wedding long since over—but I can still make out the gleam of string lights, the corner of a white tablecloth.

The laughter trails farther away, like the party's moved deeper into the plantation. But I can still hear it, and it infuriates me. Someone in that party tossed a champagne bottle over the fence, carelessly striking Louisa. Now fire roils in my belly.

Faster than I could've thought possible, I've climbed the gate.

"HARRIET, STOP!" Dawn bellows, but I'm beyond help.

At the top of the fence, built rusty ages ago by master enslavers, my calf catches on a spear tip. It impales the muscle, but weirdly, there's no pain. In the panic of my rage, I leap from the top of the fence.

Crouching in the grass, I survey the damage.

Empty bottles litter patchy grass. White napkins flutter in the wind, and cigarettes scrunch all over the place like ashen worms. The party might've started out expensive and classy, but that's sure as hell not how it ended. They've wrecked this field.

The lights of the Big House flicker, and, in the distance, a bonfire's flames lick the sky.

You can't set bonfires on historic land.

When these plantations were built, master enslavers were so terrified of fire that they built their kitchens in outbuildings. Enslaved women had to hike from those huts to the Big House to serve their food, because everything about an old plantation is flammable. Landry Heathwood would rather see these plantations destroyed, but that's not right. Without them, the people who struggled here, who lived and died here, will be utterly lost—their already maligned memories turned to ash.

Beneath my feet, broken glass crunches. Even barefoot, I don't feel a thing.

"Hey, we can't be here," Dawn says, sounding scared.

Then he spies the mess of the field and groans.

"This is not okay," I murmur. "This is—*grotesque.*"

For the rage monster, the words are a battle cry. She's scrabbling at my voice box, reaching for my brain's controls. I won't be myself for much longer.

Before I change, a thought echoes in my head: I wouldn't be so furious if only Layla hadn't let me down. Hadn't brushed away our friendship like a troublesome fly. I thought she understood what mattered, and I made every effort to reach her, to bring her into the Black experience of the past. But like so many other white folks, she disappointed me. This grotesquerie is not her fault, and a single straw shouldn't make such a difference when racism is one unholy, humongous haystack. But to me, in this moment, it makes all the difference in the world.

If only Layla—

"Harriet? We've got to get back. *Harrietta?*"

I shrug Dawn's hand off my shoulder.

Sunny Blake and the Hartwells threw a plantation wedding—but I'd made some peace with it. I'd accepted, at least, that I couldn't stop it.

But laying waste to this ground? Littering broken bottles across these acres? It's unconscionable.

Before I know what's happening, I'm tripping barefoot over the ground, scooping up glass. A Heineken breaks in my hand, shards stabbing my wrist. I might as well be made of bronze for all I feel it.

My heart thunders in my ears, and once again, I'm running, this time with an armful of trash, while Dawn shouts after me in dismay.

To the east, I spot the revelers—the small group that stayed behind after the wedding was done. They're a mess. Collars undone, red-faced, and howling like hyenas. A girl balances precariously atop a young man's shoulders, waving a liquor bottle over her head. The red light cast by the bonfire's flames swirl around them. Music blares.

Sweet home Alabama…

Rationally, I understand that the white wedding-goers aren't disrespecting this ground consciously. Their problem is that they didn't *think*, in the same way white people never, ever have to think. Never once did the dumbass who threw that champagne bottle over our fence consider that he'd be striking a work of memorial art. Never once did they consider that a family might've poured their whole hearts into restoring the plantation next door. They don't feel the dead beneath their feet, and they certainly don't understand that they're dancing on our graves.

God help me, I hate them for it.

But I'm not running for the party, vile as it may be.

With every stride, the Big House grows brighter. I'm aware that I'm shouting only because my throat is raw.

I hear my own voice, carving words out of the flesh of the night.

"*Goddamn it,* Layla! What have you done? What the *hell*—"

The Big House shivers into view, its front door thrown wide. A woman appears on the threshold. *Mrs. Hartwell.* I can't hear the words I'm shouting above the roaring in my ears, like a drone of furious bees, but my blood spells out my horror: *WHAT GAVE YOU THE RIGHT. YOU HAD NO RIGHT!*

Terror lurches across Mrs. Hartwell's face. To her, I look like a predator, but I don't care. I drop my arm's worth of broken glass at her feet.

And I see red.

It's worse than any red I've ever seen behind the wheel of a car. It's darker, bloodier, crimson as a poisoned tide. Vertigo tilts the earth, bonfire smoke addles my mind, and then it's all over.

With my mouth open to scream, my neck straining, and my hands in fists, the world falls away.

Still hollering, telling it like it is but telling it wrong, telling it awfully, *but it's stronger than me, I can't tell it any other way*—I'm blacking out.

Going, then gone.

CHAPTER 31

WHEN I COME to, there's pain.

It's hot and centered around my left calf. My leg burns stiffly, like a log aflame. My attack of rage has cleared out my sinuses but left a fog in my brain.

I'm in a hospital bed. The plasticky, over-bleached sheets rustling. Dread sews icicles inside my veins.

What have I done?

I look for Dad, or Dawn, or even Layla, but the hospital room's empty as a cage. I shrink small, then smaller, trying at first to disappear and then simply trying to remember, to slip back through the time's tight crevices to recover the moments lost in my blackout.

Louisa was bleeding. (No, not bleeding—dripping, her face sticky with champagne.) The gate between Westwood and Belle Grove was too high, too spear-tipped for me to climb. (No, not too high.) There was the smoke of the bonfire, and the woman at the Big House, and the words that shot out of my mouth like live rounds—

Shame washes over me like a breath off the desert. I'm gasping now.

Brokenly, the words I screamed echo back.

WHAT GAVE YOU THE RIGHT. YOU HAD NO RIGHT.

"No." I press my hands to my head.

This is not the memory I'm fishing for.

What I'm remembering in this hospital room are my mother's last words.

After she vomited and looked with such venom at me, Mom said:

I look back on my life and feel nothing but regret. She spoke through cracked lips.

I never should've brought you to Westwood. We never should've come South. We worked so hard, and for what?

This country will never change. It'll stay as racist as the day it was born. It wasn't easy, either, trying to raise a baby and make history at the same time. They say women can't do both—I understand that now.

But it wouldn't have mattered, having you or not.

A waste, Harriet. It was all a waste.

In a sunken face, Mom's eyes weren't hers anymore. They were small and beady and fever bright.

I wasn't supposed to come to the hospice that day. Mom didn't want to see anyone. But the charge nurse took pity on me.

In movies, the words spoken on a deathbed are a gift. What I learned on that day—and then, somehow, forgot—is that in real life, last words can also be a curse.

Despite her cheerful-seeming life, despite her doggedness in the face of racism, in the face of fundraising challenges and restoration mistakes, Mom believed that Westwood was a failure. Believed we'd wasted our lives.

Moving across the country isn't easy for a kid, and watching your parents work every waking hour is harder still. Westwood was such a problem in those early years. Buildings collapsed, roaches infested the wood, and snakes, unused to human beings, darted out of every pothole. It was a nightmare, sometimes, but we survived it—we triumphed.

Or so I believed.

I mean I *had* to believe in our mission to keep giving tours, to keep caring, to keep on through what has been yet another terrible decade to be Black.

A waste, Mom said. *All a waste.*

In the hospice, I ran.

I ran away from my dying mother, who no longer resembled the gentle, charming woman I'd loved all my life, with every *ounce* of my life. I ran straight to my car, where my own rage rose to meet hers and my hands began to shake. I struggled with the ignition, slipping in and out of a furious haze.

You don't know anyone, not really. Even when you think you do.

Now, in another hospital room, I cry for what I've done, and for what she did, and for the ruins of a relationship that once was beautiful, and that could've stayed that way but for tonight's bleak archaeology.

Mom believed we'd failed with Westwood. That we'd made no difference at all. That it was impossible.

And so, these months I've spent trying to cancel Belle Grove were never worth a dime—and Mom knew it. All along, we were only ever chasing dragons and tilting at windmills, making fools of ourselves with these impossible dreams.

Alone and aching, I weep for shame.

• • • • •

I'm not alone for long.

Dad comes in with a nurse, who changes the wrapping on my leg. She won't quite look at me as she explains that the fence cut me deeply, severing a vein. The Heineken bottle punctured my wrist, too. As she speaks, Dad looks so serious—so afraid.

After she's changed my bandage, the nurse hurries out.

It begins to sink in, through the heavy fog in my head, that the hospital staff thinks I may have hurt myself on purpose. Or worse—tried to hurt someone else.

"Dad," I whisper, scared.

Scraping linoleum, he draws up a metal chair.

"Hey, now, it's okay. I'm here."

"I blacked out," I say. "A bottle flew over the fence and hit Louisa, and then I was at Belle Grove, picking up their trash, and then—"

I look back on my life and feel nothing but regret.

My words peter out.

Hesitantly, Dad touches my hand. "Mrs. Hartwell called the ambulance. We're lucky she didn't call the police."

"Was Dawn—is he...?"

"He's fine. But you put him at risk, too."

Dawn could've died tonight, had Mrs. Hartwell called the police. Or he might've been arrested. The thought of him in jail, after what happened to his father, guts me.

"Listen to me, Harriet Douglass," Dad says. "You need to convince me, right now, that you're not a danger to yourself. That this is a nervous breakdown, not an attempt on your life. I don't want you hospitalized, but as your father..."

I groan, knowing I screwed up today—in the history of the world, has a teenaged girl ever screwed up so badly?—but the Hartwells screwed up, too, and so did Sunny Blake. For that matter, so did St. Anne's, planning to host their prom on Belle Grove land.

"It was a perfect storm," I tell Dad. "I'm so sorry, but it was. I promise it won't—I won't let it happen again."

He studies me, then nods once. He won't let me be institutionalized. If I were white, or white-presenting, it'd be a different story, maybe. The medical system could be trusted to help me, not harm me. But that's not the world we live in.

Even when it was time for Mom to transition to hospice care, Dad resisted institutionalizing her. He worried staff would disregard a Black woman's pain. And in fact, as we discovered later, the hospital did mistreat her. She ended her life as many Black folks do—in the belly of a beast that's sustained racism for centuries, and that can never be trusted, no matter what kind of life you've lived.

"You need to tell the doctor that you cut yourself on a broken bottle, and because you were bleeding, you ran for help. The Hartwells were closest.

"It was an accident, you understand? Not an episode. You were never angry, not even for a second. If the medics heard shouting, you were only very, very scared."

I'm nodding vigorously. When I leave here, I'll do whatever it takes to bury the rage monster for good.

"Where's my phone?"

"Here."

I snatch it from his hands, immediately scrolling through my texts. Looking for Dawn.

For some reason there are fifty-nine stacked TikTok notifications, which I couldn't care less about right now. The whole viral video plan seems naive to me now—a message in a bottle that'd never reach land.

Dawn:

tell me you're okay.

I want to rewind to that moment on the couch, his cheek against my hair, my head in the crook of his neck.

It hurts my wrist to hold the phone—my fingers cramping—but I fight through the pain to send my message.

Me:

i'm okay

and I'm so sorry.

Dawn:

i'm coming to see you

what hospital are you at?

Gripping the phone, I start to cry again.

Because it's finally happened. Dawn's finally seen me at my very worst. He knows now that I haven't been blossoming like he has in these last years. Like a choking weed, I've only gnarled and grown thorns.

I've always been ashamed of the rage monster, the swamp person I've become. That's the real reason I've avoided my friends, putting walls between myself and the world. I should've kept those walls up for Dawn, and Layla, too.

My remorse has so many layers now, it's all consuming.

Me:
don't come
talk later, okay?

Dawn:
okay h-etta but listen
i love you
i love you okay?

Just like that, my heart snaps clean in two.

Because Dawn *shouldn't* love me, the girl who dragged him to Belle Grove in the middle of the night.

"Remember," Dad says. "Not a word to the doctor about blackouts. Not a word about your rage."

Finally, the doctor waltzes in—a tall white man—and I tuck my phone under the hospital sheets.

Dad grips my hand.

The doctor checks his chart. "Okay, Harriet. Can you tell me what happened?"

I open my mouth then, not to tell it like it is—but as I wish it could've been.

CHAPTER 32

T HE DAY AFTER my rage blackout, Dad schedules an emergency appointment with Dr. Maples. It's awful to go into her office under these circumstances. Above all my other emotions, the one that burns is shame.

At least the Klimt looks much better on painkillers.

"Start from the beginning," Dr. Maples says, her expression unreadable.

I tell her all about the blackout at Belle Grove, how I scaled a spear-tipped fence and yelled in Claudia Hartwell's face. How I dragged Dawn Yates into something dangerous. How I let her and everyone else down.

But I don't tell her that my missing memory of Mom finally surfaced. When I even think of speaking those words to anyone—to Dad, or Dr. Maples, or even Sonya—my chest compresses, constricting, like I'm grieving all over again. Not for Mom this time, but for the loss of the woman I thought I knew. With one stroke of memory, my entire conception of her's been revised. In one night, all my monuments were toppled and set aflame.

I look back on my life and feel nothing but regret.

And, worst of all, *It was all a waste.*

How did I miss my mother's unhappiness? While she smiled at fund-raisers, charming our donors, was she wearing a mask? Did that mask ever crack—and did I somehow miss the signs?

"Before your blackout, were you able to try any of your techniques? Or were you completely overwhelmed?"

"It all happened so fast. And I'm still no good with those techniques, anyway. I've tried talking to the rage monster, but it just doesn't work."

My therapist looks thoughtful. "Tell me what you told her. Word for word."

"I mean, I popped all the way off at Belle Grove. Shouldn't we talk about that instead?"

"We'll get there. Tell me about your self-talk first."

The last time I tried speaking to the rage monster was when the deliverymen showed up at Westwood with that red carpet.

I squint, trying to remember my exact words. "'Hello there, Ms. Rage Monster,' I said. 'I really need you to leave.'" I grimace. "Like I said, it didn't work."

Dr. Maples sighs. "I should've been more clear before. You can't call your fury the rage monster. It's too combative. You need to embrace her with all the self-compassion you can muster."

"But I *hate* her?"

"There's nothing monstrous about a defense mechanism. At some point, you needed your anger to survive."

"When? When has rage ever helped anything?"

"Think. If you weren't angry after your mother died, what would you have felt instead?"

I close my eyes. "Heartbroken. Dead inside."

"Dead inside," Dr. Maples echoes. "Those are strong words. Could your rage be your life force? Your will to live?"

"I don't see what this has to do with last night. I thought I could handle the plantation wedding, but I couldn't. In a couple months, they'll throw a plantation prom. What'll happen then?"

Dr. Maples presses her lips firmly together. She's never been further from smiling at me than she is now. Normally, I'd crack a joke or something, but I'm not myself today. It's like every blackout eats a piece of me.

"Harriet, practice with me. Say, *I'm grateful for my anger. Thank you for helping me the best way you know how.*"

"Seriously?"

She nods.

"I'm—grateful. For my anger. Thank you for helping me."

"It sounds sarcastic, but you're getting closer. Try placing your hand on your heart, and say it again."

"Hand on my heart? How will that help?"

Dr. Maples demonstrates. "It helps because it feels like love. We are more than what we consciously remember. When you were a baby, your mother would've put her hand on your chest just like this. To show yourself that same unconditional love is powerful."

As it turns out, I can't manage sarcasm, holding my hand to my chest. I can't be cruel. It's too earnest a gesture, and it *does* feel like love.

For a moment, I hang my head. My eyes burn, and tears gather but don't fall.

"As for the future, I'll need you to be somewhere else on prom night. Go to a friend's house, okay?"

"I'm so tired, Dr. Maples."

"I know. We aren't designed for long bouts of intense emotion, be it sadness or anger or fear. When I was battling cancer, there were so many times when I wanted to give up. When it felt like my body couldn't take any more."

"What did you do?"

"I leaned on others. My mother, my doctor. Who will you lean on, Harriet?"

The first person I think of is Dawn.

But also, I can't bear to think of Dawn.

I love you, he wrote. *I love you okay?*

He's been texting all day, but I haven't answered him. I know it's unkind, and I know that he'll worry, but I can't deal with whatever's between us just now. He wants to be the one I lean on, but I don't trust myself around him anymore. And he says he loves me, but can it be real?

All these years he's carried me around like a photo in a locket, but does he love the real me? Or only a memory?

In Dr. Maples's office, beneath the Technicolor Klimt, I decide that Dad's enough support for me right now. When it comes to Dawn, I'm going to just... wait.

If he has any sense of self-preservation, he'll realize that he's better off without me. He'll text a while and then stop, disappearing from my life like he did before. It's not too late for him to decide to leave. I'll give him a chance to do it easily, with no hard feelings.

It scares me to think of losing him. Equally terrifying, though, is the thought that he might choose to stay.

CHAPTER 33

A T HOME, I stand in front of my full-length mirror, smudged with old handprints. My calf's still bundled in thick white gauze, the wound growling at me like a zombie. In the mirror, I look like the doomed heroine at the end of the horror movie, about thirty seconds before she's eaten by a ghost.

But I don't want to be a ghost snack.

Even now, without any hope of the future I dreamed, without even the memory of the mother I thought I knew...I want to live.

Make something of my disaster of a life.

Could your rage be your life force? Dr. Maples asked.

For years, the rage monster's been with me like an extra heartbeat, haunting my every move. I never considered that she might be looking out for me. Protecting me in her own screwed-up way.

"I'm grateful for my anger," I tell the mirror.

Somewhere in the black of my pupils, my anger is listening.

"Thank you for trying to help me the best way you know how. But please, you have to—"

Get out of my life, I nearly say.

Except that's not compassionate. And Dr. Maples says fighting feelings only feeds them. Once I might've argued with her, but I could've been institutionalized last night. I could've died.

So I get hold of myself. Start again.

"I'm grateful for my anger."

Oh, yeah, bet you're real grateful you can't drive anymore. Or act like a normal teenager. Or trust yourself, like, ever.

"I'm *grateful.*"

Keep telling yourself that.

I shout: "I'm *GRATEFUL.*"

Damn, girl. I heard you the first time.

"Well, good. Because I mean it. I'd rather be mad than dead of grief. But I need some space, okay?"

The rage monster laughs; I squeeze my eyes shut. Like, where am I honestly gonna get space from myself?

"Screw this."

The rage monster laughs harder.

A rapping gives me one hell of a jump scare, but it's only a knock at the door.

Jeez, perfect timing, Dad. "Come in!"

Only, it isn't Dad who appears.

It's Layla Hartwell.

As always, she looks like she's stepped out of a magazine. In the weeks we've been apart, I'd forgotten how beautiful she is. In a floral dress with cutout shoulders, she looks like she's swallowed the sun.

"Wait," she says. "Before you say anything, just hear me out."

She pulls a folded piece of paper out of her leather handbag and starts to read.

"Dear Harriet Douglass." Her eyes flick to mine, then back to the page. "I'm sorry for letting you down. I chose my mother over you, and I told a lie. I don't expect you to forgive me."

Good, the rage monster snarks. But I'm frozen in place.

"I'm sorry for what happened at Belle Grove last night. Somehow, I convinced myself that we were overreacting, that the party wouldn't be so bad. Sunny was paying top dollar, so I thought her wedding would at least be classy.

"But then—when they started building that bonfire..."

Layla and I wince at the exact same time.

"The wedding guests *trashed* our grounds. They sang racist songs. And they drank until they were sick. It was a disgusting display of privilege, and I hate that I allowed myself to be part of it."

I open my mouth to interject, but Layla holds up a finger.

"Please hold your questions till the end," she says primly.

Her hand, gripping the paper, is shaking.

"I don't know how I convinced myself that Claudia's opinion of me mattered more than what's right. Sometimes, I'm so desperate to be loved, I lose myself a little. And this time was especially painful because...well, because..."

Layla's blue eyes sparkle too brightly.

"Don't you dare cry," I warn her—though my own voice is thick with something suspiciously like tears.

"I won't, okay." Layla fans her eyeballs with her hands, like that's going to make any difference. And it's that silly, mascara-preserving gesture that reminds me how much I've missed her.

"I loved our friendship, H. Even though we didn't know each other very long, it felt like we'd known each other all our lives. I truly think you were one of the best friends that I ever—" She hiccups. "That I ever had."

Quietly then, she folds up her speech.

Looking at her, my diaphragm won't quite fill with air.

I remember how Layla stood up for me against Dr. Heidel, and I remember painting the Westwood sign, and watching *Star Trek* late into the night.

I'm not made of bronze. I *want* to forgive her. But Vacation Karen's voice echoes inside my head: *My best friend is Black, young lady!*

"Did you really want to be friends with me, though?" I ask softly. "Or were you hoping that, like, having a Black friend meant you'd be off the hook for Belle Grove?"

Layla's face crumples. "I would *never* use you like that. I wanted to be your friend because you're *awesome*. Full stop."

"I tried to tell you what it means to live on a plantation. I tried my best, and you threw it in my face." For the first time since she appeared, anger thrills across my skin. "I should've known better. You rich white girls are all the same."

"If that's how you feel, then why did you want to be *my* friend?"

"I didn't!" I cry. "You just kept forcing it and forcing it, and then, one day…"

"What?"

I take a breath, slowing myself down. "Do you remember when we talked about my mom? About both our mothers."

Layla nods.

"You told me how much Claudia hurt you, and I understood—because when she was dying, my mother hurt me, too."

I expect Layla to ask half a dozen follow-up questions, as is her wont. But all she says is, "I know."

"You *know*?"

"I mean, I could sense it. When you lied about your mom being in France? That was when it clicked: We're the same."

"Not the *same*."

"No, but there's something, isn't there? Something between us?"

I stare at Layla; she stares back. Just like in the swamp outside St. Anne's, we share a moment, precious as a jewel.

We could've been good for each other.

"So," Layla whispers. "Do you forgive me?"

Oh my God. It's like Layla was sent to Earth specifically to exasperate me.

"You know we can't be friends anymore, right? Because you betrayed me?"

Layla's face falls. "No, of course, I know that."

"I mean, I have a major anger problem. I can't be around unreliable people."

"I understand, one hundred percent." She shifts. "And actually, that's not the main reason I'm here."

"It isn't?"

"Nope." She pulls out her phone. "Believe it or not, I've come on behalf of the internet. Have you been watching your analytics?"

I gesture to my leg. "I've been way too busy ruining my life."

"So you have no idea what's happening on TikTok."

"Have you been stalking me?"

"Harriet, you're *blowing up.* Part twelve just hit the hundred thousands."

I twitch. "A hundred thousand what?"

"Views, H. You have over two hundred thousand *views.*"

Tentatively, Layla holds out her phone, and my eyes hook on two numbers.

110,678 likes; 290,000 views.

Heat crawls up my neck, because I absolutely did not expect this. Last time I checked, my views were middling at best.

"What happened?"

"Sunny's wedding happened! You're not the only one who's angry about it. Even the tabloids are throwing shade."

My pulse speeds up, but I can't let myself hope.

It was all a waste, Mom said.

And yet, at the end of each day, she played "The Impossible Dream."

"You've got gorgeous engagement. With a little nudge, you could go viral." It takes me a second to realize that she's dead serious. "But first, you've got to jump platforms. I hate to say it, but this is a job for the *Hell Beast.*"

"You mean like the Devil?"

"No, *Twitter.*" She smiles crookedly. "So what do you say? Want to give this thing a nudge?"

"I don't know, Layla. It's been a rough couple days."

"I know, but this is a golden opportunity to cancel Belle Grove. You must see that."

My body tenses, because *cancel Belle Grove*—those have always been the magic words.

"Hypothetically, if I wanted to go viral...what would you suggest I do?"

"Simple."

My phone pings; Layla's texted me half a dozen photo attachments. Swiping through them, I'm so shocked I nearly drop the phone.

"Is this for real?" I demand.

"Yep. I took them myself."

They're photos of the wedding's aftermath: of broken bottles and snubbed-out cigarettes and the dirty remains of a bonfire. In the harsh light of day, the plantation looks even more trashed than it did last night.

"When you post these on Twitter, tag the CAA talent agency. Then cross-post to your TikTok—and tag *Miramax.*"

"Miramax?"

"Sunny and Randy are doing a double-header with their production studio. When you've done all that, relax. Let Twitter do what Twitter does best."

"Which is what, exactly?"

"Piss people off."

I scroll through the rest of the attachments, most of which are photos of the wedding proper. And I have to say...it's not a likable wedding. Sunny can't stop smirking, and her guests look as smug as it's humanly possible to be. (Her groom, meanwhile, looks terminally bored.) They're surrounded by all-Black help—by servers and waitstaff wearing old-timey uniforms. From the pictures, it's obvious: Everyone at that wedding was playing plantation.

My God.

The Internet's gonna eat this up.

"Layla. You really took all these photos—for *me*?"

She flips her hair. "Someone needed to document what happened. The whole ugly truth."

I want to hug her, but my mind's running a mile a minute.

If I post these photos, outrage will ring from sea to shining sea. Belle Grove really might be canceled, and the plantation prom, too.

But—

"I can't," I say, remembering Mom's last, hopeless words.

Layla stills. "I know it's scary. But you can do this, H. And you should."

By myself? I nearly croak.

"Not by yourself." I jerk, because somehow, Layla's read my mind. It's always been weird like that with her. "With *Dawn*."

Ashamed, I drop my eyes.

Layla gasps. "You guys are still together, right? You didn't, like—push him away?"

Are California girls psychic? Is that a thing?

"Dawn and I are just in a sort of—holding pattern."

"Uh-huh."

"Look, I dragged him into so much mess. He deserves a chance to walk away."

"Oh my God, he does *not*. You need to get a grip, H. Dawn Yates is one in a million. And, like...so are you." She pauses. "Wish you'd remember that."

Layla adjusts her bag, and I realize: I don't want her to go.

We can't be friends. I know this. Still, there's something about Layla Hartwell that I can't resist.

"See you at school, maybe?"

"Actually, no. Tomorrow I'm going back to LA."

"But what about school?"

"What about it? I'm failing most of my classes anyway."

"Is your mom going with you?"

"No. Mom and I had a real dust-up this morning. I finally told her that I stole the guest list, not you. She doesn't want anything to do with me anymore."

UM. Why the hell didn't she lead with that?

"You really did that? Told the truth?"

Layla nods, and I find myself picking at my bandage, entirely at a loss for words.

Okay, not entirely. "Layla Hartwell, I freaking forgive you."

She smiles so brightly, it's blinding, but I hold up my hand.

"I still need some time, okay? But thank you for doing the right thing. I really—" I swallow hard. "Just—thank you."

She nods, her eyes finally overflowing with tears. "I can give you time. Probably too much of it. Because I don't think I'm coming back here, H. I really, really hate the South."

Outside, the chickens clatter, reminding me of this place I inhabit, this land that I've been raised to love and protect.

"It's the kombucha, isn't it?"

She snorts a laugh. "Yeah. It's honestly terrible."

"Okay, then." In farewell, I part my fingers. "Live long and prosper, Layla."

She matches my sign, then turns to leave with heavy footfalls. She knows as well as I do that this is goodbye. There's too much between us now. Too far a distance between Westwood and Belle Grove. We made a valiant effort, but in the end, we weren't enough.

But maybe, someday—

"Post the photos," Layla says at the door. "It's the right thing to do."

Then she's gone, and I face the mirror alone. With those photos in my messages, my sense of purpose comes roaring back, white-hot and blazing like a star.

This is a golden opportunity, Layla said.

I let myself be distracted by loss and by rage. I lost my grip, momentarily, on the impossible dream. But I was born to march for this cause, and nothing can take that away from me.

Not even Mom.

An autumn wind swirls inside the great memorial bell, conjuring the ghost-breath of a familiar sound.

And I know, with reverberating clarity, exactly what I must do.

CHAPTER 34

YOU DON'T NEED me to tell you there's a black mirror in your pocket, a portal through which you can disappear. Inside your phone, you're just a soul underwater, untethered from anything but the algorithm's riptides. Here, unseen inhuman forces dictate our fate: what sweaters we buy, how many #ads we see, whether our news is real or 100 percent lies. If our digital life were a horror movie, it'd be *cosmic horror*, for sure.

On TikTok, it takes me only seconds to realize that Layla was telling the truth. My video's gathering views at the speed of light, dragging my name, and Westwood's, right along with it. The cold mirror world has turned its face in my direction, and I feel as if I'm staring into the harsh, judgmental light of an Arctic sun.

Quickly, I navigate to Twitter, aka the Hell Beast, where Layla wants me to post her photos. I'm surprised to see that I already have a presence there, in reposts and screenshots from TikTok. At first, the sight of my own face on this infamous site embarrasses me so much my cheeks go numb. But then, after infinite scrolling through the comments, the reactions, the pure, internet-crystallized outrage, my horror slowly morphs into hope.

Peak white privilege, right here, tweets a reporter beneath a screen shot from part three.

And it goes on like that:

Tell me you call your housekeeper "the help" without telling me.

Whiteness is a helluva drug.

Um, can we cancel Sunny Blake already? Like, what's the holdup?

PREACH little sis!!!

This kid works at a slave museum, and she has SOMETHING TO SAY.

Why, yes, @southernleah52: I *do* have something to say.

As I scroll, diving deeper, I'm overpowered by the urge to reply. It's like air hunger, burning my lungs. I want to shout into the abyss staring back at me. I wonder how it would feel to take a breath of water and scream.

All I have to do is tweet Layla's photos from the Westwood account, but doubts churn. Like Mom always said, *The internet is forever.* What if I slip up, posting these photos? Cancel my own self? On the other hand, don't I have a *duty* to post, to show Sunny and Randy and their famous friends desecrating our land?

My dopamine receptors work overtime, reading all the supportive tweets. But not everyone is playing fair. There's nasty stuff, too.

This is one ugly feminazi, somebody writes.

And, *Her skin's so dark she don't have nothing better to do.*

And, *This is what reverse racism looks like.*

And, *How can she be so disrespectful of a woman's WEDDING DAY????*

Big yikes.

From the trauma menu of fight, flight, or freeze, my body selects *freeze.*

For long moments, I can't decide what to do. Then strains of music float back to me, lyrics from "The Impossible Dream."

In this world, there are some causes worth marching into hell for.

Armored now, I quit wasting time.

Um, guys, I write from Westwood's Twitter. *Check out Belle Grove plantation the morning after Sunny Blake and Randy White's plantation wedding.*

I read it over once, throw in a few tags, then press, *Tweet.*

Then: I sit back.

It's done.

Nooooo, one of Westwood's new followers instantly replies.

It spirals from there.

HOW ARE PLANTATION WEDDINGS STILL A THING???

(I'm elated, vindicated, heart soaring.)

Hang on, imma need yt folks to answer for all this.

Despicable.

(I'm nodding.)

What's the big deal, tho?

(Hol' up.)

Sorry—can someone tell me why this is in my feed?

(Tell me you're yt without telling me. . . .)

NOT ON MY WATCH. CANCEL THEM.

(THANK YOU!!!)

Hands trembling, I step off the Twitter roller coaster; I navigate back to TikTok, where I feel safer.

For a solid hour, I do nothing but watch my likes climb: 150K becomes 200, and 200 becomes 250. The rate is exponential, maybe, but I don't mess with math.

My phone pulses with notification after notification. It's astounding to think that there's a face behind each of those numbers. A human being taking the time out of their finite life span to interact with me.

A terrible cry lives in my chest. It's been building for such a long time—not for years, but for *centuries.*

All my life I've wanted a megaphone. A way to shout to those people across the racial divide. A *voice.*

Well, I've got one now.

And I've never been so scared in my whole damn life.

• • • • •

That night, I say good night to Dad (the poor man, oblivious of the portal's goings-on), take a painkiller, and settle into bed. I should sleep, but instead I'm gazing at my phone's mesmerizing underwater lights. I haven't replied or responded to anyone since I posted Layla's photos, but I'm itching to. I consider whom I might answer. What I might do to blow more oxygen at this fire. Whether it ever makes sense to feed the trolls.

And then something smacks into my window. I jump, triggered after Louisa, but the sound was soft and sandy.

A beanbag?

I'm out from under my covers in a hot second. I peer down at our wraparound porch. Someone's there.

Someone with a fade.

A smile twitches on my lips. I've been ignoring Dawn's texts and calls, giving him a chance to let me go if he needs to. To ghost me like he did before. But he hasn't, not yet.

From below, he spots me. He holds up the object he threw: a rubber frog with cartoon eyes.

Then he hums the theme from *Us*, the horror movie we watched before my blackout. It's a superslick remix of "I Got 5 On It."

Adorable.

I open the window, whisper-shouting, "What're you doing? You'll wake Dad."

Actually, he won't, because Dad's in his cryo-sleep chamber. But it's the principle of the thing.

"Are you aware, Harrietta, that you've been extremely rude, ignoring my texts?" He clucks his tongue. "*Declassé, ma cherie.* You wound me."

"How come you're here, then?"

He stabs himself with his fist, and then rotates his hand like a twisting knife.

This boy is so dramatic.

266

But then maybe so am I.

"Can I come up?"

"You shouldn't."

"Why?"

"Because I'm no good for you. Like, I'm a mess."

"Please. I see you on Twitter, kicking ass and taking names. A brother *might* think you're too famous to hang with me now. Too busy, or whatever."

The hurt in his voice startles me. "Dawn, just come in. Hurry up."

He holds the frog up, like saying, *wait*. Then he comes around the side of the house and lets himself in with the key I gave Auntie Yates. I count his footsteps as he comes up the stairs, nervously adjusting my *Jurassic Park* nightshirt.

The door creaks open, and Dawn is here, wearing an expression I've never seen before. It's stern, angry. But not the undirected anger of the little boy I knew. A grown and muted kind of anger. When he shuts the door behind him, my stomach flips.

"Of course I'm not too busy and famous for you," I blurt out. "I was giving you a chance to walk away."

"Why would I want to walk away?"

"You could've died at Belle Grove."

Annoyance flickers in his eyes. "Don't patronize me."

"But if something happened to you, and it was my fault—"

"The universe doesn't revolve around you. I make my own choices."

"I know that."

"Don't act like it, though. You can't ignore my texts after everything we've been through. You just can't, Harrietta."

I flash on Dawn at the influencer con, looking uncertain in his bright white tux...and shame swallows me whole.

Dawn Yates is a man now, and behind his wicked smile there's a self-possessed certainty. He decided to run to Belle Grove after me; he decided to keep caring, even knowing what the rage monster's capable of.

It was stupid and childish to try to push him away.

"How's your leg?" he asks, chilly.

God, but I hate that he saw me black out.

Hate it, hate it.

"Dawn, I'm—"

"I shouldn't have let you jump that fence. When you were with Louisa, I knew I should pick you up and bring you back inside the house. But I didn't, and you got hurt."

Now I'm offended. "Excuse me? You had no right to *stop me.* Anyway, you couldn't have picked me up."

He frowns. "Yes, I could have."

"Could not." My voice is hands-on-hips childish. Trust Dawn Yates to send me spinning back in time.

"I could *too*—" He shakes his head, stopping himself. "You know what? It doesn't matter. We both have regrets. Let's leave it there."

"I don't like it when you big-brother me. Telling me not to take a gap year, threatening to pick me up and take me home."

"Maybe if you acted right, I wouldn't have to."

I rear back. "If that's how you feel, you should definitely go."

His eyes darken. "I know you're going through a hard time. But—why can't you trust me more? I came home for you, and you keep throwing obstacles in my way. Since the very first day."

"I invited you to that influencer con, didn't I?"

"If Sonya weren't in Italy, would you have called me for backup? Or would you be avoiding me still?"

The truth is: probably.

But God knows I have my reasons.

"You didn't come back when I needed you. Mom *died*, and you didn't even come back for her funeral. Why should I count on you now? You still live in DC. You could go home anytime. Forget about us all over again."

I'm breathing hard, and so is he.

"You're right, I *could* leave at any time. The brochure is done, and I have plenty of photos for my portfolio. I'm no fan of Louisiana."

I throw my hands up. "So what are you still doing here?"

He softens, and the knot inside me relaxes, just a little.

"See, what had happened was, my girlfriend went viral after this one crazy night. With this video we took? But then she wouldn't text me back. It was, like, some kind of test, I guess."

Without quite meaning to, I step closer. "So, that *girlfriend*. You were probably pissed she turned out to be—I don't know—"

"Full-on *wild*? With zero regard for her life or mine? Yeah, that was a shock. *That* I had to process."

I wince. "And where'd you land with that?"

The smile spreads now, slow and wicked as can be. "I landed about where I expected to. On her doorstep."

"But you're still mad at me."

"Actually, it's kinda hard to stay mad at someone wearing a dorky *Jurassic Park* T-shirt."

I glance down at the worn cloth. "It's a horror classic."

"It suits you. Especially because, when you're mad, you turn into a tiny velociraptor."

I scoff. "I do not."

"I saw you hop that fence to Belle Grove. That was velociraptor shit for real."

I'm scowling, but Dawn only smiles. He closes what remains of our distance, then rests his hands on my upper arms, rubbing like I might be cold.

Now Dawn's here, I can feel again the tether that connects us—that's always connected us, since we were two kids growing up on plantation land, trying to learn how to live with the weight of it.

"When summer's over, I'll have to go back to DC. But I'm not leaving you here. What's going to happen is, you'll come with me. You'll take a gap year away from these plantations, where you can think clearly. You'll do something phenomenal, like you always do, and then you'll go off to college."

I marvel at this new kind of time travel: not into the past, but into the *future*. "And then what?"

"Well, long-distance dating is hard. We'll probably have to say good-bye for a while. You'll go off to change the world, because I know you've got that ambition in you. Not me, though. I'll settle down, make enough money with my pictures to buy Auntie Yates some comfort. I'll grow old saying, you know that Harriet Douglass? I knew her once."

I roll my eyes. "Please."

"Or maybe we'll stay together—commit to this for the long haul. Next year, we'll see who we are to each other away from these fields. We'll see what we *mean*. And who knows? Maybe we'll mean forever."

My stomach fizzles, full of fairy-tale hopes. Dawn Yates is so close, and I can have him if I want. He's told me, in no uncertain terms, that he wants me, too—and not just some of me. All.

"I left you behind once." Dawn's voice drops low. "I won't do it again. I'll carry you if I have to."

I wrinkle my nose. "I mean you can try."

Before I know it, he's holding me under my arms a perfect foot from the ground, and we're spinning in a circle, like dancing.

There's another kind of portal in this world, soft as hands. Dawn and I fall in headfirst, kissing until we're swollen, out of breath. Holding each other until the space between us disappears.

My phone buzzes, pulsing with endless notifications, pulling me into an unknown future, an uncertain destiny.

I have a feeling my Twitter post is picking up some serious steam.

Just now, though, neither of us gives a damn.

CHAPTER 35

BY MORNING, MY phone's ringing off the hook, and with a glance at my screen I know why: I'm trending.

#PlantationWedding is literally *trending*.

Also, and possibly more shocking, Dawn's still here.

He fell asleep in my bed, and now I have no idea what to do with him. How to get him out without giving Dad conniptions. We didn't do anything more than kiss, but what are the chances Dad'll believe that?

Sleepily, Dawn blinks his eyes open—and smiles. He studies my face in a way that sends vibrations thrilling over me.

"Don't freak out," I say. "But."

He bolts upright in bed, strong arms flexing. Immediately, he's tapping his phone.

"Oh, whoa. Harrietta, did you see...?"

"Yeah. This is *freaky*. But, Dawn, you have to get out of here."

"Do I? I was planning to clean up your kitchen anyway. Maybe make pancakes."

I pull a face. "You've got to stop making breakfast around here."

"You can take that up with my grandmother."

My phone rings again, the number unknown. I don't answer, but look at Dawn with wide, frightened eyes.

Then a text comes in.

Graham:

#plantationwedding is trending???

Ok I'm picking Sonya up from Louis Armstrong today

Can we come over? I think we'd all better come over.

Sonya. In all the excitement, I'd forgotten she was coming home this afternoon.

Nosily, Dawn reads Graham's name over my shoulder. "Who's that? Who's *Graham*?"

The hint of jealousy brings out my own wicked smile. "A friend. Not what you think. He's trying to be supportive."

"Invite him over, then. With that worm business, it made a big difference to my friend to have his boys around. Kept him from getting overwhelmed."

"Can't you just stick by me?"

"Sure I can."

Down the hall, the bathroom door slams.

Dad's awake.

"Now's your chance," I whisper to Dawn. "Make a run for it."

He picks up his feet and hustles, winking over his shoulder at me.

Graham:

Harriet? Should we come over?

I'm trying to change. Trying not to let rage, or her invisible sister, fear, control me. Shutting down was the easy choice, but it only ever warped me.

What's the harm in inviting Graham and Sonya over?

I mean, I really do need all the help I can get.

Me:

okay y'all come over if you want

That one simple text feels like free fall.

Graham responds with a series of celebratory GIFs, and Dawn clatters in the kitchen. It's a small miracle that he made it downstairs before Dad spotted him.

"Harriet?" My father howls from the bathroom. "Want to tell me what's going on?"

Shit. Guess Dawn wasn't fast enough.

I bolt for the bathroom, where Dad's standing in an old white robe, phone in hand.

"I'm getting emails. Tons of them. And then like eight grad students texted me, too, and come to find out, *Twitter* is talking about us. About Westwood!" His eyes narrow dangerously. "Explain yourself. Right now."

I brace myself. "So, Dad, don't freak out, okay?"

He grits his teeth. "What did you do?"

"I made a video. A series. I guess it went viral."

"How?"

I shrug. "No one really knows how these things work. I guess the twelfth video in particular struck a chord? I mean, did you watch it?"

"Oh, I watched it all right. What were you thinking, spewing that noise? You think that makes us look professional—one of our tour guides *slamming our tourists*?"

"Ex-tour guide, Dad. You fired me, remember?"

"You have no *concept* of our mission. No respect at all for what your mother and I have built!"

I never should've brought you to Westwood, Mom said. *We never should've come South.*

"I built Westwood, too, Dad," I mumble. "I've been working here, too. Like, for years."

"What's happened to you, Harriet? Why are you acting this way? What happened to my—"

We both know what he was going to say.

What happened to my excellent daughter.

Something inside me shatters like a bone.

"What happened to me? Are you for real?" I demand. "Westwood happened to me, Dad. If you wanted your perfect, excellent daughter, we never should've come here. Even Mom regretted it, in the end."

Dad looks like he's seen a ghost. "What did you say?"

My mouth dries up. I don't want to talk about Mom's last words. As a matter of fact, I never meant to share that re-memory with Dad—not ever.

"Hey, Mr. Douglass?" Dawn shouts from the kitchen. "Want me to fix y'all some pancakes?"

Dawn's throwing me a lifesaver; I grasp it with both hands. "Pancakes would be great, thanks!"

"Get out of my kitchen, son!" Dad hollers. "I need to talk to my daughter."

"Come on, Dad, he's been helping us all this time."

"I already asked Auntie Yates to stop. It was a nice gesture, but we don't need their help."

"Oh, we don't?" Ticked the hell off, the rage monster scrabbles at my windpipe. "Every morning, the kitchen's filthy. And you're too tired and sleepless and *depressed* to clean it up. I couldn't take it anymore. We *do* need their help."

Dad has the grace to look abashed.

"Excuse me for shouting, Dawn," he calls. "Just come back in an hour, won't you? Just give us one hour, and I'll make *you* eggs. What do you say?"

Silence from downstairs.

Then, "Harriet? Do you want me to go?"

Dad glares. "You and that boy. You and the *internet*. Is it too much to ask that I know what's going on under my own roof?"

"I'll explain everything," I tell him, because Lord knows it's time. "Dawn, you can go. We'll have breakfast in an hour."

"Long as you don't order it. Fast-food pancakes ain't even worth it, Harrietta!"

I lean over the banister. "Home-cooked, I swear!"

Dawn sets down a fry pan with a clang. His footfalls tell me he's headed out the door, just like I asked.

Meanwhile, Dad studies me closely, clearly pissed beyond words.

"Why don't you get dressed," I say, trying to keep him calm. "I'll work on that breakfast. Okay?"

He points at me. "You better not leave this house. And don't tweeter at anything, you hear?"

I wince at the word *tweeter*.

"Yeah. I promise."

He only scowls harder.

● ● ● ● ●

When Dad comes downstairs, his expression's still tight and angry. He's wearing a shirt that says, WHAT DO YOU CALL A VEGETARIAN VIKING? NORVEGAN!

Just the worst.

He makes a production of pouring his coffee. Of sighing heavily, like I'm a burden or a chore. For my part, I'm as irritable as a hungry Rosemary.

Why does Dad have to be so technologically illiterate? Why can't he see that people finally paying attention to Westwood's online presence is a good thing? And okay, I mess up a lot, but would it kill him to appreciate how hard I'm trying?

Scowling myself now, I await his opening gambit.

"So you think your mother regretted coming to Westwood."

I didn't expect Dad to begin with this. The whole Twitter trending thing seems much more time-sensitive.

"It's not a big deal. Just something I remembered."

He sips his coffee. "Your mother never said she regretted coming to Westwood. She would never. Not to you."

"You're wrong." I'm snarling now. "I finally remembered what she said to me the last time I saw her. Some part of me must've always known, because I've been so angry...at the world. But maybe also at her."

Dad's voice sharpens. "What did she say? Tell me her exact words."

"She looked back on her life and felt nothing but regret." The memory's rancid on my tongue. "She said we were stupid to come South. That we worked so hard for nothing." I tense, nearing the hardest part. "She said it wasn't possible to raise a baby and make history at the same time, but that it wouldn't have mattered whether she had me or not. Because it was all a waste."

Dad closes his eyes.

Does he believe me?

I need him to believe me.

"Damn it," he breathes a rare curse. "You're telling the truth, now?"

My punctured calf itches beneath the bandage, and suddenly I'm trying so hard not to cry, I'm getting a headache. A real barn burner.

Dad stares out the kitchen window. You can spy two Lost Children from there. I wonder which has caught his eye: Louisa, or Charlie?

"Harriet, at the very end your mother was clinically depressed."

At first, I'm not sure I heard right. "Excuse me?"

"After the chemo, she wasn't herself. The doctor prescribed anti-depressants, but they never seemed to help."

A missing piece of the jigsaw slides into place, answering questions I didn't even know I had.

Like: Why would the doctors and nurses think my mom, of all people, was an addict? She was as cheerful as a television mother. A regular ray of sunshine, even when she was suffering.

If she was depressed, maybe she didn't have the energy to charm the hospital staff like usual. Maybe she didn't have the energy, anymore, to project Confident But Non-Threatening Professional Black Woman.

"Your mother said lots of things just before she died. She even threatened to divorce me."

"She did?"

"Yes, but she didn't mean it. The woman who spoke those words to you wasn't your mother. And that is *not* how we'll remember her."

She wasn't your mother.

"It's the truth, though, isn't it?" I whisper. "She could've done more for Westwood without a baby to raise. Or maybe... maybe she was always destined to fail."

"*No.*" Dad slams his palm against the table, startling me. "Your mother was proud of what we did here. On every level, Westwood was a success for our family—it was a success *because* of our family. In those early days, when the buildings were in ruins and the land was so god-awful sad, your mother and I couldn't have pressed on without you. If we'd come alone... we wouldn't have been able to see it through."

Dad's drawing back the curtain that separates parents and their children, revealing the secrets they kept. I'm hanging on his every word.

"The land was haunted—you could feel it in your bones. The only thing that made it bearable was *you.* A child, laughing, living, playing. Enjoying the trees and the fields. You and little Dawn breathed life into this place. You have to know that *you're* the reason Westwood became what it is today. Don't you?"

"But Westwood—it never changed anything. This city's just as racist as it's always been. St. Anne's is even planning a plantation prom."

"You've got to be patient, Harriet. Real change takes time. Understand: We're not in this for ourselves. We're fighting for our *descendants.* Your children and grandchildren."

"But Dad...the last words she ever spoke to me. They were so cruel."

"She didn't mean them."

"But then it isn't—I mean, it's not—"

Not fair, I want to say, but don't.

"She was in so much pain." Dad's expression softens. "She couldn't see the light anymore—only darkness. If she'd lived, she would've apologized to you, and held you, and told you how proud she is of the work you've done here. And if you've been carrying all this on your shoulders, all this time...well, it's no wonder that—"

My mouth stretches into a grimace. "No wonder I'm such a screwup?"

"You're not a screwup. Just a little—militant? *Uncontrolled?*"

That's all professor code for unhinged, but hey. It fits.

I don't know how to square my mother's last words with my memory of her. It tears me apart that she wasn't herself in the end.

That's not how we'll remember her, Dad said.

Like history, Mom's words can't be taken at face value. They require interpretation, and the wisdom of time.

Not how we'll remember her.

A ten-pound stone lifts from my chest; I suck in the first clear breath of air I've taken in years. Of course, this re-remembering will take time, too.

On the next exhale, the stone settles back into place, and my breathing is once again shallow. But what a difference it makes to know that peace is out there, waiting.

If I can only find the courage to claim it as mine.

CHAPTER 36

DAD ROLLS UP his sleeves. "Now, pancakes."

"I'll make them. I found those cookie cutter shapes—"

"You're not making anything. I'm going to start cooking again. Cleaning, too. I'm not going to be a reason for your boyfriend to come over every morning."

"He's not my—" I start to say. "Actually. Maybe he is."

Dad turns toward the stove, but I catch the smile, as sad as it is pleased, that flits across his face.

"You need to see a therapist, Dad," I say.

He doesn't turn around. "One of these days, I will."

"You made me see one as soon as I started having problems. When will you be depressed enough to take care of yourself?"

I'm on dangerous ground, and I know it.

"Remember you're the child here," Dad grouches. "It's not your job to worry about me. Or tell me what to do, either."

I flash back to Dawn and me, talking in the Welcome Center.

I can't believe you asked me to stay with you in DC. Like we're grown-ups or something, I said.

And Dawn, legitimately startled, answered, *We are grown-ups, Harrietta. The future is now.*

"I'm almost eighteen. I'm not a child anymore."

Dad turns to look at me, and his face is utterly bewildered.

Like he expected to see ten-year-old Harriet sitting here. Not me.

"Technically..." His jaw works, like he's chewing over his thoughts. "I suppose that's true."

"Dr. Maples would say you're in an avoidance pattern. You know you need therapy, but you won't make the appointment. You can't commit to taking care of yourself. But would you do it for me? Because I asked?"

Dad's eyes skate away. "I'll do it sometime."

I press a little harder. "Would you do it for Mom?"

"Harriet." Dad's voice is pained. "Mom's not here."

"But you know what she'd say if she were, right?"

Dad doesn't answer me, and I can't keep pushing him. His mental health isn't my responsibility. All I can do is make suggestions and hope for the best.

While he cooks, my phone will *not* shut up.

At this point, the constant ringing, buzzing, beeping is some kind of *Saw*-style torture. FOMO is kicking in on a biological level, and whenever I pick up my phone I find myself gazing lovingly at my own face, a new experience for me. It's as if the sheer number of likes have made me more likable, even to myself. Psychologically speaking, everything about the viral experience is like playing with fire.

"We can delete the clocktok video, right?" Dad says, pouring batter into the pan. "We'll delete it, and then we don't have to worry about this viral thing. We can just focus on getting better. The both of us."

Oh my poor, poor dad.

"You can't really delete something once it's been shared, is the thing."

His eyebrows drop back into a glower. "I just don't know what to do,

280

then, Harriet. I don't think I can protect you from this internet business. Can't protect Westwood, either."

I squint at my father, who's never considered the upside of going truly viral. "So, Dad?"

Miserably, he rolls his eyes to me. Like: *What* now?

"Remember how I told you that things have changed since the old days? That it's safer, now, for Black folks to get good and mad—at least, online?"

Doubtfully, he nods.

"Well, my TikTok might've seemed nuts to you, but on social, people are *loving* it. Last time I checked, Westwood had *fifty thousand* new Twitter followers."

Spatula in hand, my father freezes. He's so jealous of the hot-shit professors with huge Twitter followings, it's wild.

"Remind me: How many followers did we have before?"

"Like, two thousand?"

Astonishment streaks across his face. "Wow."

"Yeah. It's a pretty big deal. Plantation weddings are a national conversation because of us. If you help me, we could maybe even—"

Cancel Belle Grove, I think, but don't say.

"Hmm," Dad says—but that's not *no*.

I try to tell him with my eyes: *This is the way. Use the force, Dad.*

Loud noises erupt from our front porch, shoes scraping across wood, laughter splashing like water. The sound of Sonya's drawl sets my nerves buzzing.

Dad's head snaps around. "What's this? You throwing some kind of party?"

I hear Sonya, Graham, Sandy, and Morgan out there so far—they must have some kind of group chat.

"Um, not intentionally? They're here about the viral stuff, I think."

"We're in the middle of a conversation, Harriet."

Before I can answer, Sonya bursts through the door. "Look who's making moves, taking names!"

Morgan traipses in after Sonya, followed by Graham, Sandy, Chase, and Asher. Behind the vintage breakfast club committee is Dawn Yates, glowing like a god. I don't know how it's possible, but he legit gets better looking every time I see him.

Still, it's Sonya who steals my breath away. In Italy, she's perfected her makeup game—her eyes outlined in kohl—and she's wearing a very cool black leather jacket. It's amazing how sophisticated she looks. How beautiful and grown.

A harsh smell rises from the stove top—in all the chaos, Dad's burned the first round of pancakes.

Unable to tear my eyes from my best friend, I rise up.

Graham and Co. part for me like the Red Sea. I wonder what Sonya sees, faced with my exhausted, battered self. I'm not fresh from the Mediterranean, that's for sure. After my unplanned assault on Belle Grove, I'm actually pretty banged up. When we're an arm's length apart, I stop, uncertain.

"How's your leg, H?" she whispers.

My eyes well. "Don't worry about it. I've been so selfish, Son. Caught up in my drama. I barely asked you about Italy. And look at you now." I shake my head. "Yale's not *ready*."

"It doesn't matter. We've got plenty of time. Peanut butter and jelly, remember?"

I nod, and Sonya opens her arms to me. I rush into them, rocking back and forth on my toes. I swear she's grown taller. Or maybe she's just standing up straight, proud in her skin.

"I missed you," I whisper.

"Lo so, bella."

I hold on until she pushes back. "Okay, Errichetta? We've got work to do. You're trending today, remember?"

Wiping my eyes, I nod. "You're right. But I want to hear about the restaurants and museums and—"

Sonya snorts. "Nobody wants to hear about someone else's museum trips. Trust."

"Excuse me." Dad clears his throat. "Can someone please explain why y'all are here?"

Graham plops down on a kitchen stool and opens his laptop. "Harriet's trending, and we're here for moral support. Also because no one from St. Anne's has ever gone viral before and it's cool as hell, my dude."

Dad frowns. This '90s Black man does not appreciate being called *my dude.*

"According to my daughter, there's nothing to be done," Dad says. "She can't delete the—the tock—"

"And she shouldn't. Claudia Hartwell deserves what she gets." Sandy sidles up to the counter, wearing Chase's football jacket.

Now Dad's frowning so hard it's a wonder his face doesn't melt.

Sandy pops her gum. "So, like, Claudia Hartwell rolls up from LA, right? And buys one of the oldest plantations in town. Only, this is the South? And you can't just do that?"

To my surprise, Sandy's seething. I don't think I've ever seen her angry before.

"Also plantation weddings are racist AF," Graham adds.

Beside me, Sonya slips her hand in mine. Asher and Morgan hover over Graham's shoulder, while Chase stares longingly at the breakfast pans.

Dawn, meanwhile, is leaning against a wall, intentionally giving us space.

"You guys," I say. "This is Dawn Yates. My neighbor. He recorded all the videos I posted. Also, we're dating."

Then there's a flurry of activity around Dawn, all because he's dating me.

It hits me, in a great wave, how much the St. Anne's kids care about me.

Once upon a time, every one of them pressed their hands into my mother's chapel memorial, and if I hadn't been such an oblivious dick, I might've realized that they've stood by me ever since.

Sure, their allyship might've been quieter and less flashy than Layla Hartwell's. But for years they checked in on me, and kept checking even when my responses were rude. I remember the worried looks on their faces when Dr. Benoit announced the plantation prom, and how Sandy quit the prom committee—for me. I remember, too, how Morgan lingered the last time I spoke to Dr. Heidel. Not waiting for a spectacle, like I assumed, but just looking out.

And what I think is: *Mom's magic worked.*

She made a difference in the lives of these kids. She truly changed their hearts and minds. But it took time for those changes to show—years and years.

"You've got all the feels right now, don't you?" Sonya says softly.

"Yeah." I dash at my eyes. "But I'll be all right."

"The best strategy is to take one interview," Graham says. "Whichever's biggest. Like that girl who put cement in her hair. I'm drawing up a Google Doc now, so we can decide which outlet's best."

"Counterpoint," Asher drawls. "What if she *doesn't* take a phone interview? If Harriet's mysteriously silent, wouldn't that be even more powerful? Like that environmentalist who stunt-ate the eel he fished out of the nuclear reservoir. Local news might roll up for that, right?"

"What?" my father barks. "What *eel*? What would the local news want with—"

"Honestly, she should talk to whoever's doing a feature?" Sandy cocks her head thoughtfully. "You know, like that guy who went viral for breaking up with his girlfriend on top of the Empire State Building? Like, if it's *Rolling Stone*, or *The Cut*, and she gets a whole spread...*that* would be bomb. And if she mentions St. Anne's, we can clip it for the yearbook."

Chase is nodding hard, letting us know he fully agrees with his girlfriend and does so in perpetuity.

"Whatever she does, the good news is—Harriet Douglass is getting into *any* college she wants," Sonya says. "This. Is. The. Golden. Ticket."

A smile blooms on my face. Trust Sonya to keep her eye on the prize.

My phone pipes up again, angrier.

"If I don't answer the phone, I'll be hearing it in my dreams."

"Check your voicemails, *please*," Sonya says. "Put them on speaker."

I glance swiftly at Dad for permission; his brows knit.

"I don't understand what all the fuss is, frankly. I mean, Harriet, you're very telegenic, but why should that video—full of complaints—make such a splash?"

Sonya speaks briskly. "With all due respect, Mr. Douglass, Harriet's video is amazing. It's full of the righteous indignation we all feel about these plantations. It's about time someone spoke the truth."

Dad looks at me appraisingly. Nothing about the words *righteous indignation* screams Black excellence to him—a man who believes careful, footnoted scholarship is the best way to make a difference.

But times *have* changed. Black folks are louder than they used to be. We have a chance, in some small instances, to be ourselves.

"Trust us, Mr. Douglass," says Asher. "We wouldn't let Harriet do anything stupid. This is the right move."

Utterly uncomprehending, Dad drags a hand down his face. "Fine. Y'all do your thing."

My eyes find Dawn, who knows right away what I need. He takes my phone from me, and cues it to play its voice messages.

"Ready?"

Comforted by the smell of him, I nod.

He presses play, and women's voices, one after another, flood the kitchen.

Hello, Harriet Douglass, this is NBC News—

Hi, is this Harriet? I'm a reporter with BuzzFeed—

This is CNN, we'd love a comment on—

If you'd just call me back—

The voicemails roll on, while Graham desperately records them in the spreadsheet no one asked for, and Sandy makes awestruck faces at Chase, who for his part is looking game but bored. Morgan's taken a seat on the couch, playing cat's cradle with a piece of black twine, but I know she's supporting me in her own quiet way. I still have the sprig of thyme she gave me upstairs in my room. Maybe it really is good luck.

Finally we hear:

Hello, this is Tammy Jones, I write for the New York Times—

"Stop the tape!" Dad hollers.

(It's not a tape. But okay.)

"Did you hear that?" He pounds the table. "Tammy Jones, I knew her in grad school, and that's—that's the *New York Times!*"

"You have to call her back." Graham's voice cracks from the excitement. "That's the interview you need to give. Ignore everybody else, but—"

"No." Morgan shakes her head over the cradle. "Give all the interviews, why not?"

Graham whirls. "Did you not hear what I've been saying this whole time?"

Morgan shrugs. "Seems like more publicity is better. And I really don't want to go to a plantation prom, so."

"But would you want to go to any prom?" Chase asks. "Wouldn't you rather, like, gather mushrooms in the woods?"

To that, Morgan responds with a mostly friendly middle finger.

"Shouldn't press speak to me?" Dad wonders. "As the director of Westwood?"

"Respectfully, Mr. Douglass, *no,*" Asher says firmly.

"Surely, if they want the historical background—"

"They don't. They want to *cancel Sunny and Randy White.* That's hot news."

"You really should get back to the *New York Times,*" Graham adds—desperate now. "And, like, sooner rather than later?"

Dad shoots me a look like, *Are you up for this?*

And the truth is, I don't know.

I set this whole thing in motion halfway accidentally. It all played out like one of those Rube Goldberg machines, where the marble strikes the pendulum that starts the tiny waterfall that knocks down the dominoes...

Like, what if I can't stick the landing? What if I rage out at *a reporter*? As in a horror movie, the world narrows, tunneling.

I sway on my feet, but Dawn's right behind me. I wind up leaning against his steady chest.

"You okay?" he whispers.

"I think I'm gonna pass out."

He squeezes my shoulder. "Shoot your shot, Harrietta. We're all here for you."

My next breath fills me with calm. My friends are here, cheering me on. Asher's watching me, a soft smile on his face. I smile weakly back, thinking how much I've missed him. Missed everyone. I've spent so many years with a giant chip on my shoulder, but maybe, just maybe, I've felt like an outsider longer than I've actually been one. Lost in my ever-present rage, I didn't register the quiet changes taking place in my own student body—maybe even in the world.

Hasn't Sonya been trying to tell me that all along?

My whole life, it seems, has led to this moment—and when it comes down to it, I'm not nearly as alone as I've always believed myself to be.

My throat tightens, preparing words for the reporter, and I can feel, already, my mother's voice behind mine—an echo of her careful politeness and compassion. And behind *her* are the voices of Westwood's enslaved. Anna, Louisa, Samuel...they're all here with me. Almost as if they were still alive.

I could hug Dawn, but it's time to bite the bullet.

Keeping the phone on speaker, I place a call to the *New York Times*.

CHAPTER 37

S O THAT'S THE story of how I went viral.

In a snap, I became super famous. Way more famous, in fact, than Layla or Claudia Hartwell. For a while there, I was plastered all over the internet, like graffiti, and everyone had an opinion about me. I felt compelled to read every last hot take, but Dawn and Dad quickly staged an intervention, confiscating my phone for hours at a time. I could ask for it, but only on the condition that I hugged my chicken first. That way, if I happened to come across anything trollish, I'd have the dopamine reserves to keep calm and Twitter on.

I highly recommend this technique, should you go ever go viral yourself.

As for my interview, it appeared in the *New York Times* on November seventeenth. The reporter, being thorough, interviewed Sunny Blake and Claudia Hartwell, too. (Randy White denied any request for comment, because it was "all his wife's idea.")

Needless to say, both white women were spitting mad.

"Why should I be canceled for having a plantation wedding?" Sunny whined. "I'm a southerner. That's what we *do*. You know what, this is some BS, I have no further comment."

Claudia Hartwell also dropped the ball.

"There's so much more to a plantation than slavery," she's quoted as saying. "And honestly, the Westwood employees have had it out for me from day one! It's harassment. Why aren't the police investigating them? What's happened to this country?"

The internet wasn't pleased. After a vicious Twitter tussle, Sunny Blake conceded defeat, announcing a social media detox and a large donation (over a hundred thousand dollars!) to the NAACP.

I'm taking this time to do the work. I apologize to any of my fans who felt hurt by my actions. I want you all to know that I'm listening and learning, and I'll be back for the premiere of my new CW show, Basic Witches.

And so, life went on.

Thanksgiving came and went, followed by winter break and the beginning of my senior spring. Like a regular kid, I did homework and took exams, watching movies most evenings with Dawn. Sonya and I gossiped about normal teenage things, like how Sandy and Chase broke up and then immediately got back together again—twice. I started spending one-on-one time with each of my friends, catching up on the years we'd lost.

But here's the best part: Amidst all the online kerfuffle, St. Anne's canceled its plantation prom. Really, they had no choice. Since I'd gone viral, the optics were just too terrible.

The new venue's the same as last year's: the Audubon Zoo, which sounds cooler than it is. For one thing, no one sees any animals at a zoo prom. You're restricted to the multipurpose room, which, though boringly animal-free, still *smells* like a zoo. So it's the worst of both worlds.

In any case, my friends and I aren't going to the official prom.

I was hanging out with Asher at Burger King when he admitted to me that he could never attend a St. Anne's shindig, no matter where they held it.

"It's not like I can bring my boyfriend to a Catholic school dance," he pointed out.

My heart sank. "Oh my God. I didn't think about that."

Asher shrugged. "Mostly, straight people don't."

That rocked me. Injustice is so thick on so many fronts—the battlefield endlessly complex.

"I apologize for not thinking of you, Ash. Let me make it up to you."

Curious but slightly cool, he studied me. "How?"

"We should throw an anti-prom."

"Like where? Venues are expensive."

"No dollars necessary." I couldn't contain my glee. "What I'm thinking will be free, and it comes with pie."

Bittersweet pie to be exact.

"Well, I'm a good southern boy. I like pie."

"Then Auntie Yates is gonna love you. Most of her community's moved on. She's getting lonesome in her old age."

"Wouldn't want to impose."

"Trust me, she'll be thrilled. I should warn you, though: She bakes this one pie with no sugar, in honor of the enslaved who were forced to cut cane. It's a whole thing."

Asher laughs. "She sounds awesome."

When I broached the subject with her, Dawn's grandmother squealed with delight.

She started baking and freezing pies right away.

· · · · ·

In late March, on prom night, the crickets are singing, heralding summer. Dawn Yates is picking me up; my father and I wait for him on the porch. I'm in a pale green dress, which Sonya helped me pick out one afternoon at the downtown Nordstrom. (Our number one requirement: that it fits me in the bust.) The department store security guard followed us around for a while, but we didn't let it bother us. Or, rather, Sonya didn't let it bother her, and told me with a look that I'd better keep things tight. She

290

didn't want anything to ruin that day, because it was the biggest of her life: She'd just found out she'd gotten into Yale.

I'm so proud of Sonya, my Italian-speaking BFF now headed to the Ivy League.

Dawn picks me up in his car, even though we're only going across the street. When he steps out, I laugh, because he's wearing that white tux again. Looking as dashing and James Bond as can be.

Dad walks me over to him, clearly nervous. In the before times, Mom would've spoken with Dawn, complimenting him on his hair, his suit. My poor father isn't cut out for this kind of high-impact social situation, but bless his heart, he does his best.

"Drive safely with my daughter, young man. I'm trusting you."

"Absolutely, sir. Thank you."

(Again, we're just going down the road.)

"Have fun, baby girl," Dad says, more tenderly, to me.

When he turns his back, I can tell from the set of his shoulders that he's on the verge of tears. Whether he's thinking about Mom, who couldn't be here, or about how quickly I'm growing up, I'll never know.

In the car, Dawn slips a corsage over my wrist.

"They're roses," he says. "I hope you like them."

I kiss his cheek. "I love them *and* you."

And then, I think Dawn Yates actually blushes.

A knot grows in my stomach on the way to his grandmother's house. I hope my friends come on time, and behave respectfully. In our text thread, I warned them about drugs, which are a trigger for the older woman. If anyone smokes so much as a cigarette, she's liable to ship us all off to Washington, DC.

But I shouldn't have worried. When Dawn and I walk through the door, clutching each other's hands, applause breaks out, cresting over waves of exuberant music. The mix, selected by Asher under Auntie Yates's supervision, is 100 percent Motown, and between that and the shag carpet, there's a feeling of traveling back in time. Sonya hugs me at the door, and Sandy twirls in a petal-pink dress. Morgan's already barefoot in the yard, gathering dandelions, and Asher is on the porch strung with fairy lights, joking around with his devastatingly handsome boyfriend.

"Want to dance?" Dawn asks.

"We better sniff the punch first. Make sure no one spiked it."

Auntie Yates comes up behind me. "Don't you worry about that, sweetheart. I may be getting on in years, but I don't miss a trick."

On a snack table, she's arranged an assortment of pies on a scale from Mournful to Sweetest. I hug her tightly.

"Your mother would be so proud of you tonight," she says. "Now go have the time of your life!"

In the yard, to the music of the Supremes, Dawn holds me close. We sway and spin and sway again. Every time I touch him, my heart stitches itself back together. Stitch by stitch, touch by touch, I'm healing at last.

As the song reaches its climax, Dawn presses his forehead to mine. We hold like that, reveling in who we've become together. And then he kisses me for real.

Out of nowhere, Auntie Yates comes up and swats him.

"Behave yourself, child!"

On the dance floor with Graham, Sonya doubles over, laughing.

When we're tired of dancing, Dawn goes to fetch me a slice of pie. I slip my heels off. A buzzing, contented feeling thrums in my belly, telling me I'm exactly where I need to be. But when Dawn comes back with two large slices (Mournful for me, Medium-Sweet for him), there's a question in his eyes.

"Did you think about your gap year? What you'll do?"

I never did apply to any college but Brown, which in retrospect was some grade A self-sabotage. But since my viral fame, I've convinced my dad that a gap year's the best thing for me. I can always apply to my safety schools next year. Dad grumbled a little, but these days, on the advice of his new therapist, he's trying to treat me like a capable adult. He's even stopped pestering me about visiting Mom's grave.

"You still want me to come to DC?"

"'Course I do, Harrietta."

I tilt my chin up. "How much?"

His expression grows dreamy. "I think we'd rock that city. A love story for the ages..."

I laugh. "Me too. And I'll think about it."

"You do that. But don't think too long."

In the way of senior lovers everywhere, we both know that time is running out. And yet, the magic of this moment—the anti-prom, full of everything and everyone I denied myself for years—will be our monument, and will last a lifetime.

CHAPTER 38

IN APRIL, I get a message in my student portal: Brown University's made a decision about my application.

I've seen kids film this moment for social. They're always wearing sweatpants and a look of agonized hope. But I have no urge to film myself. I already know what's about to happen. I don't have the grades for Brown, or the AP credits, either.

Listlessly, I click the link.

Then I start screaming.

Dad comes running, wearing a T-shirt that reads I'M SICK OF REPEATING MYSELF. SIGNED, HISTORY. I honestly sort of like that one.

"Dad! I got into Brown!"

"Harriet Douglass, you did not get into Brown."

Swear to God, that's what he says.

"Why does it say *congratulations*, then?"

Dad reads it for himself: *Congratulations! You've been accepted into Brown University's Class of 2027!*

"What did I tell you?" I howl. "Somehow, I got in!"

"Listen, I'm proud of you," Dad says dourly. "But you didn't have the grades for this school. Clearly, they recognized your name from that contagion."

"From when I went *viral*. And who cares? It's my first-choice school. Also, the only one I applied to."

Dad shakes his head miserably.

"Maybe I didn't get into Brown the way you wanted me to. But I did get in. So...can you go back to the part where you tell me you're proud?"

Dad opens his arms to fold me into a hug. "I am. I'm very proud of my *nontraditionally* excellent daughter."

Argh! "You can just say excellent, it won't kill you."

"Okay, then. *Excellent* you are."

For weeks after, I'm walking on clouds. Dawn understands that I can't take my gap year anymore, as fun as it would've been, because I improbably got into the school of my dreams. He's very understanding; he promises to visit me there. If he's disappointed, he hides it well.

Meanwhile, I'm no longer as viral as I was before—a sweet relief. The plantation think pieces peter out as the internet moves on to other scandals. For a while, everything seems, well, perfect.

And then Claudia Hartwell throws another plantation wedding.

This time, I stay the night at Sonya's. While I sink into a movie about time-traveling ghosts, a familiar feeling settles on my chest, lightly at first: despair. I'm haunted by the conviction that nothing I did this year made any real difference—that even going viral never mattered.

Because Mrs. Hartwell isn't *canceled*—far from it. This summer alone, she's throwing three plantation weddings for the type of people who hate cancel culture so much, they only get their chicken from Chick-fil-A and their crafts from Hobby Lobby. I assume they also listen to a lot of Joe Rogan.

I guess I'm the last person to realize it, but: Social media activism doesn't change much. After a brief disturbance, the digital waters settled, and everything went on as before. So what am I supposed to do? Should

I just accept the things I cannot change? And if I do—what'll happen to the rage monster? Even after my viral moment, she could still eat me alive.

By summer, I'm more determined than ever to leave this place, with its million and one ghosts. Like my ancestors, I'm ready to go North.

I'm on my laptop in the kitchen, preparing to officially accept my spot at Brown University, when I discover something unsettling. Something I'm kicking myself for not thinking of before. Northern or not, Brown, too, has its deep, dark secrets.

I click a link, navigating to a webpage for a campus memorial.

Squinting at my laptop's screen, a headache wraps me in its vice.

The memorial is an iron statue, a gigantic ball-and-chain. I hope and pray that the tombstone, transcribed on the site, doesn't say what I fear it will.

This memorial recognizes Brown University's connection to the trans-Atlantic slave trade and the work of Africans and African-Americans, enslaved and free, who helped build our university, Rhode Island, and the nation. . . .

Rhode Islanders dominated the North American share of the African slave trade, launching over a thousand slaving voyages in the century before the abolition of the trade in 1808, and scores of illegal voyages thereafter.

Brown University was a beneficiary of this trade.

A chasm opens in my chest; I feel like the stupidest girl alive.

Of course there's no escaping the slaveholding South—not even by going North. It makes total sense that Rhode Island, a *port town*, thrived as a result of the transatlantic slave trade, importing human beings.

Well, would you look at that, the rage monster growls.

Like a monster in a sequel, she's woken up again.

But at least there's a memorial on Brown's campus, right? It's better than what the Hartwells are doing, erasing history completely.

Wonder when they put it up, though.

I lean forward again, to study the plaque. It's dated 2014.

So, like, *yesterday.*

Red creeps around the edges of my vision.

I push it away, but it comes back in waves. I could still go to Brown, but my heart's heavier now. I fixated on the campus because of its beauty, but not one beautiful inch of its grounds will ever be un-shadowed by tragedy. Not to me.

You should've known there's no escape, the rage monster whispers. *Not there. Not anywhere.*

On his way to the kitchen, Dad witnesses my distress. "Oh no. What's the matter now?"

Like the Ghost of Christmas Past, I point silently at my computer.

He scans the text, then looks down at me. "You really didn't know? Most of the old universities built their original endowments on the slave trade."

Feeling impossibly naive, I close my eyes. "Maybe I should leave the country."

Dad chuckles. "Other places have their histories, too. Learning to live with the past is part of being human."

I glance again at the ball-and-chain memorial. It's meant to be a metaphor, but I don't like it. Maybe because it makes me think, more than anything, of Dawn's father, picking cotton for twelve cents an hour. That's happening now, in the present. And that means the statue at Brown isn't really a metaphor at all.

I lean back in my chair. "I don't think I'm going."

"What?" Dad snaps.

"I don't think I'm going to Brown. Maybe next year I'll apply to an HB—"

"Don't say it," Dad warns. "Please, no."

"*HBCU.* They're great schools, Dad." I snort, exasperated. "Why are you so prejudiced?"

"I just want the best for you, and those institutions don't have the same prestige. You have a chance here to attend an Ivy League school!"

"Yes, and . . . I don't want it? Like, all that prestige isn't worth it to me, if John Brown built it with slave ships."

Clearly in excruciating pain, Dad grimaces. "Howard. I could see you at Howard."

"*Thank you.*"

"And I have some wonderful colleagues there. But, Harriet, if you study history, you'll need to get a graduate degree somewhere. If you want to be competitive, you'll have to sacrifice some of these principles."

"The world's changed since you were in school, you know. You and Mom sent me to the world's whitest private school to give me the best chance to play the game. But what if the game's different now? What if I don't *have* to chase the best, whitest everything to succeed?"

Dad's looking at me like I've lost my mind, but I'm sure I speak the truth.

"I know you don't understand it, because you're kind of—no offense—old? But trust me on this."

His shoulders drop. "Well, the decision's yours to make, Harriet. You're grown now."

Right away, I text Dawn the news. BROWN OUT, GAP YEAR DEFI-NITELY HAPPENING

ready or not the Harriet show is coming to DC this fall!!!

In response, he sends me fireworks. And hearts. And a photo of the two of us at anti-prom that I've never seen before, looking like we really *do* mean forever.

Overwhelmed, I cover my mouth with my hand. Right this moment, I feel as #blessed as any basic influencer. A person could get used to it.

"So, I've been thinking," Dad says. "It's about time you came back to Westwood as a tour guide."

"You mean it? *Why?* No offense, Dad, but I'm obviously a loose cannon."

"I heard you on the phone with the *Times* reporter. I saw how you handled yourself, when the stakes were high. You've grown."

A bubble of feeling blocks my throat. Dad wouldn't give me back my tours unless he truly believed in me.

"I'll leave your badge in the office. We'll discuss your schedule later. Okay?"

I knit my brows, remembering Vacation Karen. The people who once lived on Westwood land, Anna, Louisa, and Samuel, are all counting on me to tell their stories responsibly, without alienating the people who need to hear it the most.

"There's something I need to do first," I tell Dad.

"Just say the word."

"I need to visit Mom."

He freezes. "Are you sure?"

"Yeah. I'm ready."

Dad starts pacing, mumbling to himself. "This is great, this is wonderful, this is exactly what our family needs."

Oh, damn, he thinks I mean *today*.

"Should we walk? Drive?"

Like he's worried I'll change my mind, Dad's already shrugging into his jacket. I don't have the heart to tell him I'm not *quite* ready. That I wanted to procrastinate as is my God-given right. But honestly, what's my holdup? I've been faithfully practicing all of Dr. Maples's techniques, especially the one where I welcome my rage when it comes. I didn't believe it at first, but a little self-compassion goes a long way. The rage monster's edges soften a little more every time I greet her.

So what am I waiting for?

"We'll drive," Dad decides.

And then we're in the car, heading for a place that feels like destiny, a heart-stop on the tour of my life.

We park at the forest's edge, then travel the rest of the way on foot. As we enter the small copse of pines, part of me wants to back out. Run home and plunge into that new horror series about reborn dolls.

But I can't disappoint Dad. I've got to prove I'm as grown as he thinks I am.

The trees above wrap me in shadows. I still hate that Mom's buried here, and not in a normal cemetery. It feels backward to bury her on plantation land, to have her body so close, but Dad says that's what Mom wanted.

Her headstone rises from the ground, straight as an arrow.

I kneel in a mess of pine needles before her stone, inscribed with the cold, historical facts: the years of her birth and early death. Dad's set candles here, and a dry bouquet of magnolias, which were their special flower.

Because it feels right, I take out my phone and cue up "The Impossible Dream."

Memories rush in: Mom smiling on the porch; Mom, diminished at home, a marijuana cigarette in hand; Mom, more sunken still, telling me it wasn't worth it, her life—that she regretted coming to Westwood. That she couldn't change the world and raise a baby at the same time. That she'd failed.

I inch closer to the tombstone, and then press my forehead against it. It's gritty and cold, not like her at all.

But the words of the song capture her completely.

Don Quixote, too, was willing to follow an impossible road, to fight without hope, to march into hell for heaven's true cause. He fought the unbeatable foe, and he never quit dreaming. Neither did Mom. She didn't die peacefully, but she can rest that way. And whenever I need her, she'll be right here.

For all the horror movies I watch, I don't believe in ghosts.

What I believe in is history, and that discipline extends beyond the cold, hard facts—it's a kind of ghost making, and it has as much to do with the future as the past. The history of my mother is far greater than her broken, deathbed words.

It's not historically accurate to claim that Westwood made no difference. The kids at St. Anne's remember Westwood, even care about it; and how many ancestor-searchers, like Mr. Goodman, have found their way here?

The rage monster gnashes her teeth; in my chest, her glowing eyes burn.

To Mom's stone, I whisper: "I hate you." Swallow. Start over. "I hate you for making everything look so easy. And for being gracious to white folks, even when they were terrible, and for making Westwood your white whale." (Black whale? Whatever.)

"I hate you for being so ugly and angry in the hospice. But most of all—" I choke, almost quitting. "Most of all, I hate you for dying, and leaving me here alone."

The words echo as loudly in my head as the memorial bell, ringing out the plain, honest truth.

Dr. Maples taught me to speak to my rage like it's a visitor—a guest.

Welcome the feeling. Thank your anger for visiting, she said—while I fought not to roll my eyes, because it sounds like bullshit, right?

Then, gently but firmly, tell the rage she cannot stay. Ask her where she's going next. Wish her well on her way.

"Thanks for visiting, rage lady," I say under my breath. "Thanks for everything you've taught me. But you know you can't stay."

Are you sure, Harriet?

I catch my breath, because the rage monster's dropped her growly act. She sounds concerned about me, and behind the concern, there's something like grief.

I remember how the rage monster shielded me from Vacation Karen's wrath on that hot summer afternoon. How she buoyed me when Dr.

Heidel kicked me out of class. How over and over again, after Mom's death, she kept the emptiness at bay.

We had some interesting times, the rage monster and me. But I've finally outgrown her. That's the truth.

"I'm sure," I say. "It's time."

And then—incredibly—my dark passenger lets go.

The rage monster loosens her claws, clambering right out of my soul. My shoulders, tense for months, release. The knots in my neck break up. The ten-pound stone on my chest shudders and crumbles, dissolving into dust.

Shaky on my own two feet, I stand. Dad's watching me, but quietly, trying not to intrude. His face is frozen in an expression of terrible hope, like something you'd see on a child's face. I'm not convinced he's breathing.

I pick up my feet and run straight into his arms.

Meanwhile, I'm bugging, because like—who knew that therapy actually works?

Thank you, white people, I think; I'm pretty sure they invented it.

"We'll come back and see her again on Sunday, can't we?" Dad asks. "And before you leave for your gap year, you can visit her, say goodbye—and when you get your cap and gown, you'll wear it for her. She'd want to see. And—if you ever get married—"

"Oh my God, Dad, you have to stop," I moan. And then, more gently: "Of course we can come back. As often as you want."

I mean it, too. For once, I feel as free as Layla Hartwell once seemed to me.

Free as a bird in a wide, clear sky.

CHAPTER 39

"AND SO, HARRIET, what have you learned?" Dr. Maples asks, while a new, unbroken clock ticks beside me. "What insights did you gain when you greeted your rage?"

"Does it matter?" I'm so happy, I'm practically gushing. "She's gone now, isn't she? It worked."

Dr. Maples frowns, and I think, *uh-oh*.

"You'll still struggle with anger sometimes, Harriet. Those neural pathways are etched deeply into your brain. But viewing rage as a temporary visitor, and not a permanent one, is a huge step."

What Dr. Maples says makes sense, though I don't think the pathways for anger are written only in my brain. As a descendant of the enslaved, I bear them in my spirit, too. The difference is, I know now that anger won't break me. It will never again seem as monstrous as it did before.

"Sometimes I still hear those things Mom said. How she regretted ever coming to Westwood. How it was all a mistake."

"You'll keep returning to that difficult moment, from time to time. It's only natural.

"But you know better than most that history is a *construction*. You can choose to remember the best things about your mother. You can make them, in your mind, a kind of memorial. When those difficult words arise, remember what matters most."

I guess I'm still a little skeptical of therapy-speak sometimes. "Okay."

Dr. Maples leans forward. "Let's try an exercise. I want you to conjure three memories of your mother—things she said or did that represent her best. Nobody in this world is perfect; no one's aligned with their best self all of the time. It would be an act of grace, on your part, to choose to remember your mother in her glory.

"Now, close your eyes."

I do.

"Conjure those memories. Whatever positive things come to mind."

Beside me, the clock ticks. At first, my mind is completely blank.

Then, like a breeze in summer, the memories swoop in:

There's Mom, unveiling the mural in the chapel, while a gaggle of fourth graders wait to mark it with their handprints.

Mom, tying a young Dawn Yates's shoes, to save Auntie Yates's back.

And there's Mom, playing hide-and-seek in the peach orchard. She darts in, and among, and around the trees, quick as a shadow—a trick of the light. But I know I'll find her, in the end. Of that, I have no doubt.

I'm awestruck, because against the backdrop of her immense goodness— her vast and generous love—those few cruel words she spoke mean nothing.

Nothing at all.

My eyes blink open, and joy rises in my chest; I can see my way through the wilderness at last, and beyond is a clear, blue peace.

Dr. Maples must see the change on my face. For the first time since I've known her, she finally—*finally*—smiles.

CHAPTER 40

I'M IN THE Welcome Center after my last tour on a roaster of an August day, letting Rosemary peck Corn Nuts out of one hand while I madly text with the other.

Somehow or other, I've wound up in a group chat with Sonya and Layla, both of whom have OPINIONS about my long-distance relationship with Dawn Yates. He stayed in town through July, but by August he had to start classes in Baltimore.

Truth is, we won't be in a long-distance situation for long. For my gap year, I've taken an internship at the National Museum of African American History in DC—not far at all from where Dawn lives. I'll be studying under a curator who specializes in southern history between 1830 and 1900, and I don't want to brag, but it's kind of a big deal.

Though it was hard, I've made peace with the idea of leaving Dad alone at Westwood. He still has his memoir to write—and that means, while she lives on the page, he still has Mom to keep him company. Even if that company is as bittersweet as one of Auntie Yates's mournful pies.

Layla:

when you first get to town, play it cool

don't crowd Dawn!!!

act like you have other places to be

Sonya:

girl what?? don't do that

set a date the minute you step off the plane and

show him how much you missed him

Layla:

make him work for it is all I'm saying

Sonya:

that's messed up no one should have to work

for love

Me:

don't fight guys

agree to disagree

Sonya:

just saying tho

Layla:

got a photo shoot in ten talk later!

Sonya (privately, to me):

always with the photo shoots smdh

Layla and I reconnected over social, but I'd be lying if I said we weren't still a little guarded with each other. These things take time. *Change* takes time. Layla is a work in progress, but after all she did for Westwood, I owe her a bit of grace. After all, Sonya gave me so much grace, loving me even when I was at my selfish worst. I'm well enough, now, to pass that spirit on.

I'm leaving town in a week, and honestly, the thing I'll miss most is leading my tours. Today I shepherded a bunch of vacationers fresh off the bus from New Orleans. They were supposed to visit a novelty alligator farm right after this, but most of them decided to linger in Remembrance Chapel instead.

"An hour isn't long enough," a white lady said. "Thank you for educating."

Of course, there was *one* tourist—there's always one—who gave me a bit of 'tude. He came with his wife, who broke down when I talked about Anna, and why we gave her, of all our statues, those great bronze wings. Her husband (still wearing his Mardi Gras beads and reeking of last night's beer) clearly resented the emotions I called up, but I sure don't know what he expected.

"Rosemary, curtsy," I say now—my phone raised to film.

In a shaft of warm Welcome Center sunlight, she bows. I'm already thinking of how I'll edit the footage. These days, Rosemary's a celebri-chicken on FowlTok.

The little bell over the glass doors chimes, letting me know I'm no longer alone. Mr. Resentful strides toward me, his face twisted in displeasure.

I glance at the tombstone I created for the Welcome Center desk, where Mom spent so many hours pursuing her life's quest.

It reads:

OAK WOOD DESK, c. 2013.
THE PLACE WHERE MRS. DOUGLASS
DID THE RIGHT THING, OVER AND OVER AGAIN.

"Excuse me." Mr. Resentful raps the desk with his fist. "I need to speak to whoever's in charge here. My wife's bawling her eyes out, and this is *not* what we signed up for." He huffs. "What do you have to say for yourselves?"

I suck in a breath, my eyes fixed on Louisa, just outside the window. A blackbird swoops out of the sky, landing on Louisa's bronze shoulder. Gracefully, she wraps her wings, iridescent in the afternoon sun, tightly around herself. Those wings are her birthright. In this harsh world, they're all she has.

I refocus on my tourist. When a smile, a real one, spreads across my face, I'm not surprised. Excitement stirs, seeing this scowling man for the opportunity he is—another chance to reach across the great divide, to grasp the star at the heart of my mother's beautiful dream.

"Hi. Welcome." My compassionate tone throws him off-balance, but I won't attack him for his guilt and anger. In another situation, in any other place, maybe I'd behave differently. But here, at Westwood, our aim is to heal the rifts between us. Since the triumph and tragedy of Belle Grove, I've found a way, while this important work needs doing, to soar above the pain.

And I'll tell you what: The view's spectacular.

"Before we start, I want to thank you for coming. I'm so glad you're here.…"

AUTHOR'S NOTE

H ARRIET'S STORY CALLS upon recent conversations we've been having in the United States about plantations and their place in our shared history. It's also very much inspired by the wonderful Whitney Plantation, the one and only plantation in Louisiana that focuses solely on the experiences of enslaved people. If you're ever near New Orleans, I can't recommend the Whitney enough—and I do, in fact, recommend *against* going to the type of plantation where glamorous furniture is privileged over the experiences of human beings. For more information about historical tourism's complicated intersection with Black history, I recommend Clint Smith's phenomenal *How the Word Is Passed*.

Throughout the book, Harriet avoids the use of the word *slave*, preferring *enslaved person*. Likewise, instead of referring to any *master*, Harriet refers to *master enslavers*. Discussion of these terms is ongoing, but I took my cue from Jennifer Eichstedt and Stephen Small's *Representations of Slavery: Race and Ideology in Southern Plantation Museums*. As they note, it's crucial to stay ever cognizant of the humanity of the people who suffered in these spaces.

The history of American slavery is an incredibly fraught subject because of the horror, shame, and anxiety it provokes in us today. But we can't blind ourselves to what happened in the past and expect to chart a better future. While the backstories behind the statues at Westwood are fictional, the facts that Harriet imparts about the experiences of enslaved people are historically accurate.

At the start of this book, Harriet's stressed out, grieving, and about to embark on a critical journey toward better mental health. You may notice that she's sometimes ungenerous in her thoughts about others. Through her point of view, I hoped to portray how it feels to be haunted by a history that roughly half the country diminishes, downplays, and denigrates daily. For each and every one of us, that's a lot to live with. In fact, it's an ongoing trauma. But always, there's hope for healing.

Whatever your entrance point into this book, I hope that Harriet's story rings out like a memory bell—and resonates deeply for you.

ACKNOWLEDGMENTS

I'd like to start by acknowledging my partner, Bill Mullen, who chose this story over a pile of others because he recognized how desperately I needed to tell it. Without him, it simply wouldn't exist. (He doesn't quite believe me, but it's true.)

Also, thanks to Michael Bourret, my agent, for believing in the project I nervously pitched to him, and for helping me find a title—and a whole subplot, too! Agenting through COVID seems like no small feat, and I so appreciate the help.

To my editor Alvina Ling: Wow! I can't believe this is our third book together. It's been so fulfilling, and this project benefited so much from your critical eye. Thank you for guiding me through every draft. Also, very special thanks to Ruqayyah Daud for her editorial comments and her helpful facilitation at every step. I'm always excited whenever I receive an email from you! Much gratitude, also, to Elizabeth Starr Baer, my copyeditor.

I'm so indebted to everyone at Little, Brown Books for Young Readers—to Victoria Stapleton, Christie Michel, Emilie Polster, Marisa Russell, Savannah Kennelly, Bill Grace, and the whole phenomenal team. I couldn't be more grateful. And the cover? It's illustrated by the marvelous Kimberly Glyder.

I've visited Black historical sites all my life, especially on childhood trips with my mother, author Jewell Parker Rhodes. I want to thank her for each and every one of them, and for leading by example. Back in the

'90s, I watched her tackle historical subjects that most wouldn't touch with a ten-foot pole. At a time when the country wasn't ready to hear it, she battled valiantly to tell the truth and blazed a brilliant trail.

I'd like to thank the Whitney Plantation for doing their marvelous work: I truly think theirs is one of the greatest museums on earth. I turned to their tour materials for much of the specific information about the lives of enslaved people, the particulars of Louisiana plantation history, and the ongoing struggles of the community on River Road.

I'd also like to acknowledge Clint Smith's groundbreaking *How the Word Is Passed* for touching on so many historical sites, including a detailed chapter about Angola Prison, where inmates really do pick cotton, as Smith recorded, for between two and twenty cents an hour.

Other sources for this novel include Jennifer Eichstedt and Stephen Small's *Representations of Slavery: Race and Ideology in Southern Plantation Museums*, as well as Tiya Miles's *All That She Carried* and *Tales from the Haunted South: Dark Tourism and Memories of Slavery from the Civil War Era*.

My thematic inspiration was the song "The Impossible Dream" from the musical *Man of La Mancha*. In particular, I love the Brian Stokes Mitchell version sung at the Martin Beck Theatre.

I'd be remiss not to mention that I attended Brown University back in the day (before they put up their memorial to the slave trade). There are some wonderful departments and teachers there—thanks to those I studied with.

I don't know where I'd be without my writer friends! A very, very special thanks to Christina Hammonds Reed, this book's first reader (truly, THANK YOU); the kind Carolyn T. O'Neil; and, as always, the incomparable, unstoppable Jodi Meadows, who embarked on a very special Tik-Tok adventure with me.

Finally, I'd like to thank the readers of this book. Thank you for braving this story, this voice, and the hard truths contained here.